In The
Upper
Country

In The Upper Country

Kai Thomas

VIKING

VIKING

an imprint of Penguin Canada, a division of Penguin Random House Canada Limited

Canada • USA • UK • Ireland • Australia • New Zealand • India • South Africa • China

Published in Viking hardcover by Penguin Canada, 2023
Simultaneously published in the United States by Viking,
an imprint of Penguin Random House LLC

www.penguinrandomhouse.ca

*Publisher's note: This book is a work of fiction. Names, characters, places and incidents
either are the product of the author's imagination or are used fictitiously, and any re-
semblance to actual persons living or dead, events, or locales is entirely coincidental.*

LIBRARY AND ARCHIVES CANADA CATALOGUING IN PUBLICATION

Title: In the Upper Country : a novel / Kai Thomas.
Names: Thomas, Kai, author.
Identifiers: Canadiana (print) 20210395087 | Canadiana (ebook) 20210395095 | ISBN
9780735243460 (hardcover) | ISBN 9780735243477 (EPUB)
Subjects: LCSH: Ontario, Southwestern—Race relations—History—19th century—
Fiction. | LCSH: Ontario, Southwestern—History—19th century—Fiction. | LCSH:
Slavery—Southern States—History—19th century—Fiction. | LCSH: Southern
States—Race relations—History—19th century—Fiction. | LCSH: Southern
States—History—19th century—Fiction.
Classification: LCC PS8639.H576 I52 2023 | DDC C813/.6—dc23

Maps by Jeffrey L. Ward
Book design by Cassandra Garruzzo Mueller
Cover design by David Litman
Cover images: (silhouettes), (woman's face) PeopleImages / Getty Images; (woman)
Magdalena Russocka / Trevillion Images; (grass plants) George Peters / Getty Images

Printed in the United States of America

1st Printing

Penguin
Random House
VIKING CANADA

For Lyris.

I got to be quite hardy—quite used to water and bushwhacking; so that by the time I got to Canada, I could handle an axe, or hoe, or anything.

MRS. JOHN LITTLE

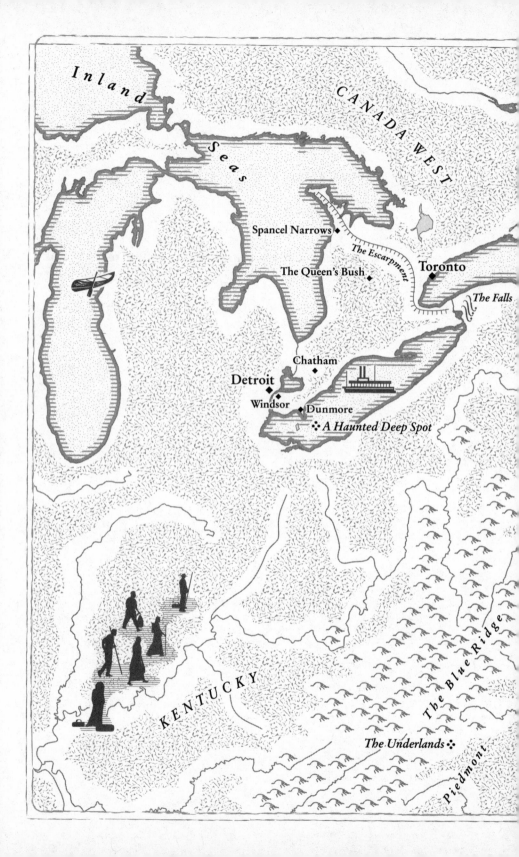

Montreal

N

Atlantic Ocean

New York

Washington

The Tidewater

Chesapeake Bay

The Rappahannock

Piedmont

KEY
◆ Cities ◆ Towns ⬧ Sites of Legend

To Africa Soil ⟶

To the Antilles

© 2022 Jeffrey L. Ward

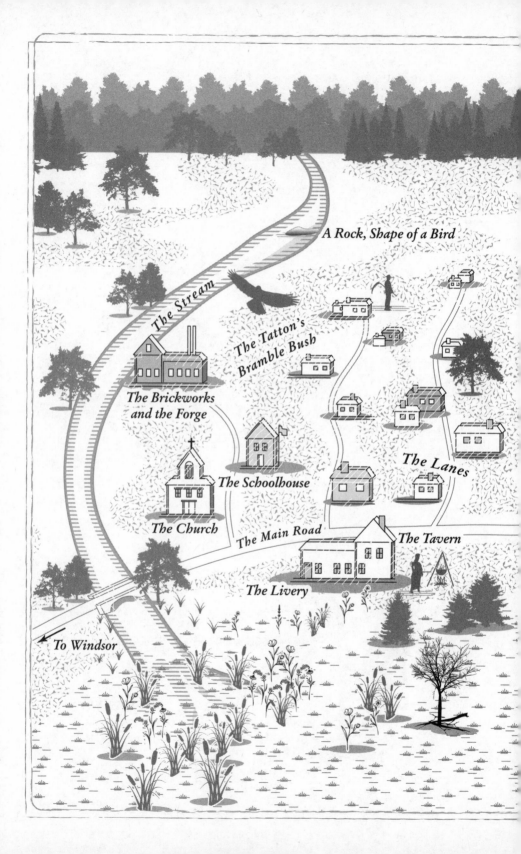

In The
Upper
Country

Prologue

A pirate on the inland sea took me south.

"It's a thing to behold," he told me. "In truth I hadn't seen free country till I saw that. You been to coloured church before, yes, but has your grain known a Negro gristmill? No. Not unless you been there. The ironmasters, the schoolteachers, even the dogs; all coloured. And the runaways flood in like spring and summer rains. Hobbling, mind you; running, holding their wounds, blood in their eyes. There in New Canaan or Dunmore, Buxton or up in the Queen's Bush. There to rest their cracked feet. Heal unseamed wounds. They have time there, at long last; doctoring sometimes, but mostly just time, and bush-wild medicine from a hand like yours. And once healed, I tell you, in those towns they have a grace in the way they walk . . . like they know for certain that they reached where they meant to reach.

"If I would be an honest man," the pirate said to me, "I'd make my life in such country. Glory and the promised land, no?"

I'm sure I scoffed. Even then, I had seen enough to know that behind every glorious thing is a whole mess of trouble.

Chapter I

DUNMORE, JULY 1859

It was dusk, and I muttered curses to myself as I made my way down the muddy green lane. Just minutes earlier, it seemed, I'd been tired and keen to finish my day with some stew and warm bread; some idle chitchat in the rocking chair, perhaps. Yet instead there I was, trodding like a fool through the mire and the quickening dark.

Mine was an unusual profession for a young woman. In Spancel Narrows, where I was born, there was a kind old bachelor named Samuel Frost, who loved hosting his coloured neighbours; many a night we brought our suppers down to his estate, dined at his great table, and then sat at the hearth listening to the old-timers. And for years, three mornings every week, my mother would hurry me along through the woods, and I would join Frost in his study while she cooked and cleaned. There, I left behind the paltry education of the crowded schoolhouse, and under his careful tutelage I learned properly to read, write, and tally accounts. I didn't realize until many years later—until I got to Dunmore, in fact—what a gift he and my mother had given me.

His teaching gave me sovereignty in my work. My employer, Arabella, would be off for days to her meetings and speaking engagements with the True Bands and the congregations as far off as Toronto; as far off as New York even. After a while it was decided I would stay at the house. There were five others there when Arabella was gone. Her brother worked days in the swamp, and he had three young children to whom he had the will, if not the time, to attend. The children's mother had not survived their escape. Their grandmother Velora used to look after the young ones, but she had begun to lose her hold on memory. She took to hiding food in corners and under loose floorboards, and dinner wouldn't be made when the brother came home from the swamp and the children from school. They would smell the food days later when it began to rot, and the children would hold their noses at one another and titter about "Granny's stinkers." Arabella would quell any such teasing if she heard it. She understood that Velora's forgotten caches were the resurfacing of an old practice: as a young slave woman she'd made a habit of secreting away meat and provisions for her family in the field.

As Arabella will often remind me, she considered me sent from above—even though my arrival in Dunmore was thought to be strange (for I came from the north when all others came southerly). Stranger still that I could read and write better than most men, coloured or white.

"I asked the Lord for a man and he gave me a hand," she would say, and wink.

So it was that I came to tend the Brimmer household. And

when Arabella returned from sojourning, her shoulders struggling to remain upright, we would spend hours by the fire, talking low beneath the snores of the household and the meandering footsteps of Velora. We'd crush mint in jars of tavern moonshine and Arabella would recline on her chair and rub the heels of her hands into her temples and burrow her fingers into her hair. She would speak quietly; hushed musings interrupted by her chuckles and sighs. I would listen. I considered these soft ramblings the addenda to her notes detailing the struggles of fugitives, the battles of abolitionists, and the news from lands near and far.

And after a while, invariably, she would give me a look—half grimace, half weary smile. "It's no easy task," she would say. "No easy task to show the world our worth."

I listened and I wrote. The next day I would look to my scribbles and I would write again. When I was done I would send my parcel to the editor in Windsor to be compiled with the articles from other contributors, and the following week we would see the newspaper in the store, or better, clutched in the hands of men and women squinting beneath caps and brightly hued head wraps, spelling out words as they learned to be free men.

By Arabella's account, sales for *The Coloured Canadian* began as a pittance; like most small newspapers, it seemed unlikely that the endeavour would survive. But by the time I arrived in Dunmore, the paper was becoming increasingly profitable. Whether this was due to donations from wealthy abolitionists or to the swelling ranks of fugitives eager to read, I did not inquire, nor did I care. She had enough to pay me well; enough too to give generously to the True Band of the church, which served as Dunmore's hub for the Underground Railroad. She never flaunted this generosity, but it was known, and she was adored for it. At True Band events, new and old arrivals to Dunmore were reminded of that special miracle whereby a slave with nothing in the world could become a man with a house, food for the winter, and work; there was always work hewing and digging in the swamp, and as a government contract this earned a man more money in a month than he had seen in his life and for labour that wasn't half as grueling as what he was used to. What a feeling, to work in free country; to move to the harmonizing rumble and trill of voices, and to see faces unified in the sweat and toil, not of terror, but of purpose.

So it was my lot as Arabella's hand that we came to need each other. She laboured tediously over writing. She worried too much about how her words would sound once read aloud, and whether people would think what she meant for them to think. I, on the other hand, did not have the virtue to care what people thought, nor the will to ask. That was Arabella's gift. She had the touch. The softening of the brow that said: I know what you have lived, and your words are sacred to me. Her high African cheekbones reminded folk of every slave woman who had ever inspired a dream of dignity in them. I, on the other hand, with my applewood skin, saucy tongue, and warring glares, tended to inspire at best a vengeful desire, and at worst, fragile condescension. All this was fine by me. I didn't think much of zeal, for I had never seen it last. I was content to be the unchurched high yellow girl who tends the Brimmer house, and no one quite knows where she comes from (though all know what is implied in that lack of knowledge), but she is there, and Arabella is probably looking out for the poor, bush-wild thing. And so I minded my household tasks. I would cook and clean until I could not put off the writing any longer, and then I would take up my station in the study.

Additionally, not as a general practice but as peculiar occasion would have it, I would be called upon to heal. Mostly this meant preparing poke salad for a child in need of deworming, or a brew of scouring rush for old folk who complained of weak bones. There were several women and men in Dunmore who were root doctors with knowledge of potions as well as poisons, so I was not overly unique. But few solicited me openly, for although Dunmore was known as the witch town, it tried awfully hard not to be. Here and there I tended more serious wounds: I had once reset and splinted the broken leg of a child who suffered a kick from a mule; twice I had stitched the cut wounds of drunken men who had brawled outside the tavern; and another time I had used pipe smoke of mullein and hops to calm a young woman who had been found screaming like a banshee in the swamp.

And so I was known, which brings me back to the business that had me scrambling down the wretched green lane. It was dusk, as I said. And I had been sent for. Young Jim burst into the house after supper, as I was reading over Arabella's latest batch of notes.

"Lensinda!" said Jim as he rushed into the study, not even

bothering to remove his shoes or properly close the front door, and the mosquitoes were always thick and fierce as the sun went down. I glared at him for that, and saw him wither, grasping nervously at his long chest. He was not yet a man, and I was normally quite fond of him, as most were; he was uncommonly bright and sober for his age, albeit a bit daft to household decency.

"There's a man," he blurted. "There's a man shot in the green lane."

I raised my eyebrows. We had heard two shots, about half an hour past. Unusual to hear gunfire so close, but not exceedingly unusual, as there were always people hungry for wildfowl. I capped my ink and rose to gather my things.

"Shut the door, Jim," I said to him.

"Simeon says to come, and quick." He spoke with hushed urgency as he fumbled at the threshold of the study. Fanny, the youngest Brimmer child, had come from the living room to stand and look into the study, cocking her head to one side.

"The *front* door, Jim," I said curtly, and he jumped and scurried past Fanny to the swinging front door and closed it, keeping his hand on it.

"I'm coming," I reassured him, "but no need to let the gallinippers eat the house alive."

I grabbed my pouch and went to the door, patting the silent Fanny on the shoulder as I passed her. I reached for my cloak. It was July, and the cloak would be hot despite the setting of the sun, but still a worthwhile protection from the bugs.

Jim waited with one hand on the doorknob, skittish, not meeting my eyes. I moved quickly but methodically, stooping to tie my boots tight.

I felt Jim's urgency, but I had questions that I could not put off, even as we made our way briskly out of the house and into the sounds of the evening on the village lane: the crickets, the clatter of dishes in washbasins, and music (someone was plucking up a banjo and moaning in harmony, a woman's voice trilling along and then laughing).

"Who is this man, Jim?" I asked, trotting to keep up with his long stride.

"I don't know," he said, and he pulled at his collar and glanced at the houses on either side of the lane.

"A man," he said quietly. "A white man who rode in with an Indian."

It took a moment for this to sink in before I stopped straight in my path. Jim was too preoccupied to notice, and for a moment I watched his back as my mind lurched over this strange piece of news.

"Boy!" I said, and Jim turned around, his face contorted.

"Don't yell so loud; Simeon says—"

I planted my feet in the soft ground. "Jim, I will raise all hell right here in front of your mama house if you don't tell me what you fetching me for."

"Sinda, I got to go, Simeon—"

He cut himself short when he caught my glare.

"Please," he said, softly now, his eyes darting around the lane again. The twang of the banjo kept on, and more sounds of supper joined in: chatter, water being drawn from a barrel, and in the slight distance, the bark and howl of the dogs. Near us, an old woman sat on a front porch, her face wreathed in smoke from a long pipe. It was loud enough, but the lanes of Dunmore were always watching, always listening. Jim had been directed to be discreet, and if he had cause for discretion, then this was indeed the worst place to talk.

"Please," he said again, with a pained expression. "In the livery," he whispered. And he tilted his head in the direction of the stable, beside the tavern on the main road.

I squinted a warning look at him and saw him flinch. He had been warned of me. Good, I thought. And I commenced to walk briskly to the stable. Jim breathed a sigh of relief and hurried alongside me.

Simeon was perhaps the only man for whom I would have come when called, especially under such dubious circumstances. And what could be more suspect? Granted, it was not uncommon for either whites or Indians to come through Dunmore. Indian men traded game meats, basketry, and leather goods for tools at the forge or drink from the tavern. A woman had once made an appearance to search out and shame the Negro father of her children in front of the man's wife and family—at congregation, no less, much to the everlasting horror and titillation of the churchgoing folk. But none of this spoke to the possibility of a white man and an Indian together; I could not find the logic of it. Perhaps the white man was a missionary on his way to the nearest Indian village. And the Indian himself—a protégé? But who in all hell would shoot a missionary? And what a bloody mess the whole town would be in if that were the case. I quickened my step.

The tavern was a two-story frame building clad in grey cedar that glowed with light from the ground level and hummed with some chatter. Swamp crew workers without wives dined here. Jim and I skirted the tavern and went into the stable. The stable boy was nowhere in sight; the rascal had probably run off to see his sweetheart in the woods, or to get a hot supper from his mother down the lane. We entered and went to Simeon's quarter horse. She was a big blue-roan whose haunch shivered as we neared. She looked at me with a large, warm eye, and I put my hand out to meet her muzzle.

"Tell me what you know," I said to Jim as he set about saddling the horse.

Jim was deft and quick in his movements as he fastened the girth. Still, I could hear the nervous quaver in his voice.

"Round end of day," he began in a near breathless whisper, "this white man and Indian ride right up to the farm."

"Did anyone else see them?" I asked.

"Probably," said Jim, "but if they did they maybe figured they was just passing through town."

He glanced at me warily, and I encouraged him with a nod. He went on:

"Me and the lads were out in the field digging drainage pipe, when the two of them ride up to the house. We seen they seen us. Didn't think much of it—figured they were old friends of Simeon. However, soon after, we start to get the feeling—well, Weems start to get the feeling that something ain't right. Can't quite say what it is, though he never can put words to it, but he almost always is right. Kept looking over his shoulder at the house until Humphrey and me start to feel the hair rise on our necks too. It was too quiet. But none of us rightly knew how to act, except to keep working till sundown, as we usually do. And so we did. And just as we was heading back to wash up, we notice a commotion by the front porch. Someone was running into the corn, and we start to hurrying across the field to see what was the matter. And then bam! One shot go off, and we stop and crouch. But we see Cassi run into the house and come out holding that rifle and we decide we got to at least run to her. Sure enough, bam! Another shot, from the corn. And we reach the porch and Cassi tell us we must go find Simeon, she afraid he might get shot. And we start to hollerin' for Sim, and rushing into the corn to find him. Finally we see some movement in the stalks and come upon him and he standing there and at his feet the white man just tumbling about on the ground in his own blood."

By this time Jim had saddled the horse, and he began to lead her out of the stable. I followed, frustrated; the story made less and less sense the more he got to telling it. Did Simeon shoot a man? Surely not—I couldn't imagine it.

"And well?" I said, hurrying behind Jim, my hand at the horse's flank. "You ain't told me nothing; *what* happened?"

"I don't know, Sinda!" he said roughly, raising his voice for the first time. He turned to me and I saw the twitching torment in his brow. Of course; he was afraid. I softened my look, feeling a twinge of motherliness toward him. He was just a boy, after all, despite his long limbs. And he had just been reminded how easily the blood coursing through those limbs could be spilled.

"I'm to make haste to Chatham to fetch a constable," said Jim. "I can drop you at the entrance of the green lane, but I gotta go from there."

"What happened to the Indian?" I asked him.

"He gone, into the bush."

It was a strange tale indeed.

Jim mounted the roan, extended his hand, and freed the stirrup for me to step in and pull myself up behind him. He took off and we rode east down the main road, into the darkening dusk. The dogs yipped at us as we passed the kennel. We heard the bellow of a man to silence them. The village fell behind us and was replaced by the rushing field of cattails on one side and the behemoth oaks on the other.

Jim rode well; he was a rangy, strong boy with grace and purpose in his movements. I smelled sweat from the still-damp shirt on his back, and the cedar pomade his mother had made popular among many of the young men, still alive and wafting from the curls at the back of his neck.

He slowed where the main road cracked open to the green lane; discernible because this was where the marshes thinned and Simeon's fields began. Jim leaned his head back and gave a loud whoop—a call, I guessed, to Simeon, wherever he was across the fields. Jim hopped off and ran a pace, like a crane landing from flight. He offered his hand to help me dismount, and for the first time that evening, I felt afraid. Walking down this path in the quickening dark, someone shot down ahead of me; who knew what villain was still on the prowl?

"Am I in danger, Jim?" I asked.

He looked at me with warmth in his eyes. "No, Simeon says there ain't no more danger, and he will meet you along the lane. But I can stay with you if you like."

"That's all right," I said, and patted his bony shoulder. "You'd best go on about your task."

Simeon was one of the few men I trusted. He was sober and sound, and his word was enough.

Jim nodded and swung his long body up and onto the quarter horse and cantered away. The sound of hooves yielded quickly to the vast rustling of the wind in the foliage, and to the clamour of frogs.

I set myself to the green lane. It was said that in ancient times this trail was the extension of the main road. The main road, now a wide trackway of compacted dirt, wood, and stones, was an old portage route, trod for centuries by the moccasins of Indians as they stepped heavy with the weight of their loaded vessels. And as I walked along the green lane and glanced back at the last of the setting sun winking through the trunks of white cedar, I could see it clearly. The green lane girdled the swamp, and as cumbersome as it was to walk through its mud and mosquitoes, it wended the most direct passage around the far deeper trouble of the wetlands.

Simeon was the only one to farm more than a small patch of garden in Dunmore. His ground was black and rich and far too wet for most to manage. Before the contract for the swamp clearing came in, most in Dunmore had subsisted on hunting, labouring on the great western railroad or on farms, in buildings, or in kitchens in other towns, and eventually through their own enterprise, as with the tavern, the forge, and the brickworks. Folk knew how to dig a rock drain—else there wouldn't be any houses at all. But to dig a ditch around one's abode is one thing; to drain whole fields properly is another thing entirely. Simeon had done so through careful planning, contracting the men at the brickworks to make him a great quantity of pipe and tile. He studied the land well and dug for drain tile so that his fields were just wet enough to keep the farm lush with Indian corn, rye, peas, greens, and potatoes. His hogs rooted through a large swath of the swamp that he had fenced for them, and they were fat and vigourous.

Simeon had arrived alone when Dunmore itself was in its early days, and he worked tirelessly for his hogs: fencing, gathering slop, building the smokehouse. Folk were happy to buy from him, and he never stopped studying that land. As soon as he raised his barn he hosted the corn-shucking bee that had become one of the most anticipated events of autumn. Each year the place was full of chatter, laughter, music, and a mountain of corn that youngsters would climb despite scoldings from their mothers. Outside, folk would lounge by the pit roast of several hogs dripping grease into the embers, and a massive cauldron of corn soup. The shucking would go from dusk to sunup the following day.

All that to say, by the time I arrived in Dunmore, Simeon

was a cherished denizen of town, and supplied a good many of the village and indeed the surrounding counties with the provisions that folk did not manage to grow for themselves. Cassi arrived more recently, and was shunned by the single women of Dunmore for her marriage to Sim. As Velora will attest, there were women laying hexes on Cassi left and right. There was even one who tried to nudge her as she jumped the broom in an attempt to have her garment touch the ground and damn her marriage to misfortune. But Cassi wasn't no fool, and she and Sim did well by each other. Though they were too old to have children, they were rightly parents to many sons through the work they gave to generations of Dunmore boys such as Jim, whose own father had drunk himself to death. Yes, Simeon was a self-made man, and in my view, one of the few who did not suffer from having something to prove.

I was not walking long on the lane before he found me. He held a lantern that I smelled before I saw it. The aroma of geranium washed over me like a memory. Then the light, yellow as teeth, came in slivers out of the corn, and I saw Simeon's cloaked figure step lightly through the squash patch until he reached the fence and lifted a beam out of place to beckon me through.

He looked solemn, especially under his dark hood, and the worn creases of his face were taut with concern.

"Thanks for coming, Lensinda," he said as I ducked under the fence beam, my gaze to the ground to avoid stepping on the gourds at my feet, already grown as big as skulls.

I nodded and patted Simeon on the arm.

"Show me to him," I said plainly, and Simeon turned and walked. I followed his cloak into the corn.

The white man was slumped on his side, curled up like a child asleep. The corn stalks around him had been broken low. Some were strewn fully on the ground, and others leaned above him like the ruins of an old shelter. The other two farmhands, Weems and Humphrey, were there, still in their sun hats. One stood as tall and lanky as Jim; the other crouched squat. They murmured to each other in the dark, as if they didn't want the dead man before them to hear. He was sorely dead, I smelled already, though I went directly to him to be sure, and leaned and put my hand gently on his neck.

"Bring your lantern low, Sim," I said.

Simeon grunted and knelt beside me, and the ground became vivid with light. The man was large, despite the smallness of his pose. One of his hands lay on the cloth of his tunic above a thick leather belt packed with a row of cartridges and the buckled sheath of a bowie knife. The man's stubbled face was purpling and his teeth showed through a lax parting in his lips. I prodded him until my fingers found a wound through the bloody cotton at the crook of his neck. It was a messy tear of flesh and bone, already cool. There was another too, lower: at the top of his belly, underneath his hand. The hole was cleaner, though his stomach had begun to bloat. I could smell the iron of his blood, the rank stink of his excrement, and the hot, sour scent of entrails, wafting.

I stood slowly, still looking at the ground around him. The

land had swallowed his blood. A coil of ship rope lay near his head, looking clean and elegant.

"Sim," I said, not even bothering to look up, "this man dead as can be."

Simeon grunted again, still crouching. "Well, I suppose it ain't much surprise," he said. "Shall we leave him and wait in the house?"

"Leave him?" I said. "Like hell. We leave him and who knows how much of him will still be here before the constable arrives?"

Simeon gave a rumbling chuckle and shrugged.

Dunmore, for all its aspirations, was yet wild. Dead things did not lie peacefully on the land for long. The beasts of the swamp and surrounding forest were always near. And hungry. Once, a boy wandered away from the village to play in the swamp. He must have stumbled and hit his head and drowned in the bog. By the time he was found the next day, the only clue to recognize him was the size of his bones. Perhaps it was a bear, or a hungry wolf. There were even tales of a giant boar that would sniff out and eat any half-dead thing in the swamp. Sim scoffed at the whole thing, saying that there wasn't any hogs in the swamp save for his, and they lived too well and happy to be roaming for carrion. But blood-hungry boar or not, he knew better than to leave flesh out at night.

"Well," he said, "let's pick him up, lads. Take him to the cellar."

The young men groaned queasily, but set to it alongside Simeon, crouching around the body.

"Here, let me help," I said, and the lads looked up at me in surprise.

"I'll take the lantern," I said to Simeon, and winked at him.

One of the lads shook his head and the other kissed his teeth, but Sim grunted and I saw a half smile on his face as he handed the lantern to me.

"Oh, now you wouldn't let a lady do something wicked like that," I scolded as they hoisted the body. I scanned the ground where it had lain. There was nothing but churned, wet soil and the rope. I squatted down and laid the lantern on the ground. The rope was three coils of thick, course hemp. Without knowing fully why, I picked it up and almost stumbled out of balance from the fullness of its weight. I stood, hefting the rope in my right hand and grasping the lantern in my left, and I followed the men through the corn.

As we made our way, I noted the lay of Simeon's land; it had been some time since I had been there. The house was a clean arrangement of clapboard and shingles. It looked hallowed, illuminated in the dark with lantern light glowing from the front windows onto a wide porch. The porch was portioned by slender roundwood pillars crowned with cornice brackets and running trim. Under the oak tree in front of the house were two tethered horses, pulling lazily at tufts of grass. Behind them, almost indiscernible in the dark, was a stagecoach.

We made our way around the house, past the privy, the brick smokehouse, and the well out back. The root cellar and the small cabin perched above it sat nestled at the back of the yard, where the cleared land ended and the grass and bush grew full between the oaks of the savannah.

Once the boys had lowered the body into the root cellar and

closed and latched the door, Simeon went above to the cabin. He knocked and entered it. Candlelight shone dimly from the crack in the door.

I began to get an eerie tingle up my spine, for it was only then that it dawned on me that Simeon was hosting fugitives. I glanced at the lads but they were bent and huffing from the exertion of lifting deadweight across the grounds and did not meet my eyes.

I heard the mumble of voices from inside the cabin, and my mind strained to figure how this development swayed the mystery at hand. I had forgotten about the fugitive presence—one might think it a strange thing to forget in a town of runaways, but it is really quite natural. They came so frequently and were so quickly absorbed into the woodwork.

Some towns were robust enough to allow for the development of boardinghouses, often for the express purpose of providing rooms for runaways. But these towns were regular towns—not backwoods Negro villages. In Dunmore, there were a few citizens with the means to host fugitives for as long as was needed. The length of the stay simply depended on the case. Many fugitives were just passing through, usually on their way somewhere else: Buxton; Chatham, Hamilton, or Toronto if they had crossed at Detroit; New Canaan, Amherstburg, or Windsor if they were heading west from Niagara. An all-Negro town seemed a sensible place to rest for a few days—sensible enough to come south off the main highway into swamp country and see what the legends were about. Some folk stayed long enough to work up the will to travel back south to rescue or petition for the freedom of loved ones they'd left behind. They might ride back down the Underground Railroad with the help of the True Band's network in Michigan, New York, Indiana, Ohio, and beyond. It was rare that we would see them again. Other fugitives would have a relation or a friend who was already established in Dunmore. In that case they would stay with them until they either wanted or needed their own home. And often enough, even if they had no previous relation, fugitives would decide to stay on in Dunmore. The True Band would get the money together to purchase a lot and gather the men to raise a house with a hearth and the women to stock it with quilts and food for a season. With all the volunteer labour and the low cost of swampland, the debt for a house was quite modest, and could be easily paid off in a few years by any working man or woman.

In the interim between arrival and whatever came next, fugitives would be put up with someone who had the extra room and provisions. Simeon had built the cabin atop the root cellar, in the shade and privacy of the oak savannah, for the purpose of hosting Dunmore's new arrivals. The cabin was a simple, well-built place with a potbelly stove in the centre that had been donated by a visiting abolitionist. There was a washbasin and several beds, and from inside one could hear the song of birds and the wind through the swaying oak, all around.

The last drove of runaways had arrived only three days earlier. They came by steamer with Hamish, a merchant and friend of the town who made his route between Milwaukee and Buffalo, stopping at Detroit, ferrying fugitives whenever he could. I hadn't seen the arrivals yet but had heard tell from Velora, who despite her ageing memory always availed herself of the town news, and would repeat the peculiar details to herself and anyone who would listen. So it was that I learned that there were six in the new group: two young women, one a master seamstress who had manufactured a set of disguises for the group that helped them stay a step ahead of the telegraph, and the other the young daughter of the older man, who was an ironmaster born in Africa; a man, younger, who was very good with horses; also the horseman's cousin, who was incredibly handsome, with eyes the dark green of a moonlit river (this according to several young Dunmore women), but who was afflicted with a terrible sadness and would not yet talk; and most peculiarly, a very old woman, older than any known to make the journey. The group was from a hemp farm in Kentucky and had made their way up through Ohio, following the iron forges as some do; they had no map, but they knew to find north, and the old man could smell out the vein of iron in the ground, so that by and by they found the next forge to rest easy for a night or two. The ironmasters are often very kindly to runaways, and will pay fairly with wages as well as a discreet place in the woods to hide out and rest. Thus the group travelled for most of their voyage by foot, through the woods. When in towns, they posed first as a minstrel crew, then as a band of decrepit beggars in the streets of Detroit. Hamish, bless his heart, had taken them at a moment's notice, and once on the open water they rode like kings atop the lumber piles. The crew dropped them where Lake Erie meets the swamp at the end of the green lane, and they trudged the path all the way up to Dunmore, where Simeon had been the first to see them.

The ironmaster and his daughter were staying with a relative of theirs on the north end of town; the horseman and his handsome cousin, with the Tattons, across the bramble bush; and the seamstress and the old woman, out at Simeon's cabin.

It was from this cabin, above the root cellar that now lodged a dead man, that Simeon emerged after a few moments, shaking his head and sighing.

I quelled my impulse to ask—I knew he would speak when the moment was right. I was beginning to get a feeling that I was not there in my capacity as a healer, but for another reason that was only beginning to dawn on me.

Simeon led us wordlessly toward his house, only a few paces away, but it felt like a long walk in the dark of nightfall, hearing the grunts and snorts of the hogs settling into their sty some way to the south, the burgeoning chorus of savannah crickets behind us, and the burps and yelps of the frogs in the swamp in front of us.

The lads stayed outside by the well in front of the smokehouse to wash up and change, and Sim and I stepped onto his wide porch, where we stooped to remove our muddy boots. His wife, Cassi, bustled out to fuss over us and then ushered us in to sit around the broad oak table in their living room. She poured us cordials and laid a plate on the table with crackers, onions, and cheese. I held my mug and watched swollen raspberries and chopped lemon balm swirl and dance lazily in the liquid.

"You hungry, Sinda darling?" Cassi cupped my shoulder and pinched me absentmindedly, like a mother.

"No, thank you, Cassi," I said, and took a sip of the tea before placing my mug on the table.

Simeon sat still with his broad shoulders back against the chair. His thick, callused fingers moved lightly around his mouth, and he gazed hard into the riverlike grains of his oak table, his mind somewhere else entirely.

Cassi sat next to him and took his hand and pressed into it, worry creased between her eyes.

He blinked and turned to kiss her hand, smiling weakly.

The room was lit with the warm, pulsing light of several lamps, and the sounds of the fields and the swamp outside were muffled by the tightly joined walls.

"Sim," I began gently, when I could no longer resist, "what in the hell went on down here?"

He chuckled and wheezed a long sigh, lightly bumping the table with his fist before working his jaw as if trying to find the words.

"Beware a dangerous tale," he murmured, meeting my eyes. "It is a knife that must be used, or left to lay."

He raised a brow in expectation. Simeon was a solemn man, and his gravitas and proverbs made most shrink. My sharp glare of impatience was all the answer he needed. He chuckled again, nodded, sipped from his mug, and then began in earnest:

Round about the end of day, I was out back putting new shingles on the smokehouse. Lads were out in the field. I heard hoof steps coming down the lane, and walked round front to see who it was. Well, wouldn't there be a man in a mail coach drawn by two horses and another man on horseback making their bumpy way down the green lane. Now, anyone from around here would know I ain't used that lane yet this year. With all the rain we had, I've taken to going around the new path through the savannah. You seen what it is out there in that green lane; only a man on a mission would be riding down that ditch in his right mind. And since they were using it they were not only men but strangers too. Musta been looking for some money, I thought. Now, it ain't tax season, and it's been over a decade since I owed any man a cent, so I stepped right in the house to get the rifle. You recall those highway robbers that folk in the county was talking about two summers ago? Well I know *they* got taken in but perhaps someone else caught the idea. Looked like both these boys were armed, and something in the way they trotted down the lane—not riding up on us in a gallop or nothing, but they weren't wasting no time neither. And the one in the back was looking all around, like he was scouting for something. The lads were out in the field like I said, so I ain't had time to get to them, and I only had but one rifle, so I gave it to Cassi, who got a better eye than me anyhow. I tell you, Sinda, you should see this woman shoot a corn-hunting coon from the porch with only the light of a quarter moon to see by—a thing of beauty, I tell you.

Said I: "Don't kill nobody lest they draw on me now, hear, 'cause it's likely some travelling salesman or someone who lost."

"If they lost why they ain't stopped in the village, then?" said Cassi.

Well, I didn't rightly know the answer to that, so I just told her that whatever the case, I'd go talk to them, and she was to spot me from the porch.

So I went out to meet them at the lane. Walking out I couldn't see the lads through the corn but I could hear they stopped digging and the man coming up in the stagecoach waved to me as he neared the entrance at the fence.

"Ho, my good man," he said to me, and right off I heard from the turn of his voice this man was from south. Way south. He was burly, but he jumped down from that carriage swift as a cat and extended his hand to me well before I reached him. Pelham something-or-other was his name, he said, and pardon the intrusion. He was speaking to me real fancy, with a hint of a grin on his face, like he knew how unusual it was for a southern white man to be speaking to me like that.

"Myself and my companion," he said, shaking my hand real firm, "we've come up from Ohio on business, and well, as you can see, we came off the main route to get acquainted with the landscape."

He waved around with a big smile, as if he was showing me land I ain't been on for half a lifetime.

Said he: "When I saw your farm, I said to my partner David: Now I bet you that gentleman has some hogs, what say you we ask to purchase some of his bacon and stock up on our road supplies?"

Now, Sinda, I looked up at David on his horse and saw for his long hair and dark skin that David was sure enough Indian, and more than that, David was looking real hard over the land, and ain't seemed the least bit interested in bacon, though he did nod and grunt and give his belly a half-hearted pat.

I ain't a man to mince words, Sinda. I looked back to Pelham.

"What type of business have you coming off the main route so?" I asked.

"Why, we're lumbermen, of course," said Pelham, and grinned again. "And y'all have some fine big trees around here."

This was plausible, I supposed. It wouldn't have been the first time surveyors came through, though it would be the first time to my knowledge they crossed the border to do so. Ain't no shortage of trees in the States, last I was there. Still, I nodded to Pelham.

"Well, allow me to show y'all what we got in the smoke-house, then," I said to them.

"Oh, that would be real fine," Pelham replied.

I began down the path to the house and Pelham kept talking, asking my name and the breed of hogs, the quality of the soil, and the yields of corn. I answered him simply, as it began to occur to me that the cabin and root cellar they might not have seen from the lane, concealed as it was by the trees, but they sure enough would see if we went out back to the smoke shack. I wasn't keen to invite them in the house, but figured it would be better than giving them the run of the place. So I showed them to the tree out front where they could tether the horses.

By this time, we could of course see Cassi, standing stock-still on the porch in perfect form, with that long baker's rifle trained right on Pelham.

"Whoa," he said. "That looks like a fearsome Amazonian, Simeon. Is she yours?"

He winked at me and then looked back to Cassi.

"We come in peace, Hippolyta," he said loudly, spreading his arms wide.

Cassi did not move. I smiled despite myself. My Amazonian wife.

"That is a fine gun you have," he continued. "My father had one like it."

This, in a tone I could not identify as gibe or genuine sentiment.

He slowly spread the lapels of his coat, revealing his belt, which held cartridges but no pistol.

"I am unarmed, madam. My rifle is in the carriage, and my companion David will stow his there as well."

With this he glanced at David, who nodded and dismounted.

Pelham continued, with one hand still raised.

"We only carry," he said, "to ward off thieves on the highway. We are simple surveyors, madam, and mean you no trouble."

Cassi said nothing, nor did she move. I let the silence lie another moment before interjecting.

"It's all right, Cass," I said, nodding slightly to her. "These fellas are interested in some pork. Why don't you head on to the smokehouse and see about some back bacon?"

I walked up to the porch, and the men stayed and tethered their horses behind me.

"It's all right, honey," I said softly to her, so they wouldn't hear. "I'll take that." I put my hand out for the rifle.

She lowered the rifle and looked at me hard for a moment, her brown eyes full of feeling that she wasn't 'bout to let loose.

"It's all right," I said again. "Ain't nothing."

Finally she placed the barrel of the gun in my hand and started down the stairs and around the house.

Her quick march knocked a rhythm on the two porch steps before the ground silenced her feet, and all I could hear was the brush of her calico dress on the grass. I was sad I couldn't do more to comfort her. She has a powerful intuition, and feeling that come up on her like a tide.

"Oh," I called after her. "And a bucket of water for the horses too, Cass."

She glanced over her shoulder at me but didn't reply.

"Come on up inside, then," I said to the men.

"Why, thank you," said Pelham, and stepped toward the porch with a leather satchel in his hand. David stayed behind him.

"Come on up, man," I said to David. "Y'all can at least have something cool to drink."

"Oh," said Pelham, pausing to look up at me from the first porch step. "David is perfectly content out here with the horses.

"You know his kind," he went on. "Never happier than in the trees and under the open sky."

David nodded and patted the side of the oak tree, and took a pipe out from his coat pocket.

This, Sinda, was the last clue I needed. This fool was just gonna sit next to the carriage and pretend like I forgot he just loaded it full of guns?

"Now David," I said, nice and loud. The rifle was still in my hands, though at ease. "At least rest yourself on the porch, man."

"Oh, don't mind me," he said, and lit a pipe.

By this time, Pelham was up on the porch with me, and extended a hand to usher me toward the door. I looked at his hand pointing toward the door of this house I built. My grip tightened on the barrel of the rifle, though he was too close for me to use it on him if I needed. He was a big man indeed, and I could see his face from the corner of my eye, a head higher than my own. I did not face him square, though, and instead looked out to David.

"David, I won't have no guest to my house sit amongst horses like a beast."

Pelham chuckled.

David nodded, smiled, and brushed the dust from his pant legs before getting up and making his way over to the porch. There was a darkening in the moments it took him to reach us. I listened to his footfalls on the grass, and to the long whine of the crickets. I could feel Pelham's gaze on me, and I thought to meet it, but I did not. I looked instead out over the corn and to the swamp, shimmering with the end-of-day heat. When David reached us I pointed at one of the rocking chairs. He sat, and struck a match, lighting up his pipe again, and then rocked and smiled at me, as if this would please me.

I grunted and went to the front door and held it open for Pelham, who nodded and stepped inside. I followed.

"Why, a lovely cabin," he said, turning around. "A lovely cabin indeed."

It was bright inside. The setting sun pierced the front windows, lighting the dust and casting long shadows from the yarrow and lupine on the table, and from the pots that hung above the hearth.

Right then, Cassi returned, marching in the front door past me and Pelham. She spanked the bacon on the table. Pelham regarded her with a curious half smile. I returned the rifle to its nook in the closet.

Pelham went to the table and opened the button of his satchel.

"Thank you so very much," he said, and he took a seat and began sifting through papers in the bag.

"Join me, please," he implored, though without looking up from his task. "Cass, how much would I owe you for this?"

He spoke her name like he was an old visiting friend. She held her composure but did not look at him, nor did she sit.

"That there's a gift," she said, looking straight out the front window. "And in return you can go on now."

I could hear from her words that her breath was starting to take her over, though she stood straight and tall.

"Why, Cass, whatever do you mean?" said Pelham, his brows creased in polite concern.

I sat at the head of the table, where I could see out the front window through David's tobacco smoke pluming above the rocking wicker chair. Pelham turned to me, as if to ask me to accord with his confusion.

"Now, look here," I told him. "You can go ahead and stop with that. You ain't no Ohio businessman on the hunt for Canadian bacon. We know a man-thief when we see one."

I was expecting this to clean the grin from his face, but it did no such thing. Instead, he leaned back in his chair.

"Man-thief," he said, and smiled wider. "Now, I assure you my role is not so unscrupulous. I am merely an officer of the court."

He dug his hand into his satchel and drew it up and pressed two silver coins on the table, pushing them toward Cassi with his fingers.

"That is for the bacon, Cass," he said. "Smelling it is making me hungry already!"

He then produced a sheet of paper and placed it on the table behind the coins.

"This here is a warrant from Lincoln County, Kentucky, for the arrest of certain fugitives fleeing service, wheresoever they may be."

Now, Sinda, you know me to be a peaceful man. And as much as I have gotten over my own slave days, looking at that man put that parchment down made me feel like I was 'bout to shake; whether for anger or for fear, I couldn't much tell. All I knew was I couldn't bear to see him see me shaking, so I got up real slow and went toward the window that faced out into the back-yard, as if I couldn't be bothered to sit still and talk.

"Listen, Pelham," I said, "I know that it ain't in my power to stop you from doing what you come to do."

I reached the window, placed my hand on the sill, and rubbed my thumb against the grain.

"That there is for the courts," I said. "Last one that came up this far from the border got arrested at Windsor and caught up in a case that ended by saying y'all ain't got no right at all to take runaways. Turns out, a warrant such as that ain't good in the Queen's dominion. After a spell in jail, the last man-thief went back empty-handed with a bill of legal fees of several hundred dollars."

At this I turned back to see him still seated at my table, looking comfortable as anything.

"Given that, Pelham," I said, "my advice to you would be to go on back 'cross that border before you make too much trouble for you *and your massa.*"

The piece about the arrest I had learned from *The Coloured Canadian*, Sinda, so I had it on good authority, yet I also knew from y'all that there had been a number of kidnappings where the slave catchers hadn't been brought to justice. Of course I didn't mention that. But the rascal seemed to know anyhow, and I'll be damned if he didn't start to laugh a low rumbling laugh— made me look back out the window and grip the sill so hard I heard it creak.

"What dignity you northern folk have," he said, and he paused for a moment, as if to ponder. When he spoke again I could still hear the smile on his lips.

"Well, all men *think* they have dignity. Which is to say"—he narrowed his eyes at me; I could tell, despite not taking my gaze from that back window—"well, one might as well just say that all men have vanity. For what is dignity other than a vain performance of self-regard? Ain't that right, Cass?"

Now here, Sinda, I might have looked at him at this point. It struck me he had been taunting my wife the whole time—I might under normal circumstances have surely glared at him. Shit, under normal circumstances, I might have done a lot more than that. But I noticed, though I tried not to react at all—noticed, through the window, in the darkening backyard, the old woman, the fugitive, coming out the cabin above the root cellar. And a moment later, the seamstress behind her. I nearly choked on my breath. They had been in there all day—why in all damnation had they chosen to come out at that moment? At the moment their hunters were so close upon them? And sure enough, there was the Indian, David, stalking them like they were a couple of does upwind. I could scarce believe my eyes and had to stop myself from whipping around to look out the front window, where I would have seen nothing but the empty rocker and a few wisps of tobacco smoke lingering on the front porch. I cursed myself for having taken my sight off him, but there was naught to do but bite my tongue.

Lucky for me Cassi found her own tongue and she and this buckra had got to talking. If I had to respond to this man I damn sure would have said some foolishness, my heart had started to pound so.

"Something sure enough wrong in your soul, mister," Cassi said to him.

He chuckled again. "Oh, but I have many souls," he said.

I saw, through the twirl of glass and the fading light, that the old woman out back seemed to be talking to David. And he, though he kept approaching, seemed to be listening.

"You handle that rifle well enough," Pelham said to Cassi. "It makes me wonder, have you ever done violence, true violence, to another man?"

I heard this, but kept my eyes trained on the old woman in

the backyard. She was pointing every which way, and then again down at her feet, and she stomped the ground and stood straight, with her shoulders back. David seemed to say something in response. She listened, then shook her head.

"True violence," Pelham continued, "is the most intimate imposition on a man's life. Even more intimate, I daresay, than a lover."

David and the old woman were face-to-face by this point. His demeanour had gotten slow and gentle. He lowered his head, and she kept talking. Then, he crouched and touched the ground, glancing back at the house. I saw his jaw move as he spoke. She nodded. He rose, and she untied something from her neck and put it in his hand.

Pelham was carrying on, but the words echoed in my head without much meaning as I watched in utter disbelief as David and the old woman made their way together, back around to the front of the house. The seamstress followed.

"The soul at such a time," Pelham was saying, "is a flighty, wayward thing. Ready to be snatched."

Cassi huffed. Said she: "Well I don't suppose I done true violence to a man, but I sure enough had it done. And I sat in death. You know what that feel like? Have death quell your heart to a slow drum?"

"That," said Pelham with something like admiration in his voice, "that is true poetry, Cass. Thank you."

By this time I had lost sight of David and the two women as they passed beside the house, out of view of the back window.

I turned to face the room. My Cassi, brave woman that she

be, looking square at Pelham. And he with that handsome grin turned slow to face me, whereupon his expression sobered to something that would have been concern if it weren't so hungry.

"Why, Simeon," he said to me, "my good man, you look like you've just seen something."

I recovered my face as best I could, and went to sit at the table. But I could not come up with what to say, my mind still running to make sense of what had passed before my eyes.

"Now," said Pelham, placing his hands on the table and giving us a light smile. "I thank you both for your hospitality. What will happen presently is that I will go on out to my carriage, and from there to the cabin y'all have out back. I will take the fugitives into my custody and either you will tell me where the others are sequestered or I will go to great pains to extract that information from the ones that are here."

Cassi started breathing heavy enough that I could hear her, and Pelham looked at her with a quizzical smile, as if he ain't know what was the matter. I felt my jaw getting real steely, and I looked at this man with a hate I hoped he could feel on his flesh. He glanced at me, his smile ever present, his eyes darting up and down me, and then back at Cassi.

"You, madam, look like you know what you are doing with that musket, but you also look smart enough to know that if you draw it on me again I will acquaint you with the unforgiving speed of a breech-loading rifle, and then you and your husband and the young men out front will hear that slow drum you were talking about earlier."

With that he reached behind his back and drew a long bowie knife, bringing it to the tabletop. His thumb rubbed gently on the hilt. My own hand went slowly to the handle of the dirk that I carry with me, sheathed in my boot.

"We know where the others are," I said to him, my voice loud and grave.

I had had enough. Enough of hearing my poor wife breathing like she herself was on the run. Enough of this paddy roller's cursed grin. We're a safe house, Sinda, not a fort. I had no notion of the meaning of the strange scene I had just witnessed in the backyard. All I knew was we weren't 'bout to get in no shoot-out with no bounty hunter. I would not see my wife or those lads killed on my land. This is Canada, damn it.

"We won't hinder you," I told him. "But we will go with you, so you don't cause a fright and get somebody hurt."

"Ah," he sighed, tilting his head toward me in extravagant gratitude. "I knew you to be a man of good sense, Simeon."

"And then," I said, looking dead at him.

Pelham returned my gaze in perfect expectation.

Said I: "You know, Pelham, there's a man in town—in Dunmore—who raises hounds. Where this man was born, in Tennessee, his massa taught him how to raise a mean dog. All manner of bloodhounds, mastiffs, bulldogs, big as boars, and furious as hell. He used to teach these dogs to get mad terrible at the heels of a running coloured man. I tell you, it wouldn't matter if a runaway be gone for two minutes or two weeks, these dogs could follow a trail like the poor fella was in clear sight.

No spruce pine or wild onion rubbed on the soles of the feet would do nothing to put these beasts off. Only one way to throw off a dog like that, Pelham, you know how that be? You don't look like one to believe in hoodoo, but I'll tell you anyhow. You go to the grave of someone you loved, and you dig. You catch that body before it get turned to soil, and you grind it between two stones until you got yourself a parcel of bone dust. This, you bathe in every morning before the sun come up. Ne'er a beast will follow you then. But that ain't this man's story. This man was manumitted, and made his way north with his kennel, where finally he settled in Dunmore. Except now, after a couple generations of dogs, they a little different. He let some of the bitches loose, where they mixed up with the wood wolves who terrorize the shepherds of Canada West. So the hounds got bigger, and more bush-wild too. Another thing, Pelham. These hounds ain't nigger-hunters no more. They the dogs of Dunmore. They the reasons the wayward, thieving buckra of Chatham may go to the other coloured towns, but they don't dare come around here to terrorize folk after sundown. These dogs, they mad for white flesh. When you leave town we'll send the hounds for you. And you best pray the lawmen find you before they do. Because then you will be stopped and taken like any old brigand. But if the dogs catch you"—I looked square at him—"you shan't be more than a stag in the savannah."

His smile had faded and almost disappeared as I spoke, but it grew again as he regarded me silently for a long moment before speaking himself.

"Well that," he said, "sounds like a fine old coon hunt, wouldn't you say!" He flared his eyes at me and began to chortle.

We all knew that with his guns and horses, and with the head start he was liable to get, he had every chance of making it to the lakeshore unscathed. And depending on what connections he had, it would be an easy matter to cross, either by barge, clipper, or private schooner, where he and his captives would be entirely out of our reach.

But then again, so too would we have every chance of catching him.

Pelham stood slow and brandished the bowie knife with a quick flourish. Cassi couldn't help but gasp. I drew the dirk from my boot, and brought the handle of it up over the table in my fist. Aye, Lensinda, I had had enough of talk, and would cross blades with the man if he gave me more cause. He smiled again.

Said he: "Let's get to it," and he stabbed the back bacon. He lifted it from the table, picked up his satchel with the other hand, and gestured toward the door. "After you," he said.

Cassi was still breathing heavy through her mouth, and trying to still her chest, poor thing, but she could not.

I let her out on the porch, and held the door open for Pelham, not letting my eye off him, nor my right hand to leave its grip on my dagger. Outside, the sun still winked toward us, but most of the fields were cast in the shadow of the swamp.

"Now, where might David be?" said Pelham as he stepped on the porch, speaking more to himself than to us.

I only realized after that David's horse was gone. Because then a shape, a woman, dashed quickly from beside the house toward the cornfield. She held her linen skirt aloft as she ran. It was the seamstress. My heart pounded.

There was a thump on the floor, and Pelham grunted and took off. I nearly lunged for him, but he was gone, running headlong down the porch steps. He stopped at the driver's seat of the carriage and pulled out that rope you now holding, Sinda.

The seamstress disappeared into the corn, and I saw the stalks waver as she made her way. Moments after, Pelham plunged in, hot on her trail.

"David!" he bellowed, but did not slow his pursuit.

We watched him, Cassi and I standing and faltering on the porch. The bacon was on the deck at our feet.

Said Cassi: "I'm getting that rifle." And she turned back inside.

Just as I began to shake my head no—for at this point, I tell you, Sinda, I was resigned to avoid bloodshed—a shot rang out, like a thunderclap, from the cornfield. Cassi shrieked and I reached for her through the threshold.

"Fetch it and stand guard here," I said, and I ran down the porch, still gripping my blade as I went toward the corn.

Another shot rang out, shaking me in my boots. What the hell was going on—they came to catch them, not to kill them. Maybe they had missed. Maybe I could still tackle him. I ran into the stalks.

Since I saw the direction they were running, catching up didn't take me long.

I came upon him—Pelham—roiling on the ground like a

beast in a trap. He tore down the stalks of corn around him. I don't think he saw me. He managed to raise himself once before he stumbled back to the ground, clutching at his neck and growling through the blood. I watched dirt cling to his shoulder as he flailed. I stayed back, for I knew he still had that knife.

I heard the lads' voices clambering for me in a panic, but I could not answer, could not look away from his boots scuffing into my soil.

A movement in front of me broke my gaze. It was the old woman, standing small and dark amid the green stalks. I took a step back despite myself, though I don't think she was looking at me. She was fussing with the rifle in her hands. Then I saw the other woman, the seamstress, behind her, put a hand on her shoulder.

"Ah, to hell with it," said the old woman. "That'll do anyhow."

With that she marched off, skirting Pelham's twitching body.

The seamstress—Emma is her name—approached me, though she kept her eyes trained on Pelham, as did I.

"Sorry for the trouble this will make you, Simeon," she told me, "but we done running."

And with that she followed the old woman out through the corn.

Must have been her movement that alerted the lads to my whereabouts, and I heard them rustling, and in a few moments they came upon me and shouted and cussed when they saw the body.

Them lads started chattering, all nervous. Asking me what to do, telling me they were all worked up, that they thought something was wrong but hadn't rightly known what to do; cussing some more; asking me what to do some more.

I couldn't say nothing. Couldn't stop looking at Pelham on the ground. I got closer to him and saw his face wet with sweat, his lips bloody, his hands gripping his wounds, and his eyes just as clenched as his jaw.

So I sent Jim for you, Sinda. And here we are.

There was silence then, Simeon's tale done, and I noticed the quiet weeping in Cassi's breath, her face wet as river clay.

I glanced between them and became aware of the fibres of rope coming off in the tight grip of my hands. I relaxed and contemplated the two of them, holding each other as close as the yarrow and lupine on the table between us.

"And what of this Indian who is out roving?" I asked.

"She says we ain't got nothing to fear from him."

"Who says?" I responded, incredulous. "The old crone? And you believe her? Sim, what cause you got to—"

Simeon interrupted me gently, speaking low and firm. "I know it don't sound sensible, Sinda, but yes, I do believe her. You would too if you seen the way he came to her in that backyard."

I looked at him sharply, trying to discern if he was addled with the shock of it all or if his judgement could still be trusted.

"Simeon," I began softly, weighing my words, "after what you've told me, why'd you send Jim for the constable?"

I glanced at Cassi to see if she understood the implication

of my question. She looked at Simeon as well, and petted his hand.

Simeon was silent, and I wondered if he himself understood. So I spoke again: "You didn't send for me to heal that man, Sim. You sent for me because I am an upper-country witch who you hoped would know how to disappear a couple of slave women far enough north that no bounty hunter or lawman would know to come looking."

"They ain't slaves, honey," said Cassi.

"Really?" I said, glaring at her. "Well, they must have some mighty good employers that missed them so bad as to have Pelham come all the way up here and get them."

Cassi looked hurt, and too exhausted to retort.

"Anyhow," I continued. "Perhaps I could help with a northerly expedition. Perhaps not. Either way, Simeon, you've precluded any chance of that by calling for a damn constable. Hell, Jim is a good rider; there ain't no way we can catch him by now."

"No, that can't be, Sinda, even if we did catch Jim," said Simeon. "It can't be. They knew the women was here. They knew who we were; they knew enough that someone must have told them. Dunmore is a good town, but not good enough to keep a secret like this. And I ain't in the business of hiding dead buckra."

"What are you talking about, Sim?" I said, exasperated. "You bury this bastard in the swamp and every trace of him will be gone by Sunday. Hell, you could even feed him to the hogs."

"Come now, Sinda," said Simeon, shaking his head.

I rose from my chair in anger, still holding the coil of rope.

But when I saw the looks of concern on their faces, I cooled. A little.

"Simeon, the last thing Dunmore needs is a murder case," I began. "Least of all of a white man. The swamp village full of witches and moonshine, where even a white man ain't safe. Shit. Canada won't allow that, Simeon. They'll take over everything: the school, the industry, church. Put down those dogs you boast of. Don't matter that it's a bounty hunter. . . . Believe me Sim, there are towns that have been razed for less."

I sat, laid the rope on the table, and looked at him pleadingly.

"This is not a thing that folk need to know. With all its pride, Dunmore will not survive the scrutiny. Folk won't stand for it. They'll leave, go up to the Queen's Bush to live more free. The end of this road finds you farming for a ghost town."

"Well, look at you," Simeon said, a smile finally creeping on his weary face. "Arabella done taught you, didn't she? Ain't been here but what, three years, and already talking about what Dunmore needs."

It was a playful gibe, but a gibe nonetheless. I glared at him.

"Goddamn it, Sim," I said. "Why am I here, then? You knew as well as anything that the man wasn't 'bout to be healed. If not to counsel you on how to handle this, why in all hell am I here?"

"I suppose," Simeon began, "in all this, folk will want the story."

He and Cassi both watched me expectantly now. And then, all at once, I understood what they wanted, and a shiver of dread and anticipation crept up my spine.

"Well," he continued, clearing his throat slightly, "whether they want it or not, a story must be had to make something out of all this mess. And, well, I might very well be wrong. But something out there in that dusk made me think you be the one to tell it."

Chapter II

It was not my first time at the Chatham courthouse, though it was my first time there alone. The courthouse doubled as the county jail, of course, and so coloured men were no strangers to the insides of its thick limestone walls. I was no stranger to them either. Before I had managed to convince Arabella that my time was best served in the study, she would insist that I join her on her interviews. So I knew the turnkey, a discontented man from Lincolnshire. I knew also the visiting hours, and timed my arrival so as not to suffer his talk of missing the ocean. I should never have told him that my mother was from the fenlands; perhaps then he would have respected the stony silence of the interior court.

The night before, two constables rode in around midnight, led by Jim. I hadn't even the time to meet the old woman before she was taken away. We heard their horses coming down the savannah path, and we went out to meet them. I had seen the two before in Chatham, and I gave the details of what had come to pass, whispering, while we all stood in the backyard. The constables, having failed to bring cloaks, swatted away bugs in the starlit dark, and cussed quietly. Once I had done with my sum-mary of events, we went together to the cabin above the root cellar, and one constable, the elder, knocked, with his body turned sideways, hand on the pistol at his belt. The younger constable held a lantern that lit up the grooves of the door. After a few moments the seamstress, Emma, peeked out. Her face was long and eerily beautiful in the light from below.

"She waits for you out by the swamp," said Emma simply, shielding her eyes from the lantern light. She pointed out to the green lane.

We led the constables through the fields until we came to the lane. Cassi saw the old woman first, and pointed wordlessly to the small form, standing on a wide, flat stone girded by the softly flowing water in the lane. The old woman was draped in cloth and stood looking out at the moon. The younger constable went to her, fumbling with the irons, but he looked back at the other, who shook his head.

"Cumon, ma'am," said the younger.

The old woman nodded and went willingly with them. I could not see her eyes under her hood.

"You might as well take the body and his carriage; all your evidence will be in there," I said to them as they loaded the woman in their coach.

"Of course," said the elder constable, quickly, as if he were planning for that.

In short enough order they had loaded everything up into both coaches and were on their way. I think they were expecting something more thrilling.

Jim rode the roan horse back to the livery and I went with him. It had been some time since I had been out so late. The rush of cool night air, the respite it brought from the flies, and the blue-green twinkle of stars invigourated me. Jim and I parted ways at the village lane—he was anxious to get home, as his mother was no doubt awake, fretting over him.

When I got in, I couldn't sleep. I turned on my mattress. I was too hot with a blanket and too cool without it and my mind was whirling. Then, just when it seemed I might doze, the Tattons' cock crowed like a jubilant madman, though it was still hours before daybreak, and I was vexed. So very vexed. First at the temperature and the rooster, and then at my own tumbling spirit. Damn Simeon for bringing me into this confounded mess. To hell with telling stories. I'd had enough of stories. No—I'd had enough of people's hunger for stories. Is life itself not enough without stories? I could have had those women halfway to Spancel by now—if the constables hadn't been called. The slave catcher could have been well underneath the roots of some old swamp tree, and no one the wiser.

But people wanted a story. And I was the one to tell it. Damn him. I could do nothing for them now.

Girl, the most that you ever could do for them is now.

I groaned to drone out the voice in my head. I wished Arabella was back. This was her purview. I was not the one to speak to an old slave woman. And yet, as I finally fell asleep, I could not help thinking of her. Of how lonesome it must be in the jail-bound carriage with a hardy sheath of wood between one and the fresh air of the marsh. And then I was lonesome. For the first time in a long time, I longed for Spancel. I was sick of this southern flat marshland, and I missed the escarpment and the eastern slope, from which one could see light on the tops of clouds at dusk.

In the morning I rose with the sun, prepared porridge for the household, and went out to the main road to catch the omnibus to Chatham.

A couple of hours later, I found myself out of the morning sun and in the strange dark and cool of the jail.

The thick smell of hay gave the jail cells the feel of stables. Fittingly, perhaps, the only seat in the hall was an old milking stool. When I took it, and blinked in the half-light cast by the high, barred window, I saw the old woman rise from her corner and regard me closely. She approached in a prowling way that threw me; for a moment I was unsure of where, or rather, on which side of the bars I had moored. I was still tired from the lack of sleep, and my head ached.

She was small, and older than I had thought; the skin of her face seemed as grooved as the folds of the head wrap she wore. Her eyes, deep set beneath her brow, shimmered as she walked through the shaft of window light to come as near as she could. She shifted the thick throw blanket that she wore as a shawl, and rested her hand on an iron bar between us.

"What's your name, girl?"

Her voice sounded like the wind, a drum.

"Lensinda," I told her. "Pleased to meet you. And your name, ma'am?"

I reached into my sack to retrieve my pen and ink.

"Your other name," she said sharply.

I hesitated, my hand pausing, clasping the ink bottle.

"Martin," I said. "And may I ask yours?"

She turned her back to me and made a cooing sound, one hand against her mouth, the other moving in a pinching motion, sprinkling what looked like dust, which fell slowly to the hay-strewn ground. She bent and touched the ground directly after. She was a strange bird indeed, and spry despite her age.

"Come back tomorrow," she said, turning to face me again.

"And another thing," she went on, raising a finger at me. "Don't ever come empty-handed again. I crave a soft pear. It's a bit early for pear, yes, but see what you can do."

I sat for a moment, dumbly, my hand still in my bag. I felt confusion for the briefest of moments before annoyance took over, prickling at my temples. It was no small voyage from Dunmore to Chatham (and back again), and I was not eager to have made it for these few moments.

"You know," I said, summoning every bit of warmth I could muster. "You know, there are many folk, black and white, who will be aching to hear your story."

She stood still, looking at me with the utmost boredom, and did not move for a good long moment. Believe me, I have been known to hold a gaze, but when she started to sniff, snort, cackle, and finally hoot, all the while staring at me, I let my eyes wander over the cold stone walls of her enclosure and felt a whit of contentment at her condition.

"Girl!" she said in the most dissatisfied tone. "The day will not come—" she whispered, interrupting herself with a cough and another cackle. "The day will not come when I care what folk *ache* to hear of me!"

And she devolved into snorts and laughter again.

"I may be down here," she said, breaking her jest to breathe, and pointing at the hay beneath her. "But I ain't down there." And she pointed past me. Due south.

I was beginning to hate every moment of this.

"And even if I was—ho! My story!" she blurted, and I feared she would devolve yet again. Instead she coughed tentatively and sobered. Thank God.

"No," she said finally. "Folk may want to hear about how an old woman shot a man down in a cornfield."

She paused a moment, staring lazily at the iron bars before her.

"Folk may want to hear about how the woman mad, or how terrible it is south of the border." Here, she looked at me with something resembling fury, and I could not abide it.

"You are not the only fugitive to cut down a slave hunter!" I snapped at her.

Her lip curled at my remark, making her countenance more disdainful than angered.

"Though you may be the only one stupid enough to get caught," I said.

I might have regretted that taunt immediately if her face had not deepened in contempt. So I continued: "You may not have known when you shot the man, but your case will go to court. This means there is an opportunity to set a precedent that affirms that actions such as yours—stupid as they are—are justified. Such a precedent would stoke a very necessary dread in the souls of all those who would hold coloured men captive."

She looked on me, unmoved.

"Don't you see?" I implored. "This is a chance to make folk recognize, or rather to make them realize . . ." I wavered, unsure of what, exactly, I meant to say. I cursed myself for speaking at all.

"How gruesome the life under the whip," she said, as if that settled some great thing. She half turned away from me and began to walk as if she had somewhere to go.

I simmered on my stool.

"My story," she mumbled, placing a hand on the stone wall of her enclosure. "Where would you have me begin?" she said, as if entreating the wall itself.

I fumbled for my pen in my sack. I hadn't expected this turn—I had been fit to give up, in fact.

"Well," I began, "how . . . how came you to slavery?"

She huffed and I saw the back of her head wrap bow as she lifted her face to the wall.

"Same as everyone, I reckon," she said. "I was born Negro in this world. So it is we come to slavery, no?"

I rolled my eyes. I had so little energy for riddles and wordplay.

"It is not the world but the southern planters that bring coloured men to bondage," I said. "Were you born to them, or taken from some other land?"

She gave a grumbling chuckle and turned until I could see a pale glimmer in her right eye.

"Not some other land," she said, "but here."

I scanned the side of the old woman's face I could see. She was looking up the stone wall, as if into the heavens. A howl from down the hall caused my neck to twitch. It sounded strangely like the Tattons' rooster—the brittle pitch of either mirth or madness; I could not tell which. When I looked back at the old woman she had turned toward me and was grinning.

"There is much you will never believe," she continued, and her smile grew deeper, more wrinkled and ominous. "Best to begin with a tale that is not meant to be believed," she said. "Tell me, Lensinda Martin, do you know of any old tales of this land?"

"Old tales of this land . . ." I repeated as I quelled my frustration—just as I thought we might get somewhere, she slithered away. But no matter; there were tales I could summon.

"It is said you are a woman of letters," she prompted.

"Is it?" I asked, warily intrigued at how she might have learned that.

She nodded, and hummed as though she was about to laugh.

"Very well," I said, "I can think of one or two. And will you barter with me? A tale for a tale?"

She smiled slowly, revealing a good set of teeth, worn but white.

"Ah!" she exclaimed. "Someone has taught you. Very good, then. A tale for a tale you shall have. I am listening."

And she sat, nimble as a girl, on the hay.

"There is one the folk of Dunmore tell to scare one another around the lane fires, when the wind howls in from the lake," I said.

She hummed knowingly, and I began.

———

Before the north was free there was many a terror that befell Negroes here. Yes, before they were tempered, the British were mean slave drivers who whipped hard as anyone. There was one especially cruel who owned a very clever slave woman. The woman was willful, and she would walk out when she pleased and be among the animals and the trees on the land. Her master despised her for this, but he feared that if he whipped her she would run, for so easily was she keen to wander and stay out for days.

And she thought often of running away. The first time she meant to do so, a crow flew up to a branch before her and spoke with a creaking voice.

"You may walk this land," the crow said to the woman, "but you cannot stay, for you are granddaughter to the sea, and the sea will not be appeased until it has you."

The woman was angered, for she found the sea to be cold and dark, and she did not like it.

"Why does the land not take me?" she cried to herself one night outside the barracks of her master's house.

A bear lumbered to her and she felt its hot breath on her face in the dark. "You would be most welcome," said the bear to her, "but you are a daughter of the water, and the water will have you."

The woman was afraid of the water and would not go, not even to the shore. And so, with a heavy heart she remained with her master, and she grew more willful, and took to wandering at every chance.

By and by at her master's house, she fell in love with another slave. And there, with cruelty in his heart, her master sought to punish her willfulness. When he saw she had fallen in love, he separated her from her lover and sent her away on a boat, sold to another man.

As she went out on the water, she howled and wept. And as one of her tears fell into the sea, it awakened the whole of the water and the waves began to whisper.

"Take comfort," said the voice among the waves. "Take comfort in me."

She took no comfort, however, and wept all the more until the sailors noticed the bottom of the boat beginning to fill with water. They implored her to stop, and they beat her, even, but she raged and howled, and the salt water fell heavy from her eyes all the more.

And the boat began to bear down into the dark and angering sea.

The sailors became sore afraid, and knew not what to do. The sea began to lick up higher and higher, and press at the wale of the boat. So afraid were the sailors of drowning that they threw the woman overboard.

She plunged in, flailing and howling, and though she went under, the water began to churn and her howls grew louder and became a rolling cackle, as loud as the thunder on the plain. Her voice whipped up a wind that roared and dashed against the boat, tearing open the hold, whereupon all aboard were swept into the waves and drowned.

The howl of the lake continued with a vengeance that struck fear into the hearts of the British, in that they could hear the echo of their own evil. This fear haunted them until it changed them so that they abolished slavery.

That is why every year in Dunmore, the old women will take food down to the shore and weep into the water, to give thanks to the woman of the lake for making free country here.

I finished the tale, and the old woman before me nodded. We both sat silent for some while.

"Did you know," she began slowly, considering each word. "Did you know there is a text, behind that fable? Yes. A text. And I know where it is."

I couldn't say if this piqued more my interest or my suspicion. A text about slaves in the old days of Canada? What could it possibly be? And how would this old woman have come across it? Far more likely that she was spinning a yarn, if for no other reason than to have someone to talk to. I pitied her.

"It's your turn," I said, not wanting to give her cause for fantasy. "Tell me of your time in Kentucky."

She leaned toward me and squinted. "Yes," she said, "another fable. Hear this, a fable for you."

The old woman began to chuckle before she stopped herself with a deep breath.

"In the hills of Kentucky," she began, "there was a rabbit. Rabbit had many beautiful wives, and many, many children. But the rutting imp lived in fear of his neighbour Fox, for every day, Fox came and ate one of his young."

My eyes rolled up toward the ceiling, as if in an effort to whisk me out of the jail. Would I ever get anything of value from this woman? She seemed to notice my torment and sobered with a somber droop in her lower lip. I summoned all my willpower to give a weak smile and nod. She went on:

"One day, Fox came and eyed a very fat child of Rabbit's, and, greedy with hunger, he took the plump meal in his claws. He chomped on the kit, and as he did he choked and his eyes bulged, and he keeled over just so. Rabbit looked upon the body and thought, 'My stars, now that he lies dead, Fox is not so much bigger than I!' So Rabbit took Fox's pelt clean off and wore it on his own shoulders. He wore Fox's pelt like a mask and coat, and he lay with Fox's wife, and she bore him children. They looked like Rabbit, but instead of Rabbit's earth-brown pelt, they had the red colour of Fox himself.

"And that is how, they say, so many rabbits became red as you."

This she spoke in a matter-of-fact tone, looking square at me. My eyes glanced at the light, creasing brown of my hands. It had been quite some time since anyone had managed to make me think twice at my own complexion. Yet somehow, this strange ending to a strange tale made me wince like it was a sound box on the nose. I blinked twice and shook off any thought of reprisal. I put back my pen and ink. Let Arabella deal with this one.

"What mean you by that, ma'am?" I asked, humouring her, as I rose from the rickety stool.

"What I mean," she began as she groaned and reclined in the hay in the corner of her cell, "is that it is no wonder men such as your father find comfort in a white woman."

My shame twitched into anger. How is it, I thought to myself, that the hue of one's skin can equally be the object of fascination and scorn? I was at my wit's end, and altogether too tired to suffer riddles barbed at my own expense. I looked at the crone again, sitting there, her legs out straight in the hay, now eyeing me, much like a fox herself.

"Good day to you, ma'am," I said.

I looked at her hard and cold now. Patience had left me. She met my gaze with her solemn eyes, and I held them until I could discern a twinkle.

"Go on now," she said. "You bring me a nice bushel of pears tomorrow and I'll tell you all about *my story*. I have dreaming to do in the meantime."

My mind whirled, and I cursed myself for caring. What was the crone playing at? I swallowed the heat of frustration in my throat. I would leave, to be sure. Leave and forget this nonsense. I had no allegiance here.

"Oh, another thing," she said as I began to walk away. "The text!" she shouted.

This had me pause, though I did not look back.

59

"Emma has it. The seamstress. You must go and ask her, yes? Bring it too."

I looked back on her for a moment. She was nearly unnoticeable in the shadows of the cell corner. She yawned, like a cat.

"Pears," she whispered to me, before the yawn had left her.

I snorted lightly, my jaw clenched. "Someone else will come for your story," I said. "I won't be back."

I walked away, the only sound the clap of my footsteps on stone. I signed quickly at the entrance, and waited impatiently for the turnkey to return my purse and my knife, and then I was gone into the light and the bustling heat of the Chatham planks and cobbles.

Chapter III

After a few brisk paces down the street I became aware of myself, as if waking from slumber. Slowly, a dilemma dawned on me: it would be at least two hours before the first afternoon omnibus—the one frequented by washerwomen with families in the villages—and I had nowhere to go to get out of the heat. I'd not planned to have so much time—not anticipated so swift a departure from the jail. I gradually came to a halt next to a market stall selling woolen textiles. My fingers brushed over the weft of a stone-grey blanket as I dallied in the wisp of shade cast by the awning of the stall. The vendor, a young woman with hungry green eyes, greeted me and I nodded and wandered off as slowly as I could without appearing aimless, or so I hoped. I tried to pause in the shade of other street-side stalls, but the vendors were ill-tempered and could see I had no intention of buying. I sweltered. The heat of the day had become oven-like, and between the sun and the baking cobbles I felt like a stew in a pot. At least it had been cool within the dark stone walls. Perhaps it was worth returning for that, and I could sit in silence for the hour or so permitted me. I almost turned on my heel before I remembered the sneer of the old crone, and I cursed my own weakness. No. I would not make myself a liar. I could not return.

After some vexed wandering, I found myself at the threshold of the root doctor's shop. He was busy with a client—a woman I vaguely recognized, from Buxton, I think. She sat, slightly slumped and perspiring, one hand on her belly, the other limply fanning the side of her head. The root doctor was stooped over his bureau, reciting the herbs as he packaged them: slippery elm, Jamaica mint, gingerroot. Pregnancy, probably. I glanced at the woman again. Definitely. I did not envy her that condition in this heat. I stationed myself behind a hanging mane of dodder before the man could recognize me.

My fingers tangled idly in the coarse tendrils. It was still stifling, even in the shop, but at least it was shaded, and it smelled of geranium and rue, moss and mugwort, a welcome break from manure cooking on the road.

In this moment of repose, a nagging thought pressed at me: Why had I left the jail so abruptly?

The old woman had snubbed me and asked me to leave. It was simple.

Had she?

Of course she had. I was sure she had. No use dithering on about it. I was not one to stay where I was not wanted.

All right. Well then, why not return?

Now?

Now, or later?

"Sinda, is it?"

I jolted out of my thoughts. I did not remember the root doctor's name, but I tried to smile.

"It's been some time. How do you do?" he asked.

He was a small man of a kind and deferential disposition. He always seemed to be lowering his head, as if to bow, and he would never face you head-on, but rather orient his body to one side, like a boxer ready to dodge; a posture that, as I thought about it, was quite common among refugees who had been seasoned with too many blows.

"Say," he went on, "if you ever have any more of that milkweed, or especially that, er, what was it? The yellow marigold—yes, especially the marigold—you'll bring it for me, won't you?"

"Of course," I murmured, and began to amble slowly toward the door. I had no mind to go back into the heat; it was a reflexive move—I was keen to be with my own thoughts.

"Those plants can't be found so well up here, on dry land, you see," he said, and then shook his head, bumbling. "But of course you know that."

I nodded and tried to smile, still inching away. I brushed against a potted clump of lemongrass that caught on the back of my frock and pulled me, gently, holding me in place for a moment.

"Say, Sinda," he began, one hand behind his ear, as was his way.

I knew what the next question would be before it came out of him. Somehow, he had heard the news, or some version of it, already. The night before flashed in my mind: the terror behind Jim's eyes; the bounty hunter curled up in the corn; the old woman, led away by constables under moonlight. But how in all hell could word travel like that? He must have seen my dismay written plain across my face, bless him.

"Lord forgive me, I don't mean to pry," he said, still scratching behind that ear.

He paused, cleared his throat, and removed a kerchief from his breast pocket to dab the sweat off his forehead. His hand returned to behind his ear, as if he needed it positioned there in order to speak.

"Well, it's just that—and forgive me if you already know this—but I myself had to commit . . . violence—yes. Upon my escape from bondage, yes, Lord forgive me."

I had not known, and found myself looking at the small man differently. His excessively gentle manner; how strange, how perfect.

"And, well, if there's anything I can do, you'll just let me know now, won't you?"

As he spoke he moved his hand from behind his ear and it formed a tight fist at his side. For the first time, he squared himself to me, just slightly, and I saw a glint in his eye.

I had released myself from the lemongrass, though its scent lingered on my hand—I could smell it from where it grasped the band of my satchel on my shoulder. I stood with my back to the open door, where I could feel the cooler air draft gently past my face and into the heat outdoors.

"Do you suppose I could sit here for a while?"

The question was out before I could think twice, and it broke his posture.

"Of course, of course. It is devilish out there, isn't it?"

He was nodding profusely as he stepped behind his bureau and pulled out a chair. He gestured to it, smiling widely. "Make yourself comfortable," he said. "And oh—" He shuffled through drawers, one hand held up as he did so. He pulled out a large tome and placed it on the bureau in front of the chair. "Some reading material, if you like."

It was a botanical encyclopaedia. I thanked him and sat, while he set about packaging orders. He didn't ask me anything further, and he would not. Men such as he knew the sacred value of silence. I perused the encyclopaedia. I pretended to, at least, while I fell once more into my thoughts.

There would be plenty like the root doctor, I realized. They would not all be so forthcoming, or so measured, for that matter. And even he—I didn't know what he might do if inspired by some zealous mob. I thought of his fist, that glint in his eye. Like retired soldiers who yearn still for war, there would be a whole army willing to leave the banality of their peaceful lives, despite themselves. It was the same impulse that led so many back across the border. No sooner healed than gone, once more into the breach, and—more often than not—never to return. Freedom is never absolute, it seems, and therefore escape, despite what they tell you, yields no final destination.

Even here in the promised land, freedom was a frail thing—hollow at the core. This notion took hold in my belly with a clamp of nausea. Simeon was right. Well, he was wrong for turning the old woman in, but he was right that a story must be told;

some sense must be made. For in the absence of sense, fear and violence would reign. My gut continued to twist as I saw it in my mind's eye: one careless liberty taken by a patrolling constable with his baton or pistol. Dunmore would not stand for it, and he would die. Then there would be retaliation: beatings, killings, people thrown in jail. Emboldened by the mayhem, more bounty hunters would surely come. What would the promised land be then? Maybe that was why the old woman ousted me, I thought to myself. Maybe she was a bringer of chaos.

But did she oust you?

Not this again.

She asked you to return.

Well then, she will be disappointed.

If you don't return, you will disappoint yourself, child.

I will be content! This is not even my town. None of this is my concern.

Hm. What is it you are so afraid of?

I couldn't tell you precisely who this little voice in my head was. An old woman—not the old crone in jail, but Hestia, a woman I knew from where I was raised, who would take special notice when I talked to myself. And then one day, she soberly told me I was speaking to my guardian spirit, and if I knew what was good for me, I would keep speaking to him. I loved Hestia, and generally I took her word, even when I pretended not to. But in this instance, I could never fully believe her. And as I came of age I began to realize that the voice in me was in fact some version of Hestia herself. If not her individually, it was a chorus of the few people I had known whom I actually respected when they questioned me. Such a haunting was reasonable enough, as hauntings go.

Once the hour was nigh, I left the root doctor's and caught the afternoon omnibus. The washerwomen packed the carriage; some from Buxton, two from Dunmore, and the rest from the towns in between. I feared gossip and chat about the previous night's murder would be in order, but most of them napped immediately, thank God. I have no idea how, because between the jolting pull of the horses, the crack of the teamster's whip, and the bumpy ruts of the old roads, the carriage felt like a boat in a storm. Yet the women had been up since well before daybreak, and they all had another half day's labour ahead of them, cooking, cleaning, minding children. They shuttered the windows and reclined in various positions of repose: heads drooping, some resting an ear on their neighbour's shoulder. Two stayed awake and chatted quietly to each other, but I could not hear them above the noises of the carriage. I suddenly felt tired myself, and dozed with my eyes open. I found myself imagining living in a peaceful, less complicated place, and from there, my mind began to muse on escape.

I had savings enough to make my own way for months. My expenses had been minimal, my work for *The Coloured Canadian* profitable enough. I would leave during the day. Dunmore was too bustling at night anyhow. Everyone was home, the tavern and the main road alive. Daytime would be best. The day labourers out, the rest tending to their homes or businesses. I could catch an omnibus such as this one. A series of them. Maybe go back up to Spancel. Or maybe to port, where I could find work and wait for sign of the pirate. I did miss the open water, for all its tumult.

I couldn't imagine a way out for Dunmore. The old crone had shifted everything into disarray. She was either mad or extremely tactical in her goals. I thought of her crafty grin, her shadowy figure in the cell. There was no pitying her. She seemed content, the more I thought of it. Content! As if that cell was exactly where she meant to end up.

And was she more or less content than the bounty hunter would have been, had he made good on his capture?

That's beside the point.

Hm. Well, point me to the point then, girl.

The point is, I thought to myself, I don't trust her a whit. And I certainly don't trust that I can pull any story from her. Arabella will be back soon—any day now. And when she returns, she will have the patience for the old woman. In the meantime, we can only pray that disaster doesn't swoop on Dunmore.

I never thought you the one to leave your fate to prayer, unchurched as you are!

I snorted lightly at this. My fate, if I had any to speak of, would not be to fulfill an obligation to Dunmore that I didn't have. I could walk away from it all without consequence or second thought. Nothing would be easier. I could stew the morning porridge, send the children off to school, pack, and be off. I might even tell Velora of my plans and she would forget before lunch. And even were she to remember, I was under no indenture there.

Nothing easier than leaving your friends—this I've known of you, for some time now.

At this thought, I must confess, I had no answer. But instead a lump began to rise in my throat and press tears behind my eyes. Why? Well, that's for another time. I brought myself back to the rollick and bump of the carriage. There were only the three of us remaining: the two Dunmorian washerwomen and myself. They began to rouse as we smelled the damp of the swamp burgeoning to the south. Though the shutters were closed, I knew we were passing Simeon's land, and the green lane. Almost there. It was a long journey—I could not imagine taking it every day.

The teamster let us out in front of the tavern. The sun was still strong, baking this part of the road into dust. We paid the man and he was off—Dunmore was his terminus on this route, and none were going back to Chatham at this hour.

The women stretched their shoulders and were also off—to their respective lanes. I tarried a moment, unsure of what to do. The main road was quiet, a strip of dirt cutting through the lush, encroaching grassland. The trees loomed all around, and the buildings were secondary to them. It was hot and bright enough to keep most of the mosquitoes away, but there was plenty of shade and a near-permanent breeze, like a cool, constant whisper from the swamp itself.

The street was empty, and I felt an undeniable comfort.

Then I heard a shuffle: a dog—two—westward down the

road toward the church and schoolhouse. One, head at attention, looking at me from the middle of the road. Assessing my colour, perhaps. The other, behind her, head down, facing the swamp. So the dogs had been loosed. Chaos, to be sure. My sense of comfort dissipated, and on a whim, I headed into the tavern.

Circe, the tavern keeper, was behind the counter carving a massive ham with her long butcher knife. She glanced up at my opening of the door without pausing in her task, as though she were expecting me.

"Well, look here," she said in her rasping drawl. "If it ain't the healer herself. What happen, Sinda darling, you lose your touch?"

I rolled my eyes with as much exasperation as I could muster and approached the bar.

"Long day, sugar? You ain't used to getting up so early."

"Hush up, Circe, and pour me a drink."

"Uh-uh, honey, it's Friday—the boys coming in later. Here, take a ham," she said with a smile, and pulled a plate from under the bar. I grimaced, but she huffed and deftly cut a slice from the ham that fell onto the dish. She fished a pickled onion and two small biscuits from jars on the counter behind her, and slid the plate over to me.

"So," she said, smiling hungrily, "how does our murderess?"

"This town, Circe." I shook my head. I dunked my hands in the washbowl on the bar, and Circe handed me a cloth and a fork. I dried myself and pulled my knife from my satchel. I cut into the meat. I was hungry, and the ham was good. It was Simeon's,

I could tell from the taste. Sweet past the brine, with an undertone of peat.

"Well, come on, Sinda, don't leave me in the lurch!"

I smiled, chewing my food. I liked seeing Circe impatient. She was normally so unrepentantly aloof. I savoured the moment; her eyes darted between me and her ham, and when she saw me smiling she huffed again.

"Why don't you answer a question or two for me?" I asked, still smiling.

She raised an eyebrow and pointed the tip of her long curved blade at me. "You a high yellow hussy, you know that?"

"Now, ain't that the pot calling the kettle black," I quipped back at her as I diced the onion.

I looked up and held her gaze for a moment. It was in good fun, our banter. We had an unspoken alliance, masked by these moments of insult. It wasn't so much that we were both of light complexion, though that was often the subject of our gibes—a performance we kept up even now, when no one was watching. Like me, Circe was alone—un-husbanded, that is. She and Arabella were my mentors in that respect. But Arabella was all warmth and charisma, and full of virtues that I could barely comprehend, let alone aspire to. Circe, by contrast, was unabashedly callous. She wielded that knife, took lovers without qualm, and had a tongue as sharp as her mind, which made any think twice before bad-mouthing her. She had arrived in Dunmore twenty-odd years before me, from the south, her purse filled with an unbelievable sum of Spanish silver. There were all sorts of stories—most struck me as spiteful and baseless—of how she had come into the money. With her small fortune she established the tavern, a spacious and well-built structure, which—as restaurant, dance hall, boardinghouse, and stables—remained, much to the vexation of the church folk, the economic and cultural centre of Dunmore. All this I respected—that respect being the unspoken subtext of our encounters.

"All right, trollop," she said, resuming her carving, "what is it you want to know?"

I relished my small victory, but had to pause a moment: I had said I had questions, but I hadn't really thought about what those questions would be. I considered as I took a bite and chewed.

"This bounty hunter—you see him yesterday?"

"Oh, I saw him, all right. And the Indian he rode with. They stopped in here—bought some feed and watered their horses in the livery."

This was news—potentially complicated news, as I thought it over. Was it possible that Circe herself had pointed the men to Simeon's cabin? She paused, as if she'd heard my thought, and pointed that knife at me again.

"Now, don't you dare ask what I see you about to ask, girl, because then you would truly vex me, and even you wouldn't want that."

She looked at me with heavy, hooded eyes, before rubbing her brow with the wrist of her knife hand and continuing on her work.

"You know Gabriel? Young lad, my hostler. He was absent last night from the stables, and this morning too. I sought him out at his home, and found him—his mama spooning him a broth, cussing me out. He had a bruise around his neck so swollen he could barely speak."

She paused to snort gently and shake her head. She met my eyes and must have seen them wide with shock.

"That's right, girl. Before they left my property they bound and gagged him, took him in their carriage, out to the savannah, and hanged him light—that's how we used to call it. Make your God-given life flash before you, till you shit yourself and the blood fills your eyes. Yes, he told them where to find the fugitives. Thank the Lord he did. They left him there—not hanged, but bound to a tree. Took him most of the night to work his way free."

I shook my head, putting my own knife down and rubbing my eyes. I felt another painful urge to escape. This whole event was getting worse the more it unfolded.

Circe went on. "I knew there was something off about those two, but I was busy with cooking and didn't pay them much mind, except to take their money. Besides, I couldn't imagine anyone would make off with a boy like that in plain daylight."

"Well," I said, looking up from my hands, "such was their profession."

"Mmm-hmm," she grunted.

She finished cutting the last strips of meat from the bone and then excused herself to go start the soup pot out back. I felt the gust of afternoon heat as she opened the door behind the bar; the long drone of cicadas seeped in from the yard, and then muffled as the door swung shut. I finished the last bites of my meal and sat in silence a moment. I noticed the creaks of Deacon's heavy steps upstairs, and the sound of sweeping bristles on the floor. Then a chorus of low barks from down the road.

Circe reentered with a waft of woodsmoke.

"He loosed the dogs, I see," I said.

She rolled her eyes and shook her head before turning to open the pantry.

"Lord o' mercy," she drawled, gathering a bundle of herbs in the basket she held in the crook of her arm. "Maybe you go talk some sense into him." She turned one side of her face over her shoulder and winked at me.

"Hell no," I chirped. "I ain't talking to anybody ever again. . . . Anyhow Arabella will be back soon. They'll listen to their queen."

"Mmm-hmm," she hummed as she surveyed the pantry, passing over the shelves idly with her free hand. "Arabella will bow them all, with that high bosom."

I snorted and covered my mouth. I may have looked over my shoulder too. Circe glanced back with a scowl.

"Oh, please, look at you. You ain't that blind, are you? You think all these mens listen to her 'cause she in the papers and shit? Like hell!"

I could not contain my smirk.

"Unmarried, respectable woman like that." She lowered her head, raising an eyebrow. "Plump, full bosom and hips like that!"

I only smiled. And Circe, as if her point was won, turned with her basket of flavourings and began to make her way to the door again.

"They hungry for her is all. And the women"—she turned at the door to look at me and wag a finger—"the women only abide her 'cause they know she prefer bosom anyhow!"

With that vulgar pronouncement she winked again and backed out into the yard. I was left shaking my head, still smiling.

I rose to leave as I'd come, through the front, but paused again as I heard Circe's unmistakable rasp, and the voice of men too, coming from the side yard. Curious, I made my way around the bar and toward the door that led to the yard, the voices from outside gaining shape and familiarity. I swung open the door. Circe stood poking the fire beneath her cauldron, and the men, whom I recognized as the three currently lodging at the inn, were shirtless by the well, their tools and packs on the ground around them. One, the big one, was drawing water, another leaned on the edge of the well, chatting to Circe, and the third sat a pace or two off toward the road, curiously out of the shade cast by the tavern. Two dogs were near him. One lay behind him, on the edge of the shade, and the other faced him, prodding a wet snout urgently at his face while the man gently rebuffed it with a hand on its muzzle.

"Hey now!" said the one leaning against the well, as I emerged into the yard.

"So this is what you ladies do afternoon time," he said, surveying me with a smirk that aligned with the tilt of his bowler hat.

Normally I would have glared, but with them indiscreetly exposed I found my eyes shifting conspicuously between them and the tufts of grass poking between the stones of the inn's foundation near my feet. No, indiscreetly was not the word, I thought to myself. They were obliged to be exposed—Circe always required them to wash up before entering, no matter the season, and since they were so obliged, it gave a brazen quality to their nakedness. They were gleefully comfortable in their flesh. The hewing and digging of the swamp work, grueling as I imagine it must be, does no small service to the male frame. To say they were well-built would be to understate the point. Even with a passing glance one could see their every movement—the slight shifting of weight, the heft of a well bucket—showed a rippling orchestra of muscle.

Circe did not look askance, as I did. To her, their bodies held no special mystery. She looked at the man on the well frankly, with an irritated scowl, as she cut a potato and let it drop into her pot.

"Boy, hush. The labour of women goes far beyond what you would understand. Quit beating around the bush—what the hell happened?"

The young man smirked again. "But Circe—beating around the bush is what I do, don't you know," he said, raising his arms like a buzzard priming to take flight.

Circe lowered her heavy eyes at him. "Mmm-hmm, well that explains why you ain't the one catching the birds then, don't it?"

The big man guffawed and the man on the ground chuckled too. The man leaning on the well crossed his arms, flexing them. He continued to smirk, but there was a pained quality to it now, a pursing of the lips.

"Enough anyway," said Circe, turning to the big man, who

had picked up his bucket and begun to walk to the hemlock stand. "Gaston, what happened?"

Gaston paused, still holding the bucket.

"Emancipation Day," he said, one hand scratching the beard under his chin. "When we told boss it was come Sunday, he insisted we break early. . . . Imagine that." He smiled, shaking his head.

"Breaking early, with full pay," he went on, "and on a week-day too. Shit."

"Well, I'll be," said Circe as she stirred the cauldron. The soup was coming to a simmer, and the steam began to wisp around her.

"He makes like he's a great friend to the coloured man," said the smirking one. His head was over the well now, lowering another bucket, and he paused to look up. "But that man just lazy as sin."

"And he ain't worried 'bout the job."

This from the one seated on the ground, the youngest one, who looked up—to my surprise—at me.

"They got salary coming in for another five years at least," he went on, looking away and nodding. "Guaranteed."

I began to inch toward the road. I didn't much feel like chatting, and fatigue was setting in. Perhaps I could catch a nap, I thought, before the children came home.

"Hey, where you off to, sugar?"

The smirking one spoke to me with one hand on the rope, a show of muscle.

Before I could respond he added, "You ain't gonna tell us about our murderess?"

Of course. All four—even Circe—glanced at me expectantly. I prepared to disappoint them. The side door opened and Deacon, Circe's manservant, poked his head out. He was a giant of a man and slow in the mind.

"Deacon, sugar, could you fetch me some vinegar from the cellar?"

Deacon grunted an affirmation and the other men nodded and greeted him.

"How you do, Deac?"

"Say, Deacon, would you bring me a clean kerchief? Thank you, brother."

I breathed easier. The interruption had dispelled their anticipation.

"I'm afraid there ain't much to tell, as yet," I interjected quickly, before they could look to me again. "See you fellas. Bye, Circe!"

I turned to leave.

"Say, Sinda!"

It was Gaston; I could tell by the rumble in his voice. I didn't know he knew me by name. I turned to look back at them.

He stood still, framed by the hemlocks behind him, and he seemed, in that moment, as brown and vast as a tree himself.

"You—you tell the duchess," he began, and paused, with a small chuckle. "And, come to think of it, the old woman herself... tell them, they say the word and I'll bring my own pickaxe and break that jailhouse wall to dust."

He tilted his head over to where their things lay in the grass, as if the tool would confirm the claim.

I nodded, unsure of how to reply.

The smirking one huffed. "How much dust you think you'll kick up before you sharing a cell with the old woman?"

"Shit—enough. Enough. Who the hell they think they are? These man-thiefs worse than murderers. A white man kill a murderer, what you think happen to him?" His tone was growing more grave and loud.

"Murder's murder, man." This, the younger one, still seated with the dogs. "Anyone murder a man, they go to jail. Ain't no bail for murder."

"Boy, you lying to yourself."

"The law's the law. Just 'cause I know it don't make me no liar."

"Hm! Negro who gives a whit about the law? Tell me this: The law matter so much, then why you here? Why you in Canada, Jack? Lord knows you broke laws to get here." Gaston's voice was reaching a roar.

"Ain't the same thing, man."

"Ain't the same thing. Well, I guess the law's the law until it ain't the same thing. Go ahead and pen that one."

"Bye, Sinda!" Circe had noticed me inching my way toward the road and interrupted the debate to wave.

I waved back and the men wished me well before resuming their squabble.

For whatever reason, as soon as I left the shade of the tavern the dogs rose and trotted beside me. I tried to shoo them away, but the one closest to me—a bushy black one who looked like a wolf—gazed up at me quizzically with yellow-flecked eyes, while the other, a larger mastiff, didn't even seem to notice my effort to dissuade them.

"All right, but I won't feed you," I said to them, and bustled off down our lane. It was louder already with the swamp crew home early—the sounds of fires crackling up, water falling over eager bodies, and murmuring, laughing. The dogs trotted, just ahead of me now, like they knew where I was going. Their backs swayed, and their paws were silent, as though they swam through the land. There was a bark up ahead, and the mastiff growled and sprinted away to sniff another—a shaggy grey mutt. The two squared off and chased each other in circles, then between two houses and through the Tattons' back field. I heard a curse, from the back porch, hurled after them.

The bushy one stayed ahead of me. I came to our porch and sat on the bench to untie my muddy boots. I looked warily at the dog, but she simply lay at my feet, panting contentedly in the shade and looking out at the lane.

I went in the front door. The dog glanced back at me but made no attempt to follow. And all of a sudden, I was glad she was there, and I found myself compelled to bring her water and food.

But I closed the door behind me, and to my surprise, I noticed an unmistakable lilting cadence from the kitchen. Arabella, for as long as I had known her, was keenly adept at the enchantment of oration. Her sermons, biblical or not, inspired—as folk often said—a great moving of the spirit. She built her rhetoric as much with her logic as with the sheer beauty of her voice. She was a singer, a passionate contralto. She would be called upon sometimes at church to lead a song, and oh, how the sinners would weep.

I heard Velora's churchwoman moan in response to whatever Arabella had just said. Their exchange made me smile, and I tiptoed my way down the hall, bypassing my usual stop at the study to get to the kitchen. I leaned against the doorframe and waited for them to notice me. They were facing each other at the butcher block table, a mound of mottled potato skins between them. Their profiles were to me, and they were talking, their eyes on the paring knives in their hands; in the dark hallway, I might have appeared as nothing more than a shadow shifting on the wood.

"I tell you, Mummy, some things people fear but they need all the same."

"Mmm-hmm. Yes, Lord, you right, girl."

"You taught me that, you know that? Through your words, and your deeds too."

"Hmm! Yes? Well amen, child, amen!"

"Yes, Ma, you did, and I'm just trying to tell people the good word of my elders: there is an earthly kingdom, and a heavenly one, and we mustn't confuse the two."

"Mmm-hmm. That's it."

"The promised land is good, yes it is, but it is also a land of battle and blood."

"Amen, girl, amen."

"Do not cross over if you are not ready to stake your claim."

"Hallelujah! Mmm-hmm. Yes."

"You know how it is, Mummy."

"I know, child. Yes-hmm, yes!"

"These folk, they're good folk, Ma. Good folk. I walk down these—sweet Jesus! Sinda Martin, you scamp! Mummy, did you see her there? How long you been standing there? Come here, girl, I missed you!"

I could not restrain my full smile. Only Arabella could go from indignant shock to gentle caring in an instant. It was one of the many manifestations of her grace.

"How I missed you, Sinda. Would you come on over so I can hold you?"

I walked over to her, and she laid her knife on the table and embraced me, swaying gently side to side. She was nearly a head taller than I, and so my neck was smothered in the comfort of her linen blouse, and the softer comfort of that high, full bosom. There was still dust on her clothes but that was cut by the pungent smell of her sweat and of the magnolia oil on her neck.

Velora chuckled and rubbed my back from across the table; I felt her strong bony fingers between my shoulders.

"So," Arabella began, clasping my hands. I felt the grit of potato starch on her skin. "You are now the woman to know in Dunmore."

I snorted and backed away, finding the stool by the pantry shelves.

"I've had quite enough of being *that* sort of woman," I said, and I perched on the seat.

I looked to them at the butcher block. Velora had begun humming and returned to chopping the taters, while Arabella, one hand on the table, head cocked to one side, fixed me with a look of utter compassion.

"What a day you must've had, dear friend," she intoned, smiling softly.

I felt my face flush—I couldn't quite look her in the eye. I was strangely repulsed by her kindness. I could not understand it as anything other than condescension. Her days, I imagined, were full of this kind of drama—this endless navigation of people's wants, their attention. And here she was, preparing dinner and consoling me.

Tom, Arabella's brother, stooped through the back door, rubbing his neck with a rag.

"Afternoon, Sinda," he said, and there was an awkward pause, and he looked between Arabella and me.

"Afternoon, Tom," I said.

"There's wood ready by the pit," he offered, and we thanked him.

"What you got planned for your day off?" I asked him.

"Not sure," he said, scratching his chest, still glancing between us. "Mayhap I'll go meet the children."

He was a quiet man, but attuned to his surroundings—I wager he could discern from the cadence of our silence that there were words brewing that needed some peace to surface.

"Can take 'em to Saison to help with the berry picking."

We all mumbled our support of the idea: the children would love it; the Tattons did say they needed some help afore Sunday;

watch out for those hounds, though, but don't mind the one on the porch.

Tom bowed his head slightly and was off to leave through the front.

I always got the impression he had pain, for what else causes such a stony silence in a man? But he seemed to have buried it so deep it would never, ever surface; I knew this because even when drunk he was subdued, like some giant, brooding lamb.

We heard his lumbering steps leave the house. Perhaps I would excuse myself under the pretense of feeding the dog. I looked up to find Arabella's eyes, full and searching, somehow without prying.

"Do you need rest, sugar?"

She didn't intend it to demean me. I knew this, but I couldn't take it any other way.

"I'm fine," I said, and continued before she could ask any more questions. "Look, there's nothing to report. I tried to talk to her but the woman is mad. I left and I won't be back. Anyhow, she'll listen to you, I'm sure."

Velora nodded and mumbled an affirmation—either "amen" or "yes'm"—and I glared at her. Her lack of enunciation offended me further.

Some small thing in Arabella stiffened. She glanced between the unwitting Velora and me, and her eyes hardened ever so slightly.

"If only there were more, and ever more, mad as she," she said.

"Ay-men!" said Velora.

I simmered.

"Then our people would be out from bondage—Lord, how bondage would be so far a memory, we would tell our children as if it were a bedtime story."

"Mm-hmph!"

"If there were more like her, our people would be dead," I interjected plainly.

Arabella looked back to me, her brows lightly furrowed. Velora huffed.

"And there would be no stories to speak of," I went on gratuitously.

I was hoping for dignified silence. Perhaps a bit of honest hurt. What I got instead was laughter, cool and trickling, like a brook. Arabella's, of course. Velora paused in her chopping, looking up at me with a bemused sort of grimace, but even that was soothed into a gentle smile by Arabella's tinkling laughter.

"Oh, now I am truly intrigued! Lensinda Martin, of the cold eyes, what could a poor old woman have said to prick you so?"

I crossed my arms, feeling the anger rise to my head.

"*If* my eyes are cold, it is only because they have been deadened by the tediums of my elders," I said.

"Ohhh!" cooed Arabella, looking to Velora, who followed suit, striking up some churchwoman chord.

"And what, dear sister, pray tell," said Arabella, hobbling over to me, as though she were a hundred years old. "What are the tediums that have soured your pretty cheek?"

She went to pinch me there and I blocked her hand, holding her at a distance. There was a moment, as she pushed toward me, my hand over hers, holding it as if I had managed to catch a small bird trying to swoop on me. And it was as though the bird's beak were real, and keen to gouge me, and nothing was more important than the protection of my face. I became suddenly aware of the blood rushing in my flesh, and I did not want to suffer anyone's look. I stared, instead, at the butcher-block table, the yellowed indent on its face, crisscrossed with knife lines, but everything around seemed to close in on me: the folds of Velora's green frock; the clayware jars of the pantry, like muddy infantrymen in line; the stove, reddened and dusty as pig iron; and Arabella, her face glowing, as if in refutation of anything that anyone had ever said of blackness. Then her hand was no longer pushing, but squeezing my own, gently, though I still held it stiffly at a distance.

"Why did you leave the woman, Sinda?"

She was still warm, still glowing, but her smile had faded into an earnest look of concern—one so attentive it could not be denied. She could look at you as if the whole world, in all its fascination, all its turmoil, was in you, and in need of attention.

I was almost seduced.

"I left because I am a free woman, and I leave when I please," I said.

To prove my point, I shuffled out of her gaze and her grip, and made my way out back. Velora huffed, and I shot her a final glare before turning to the door. Outside, a gust of afternoon air softened my scowl.

Our yard—Arabella's yard—was unusually secluded. The Tattons' meadow crept on us to our south, like a sea of brambles, low- and highbush fruits. The action of the meadow extended upward too, buzzing with all manner of insects, hummingbirds and songbirds, and far above them, the white-bellied hawks. At night the meadow was alive still with fluttering moths, like flakes of white ash, and bats, and the barred owls, whom I rarely saw but heard from the woods at the tip of the meadow, till the morning.

Just the week before, as he did each year, Tom cut back the raspberries with the scythe, and even in this act, he moved slowly. The crescent blade hummed as he swung it in its wide arc and then sang out a faint metallic vibrato as it cleaved through stalks of grass and bramble.

I drew a bucket from the well and brought it around front, but the bushy dog was gone. I looked around, searching for her black form. The lane was empty again, and quiet, save for the chorus of the meadow. As I glanced down at my own bare feet, now flecked with mud, I felt overcome by a powerful bout of loneliness. How wretched—to be pining after a dog. What was there for me here?

There is everything there will be here.

Shut up, I thought, just shut up. I am at my brink.

Hah! Good. At long last.

I moaned in exasperation and toted my bucket around back, where I could use the privy and then bathe on the wide stone behind. The cold water would dispel my thoughts.

I avoided further contact with Arabella and Velora and went to bed early that evening, even before the children were home from berry picking. My cot was in the study and afforded me some privacy. Arabella entered at a point, waking me from a light slumber.

"Brought you some dinner, sugar," I heard her say quietly. I could feel the touch of lantern light from the hallway on my face but I didn't open my eyes, nor did I reply. I heard her steps retreat, and the door closed. Good. I was full enough from the tavern lunch and exhausted. I needed sleep, and I could already feel the next day, as though it were seeping in through the night around me.

In the dark, I arose to piss, praying that it would not yet be morning. I reached the backyard and took in the sky—a vast dome of fading stars, the spaces between them already more blue than black. I felt like weeping. My eyes ached, and somehow I was no more rested than had I dozed for a mere moment. The Tattons' cock crowed like a gargling daemon, as if to seal my doom. I yawned, which did prompt several tears from my eyes. I let them run down my cheeks, hanging my head back, offering my neck to the coming dawn.

It would be sweltering again, I could feel. The sky was cloudless, and it was warm already in the half-dark. The dew on the grass, on my feet, was the only cool thing, and it would soon be gone. I cast off my cloak and twirled myself around with my arms out, head back, and toes delving into the earth. Then I crouched and ran my hands through the low grass, palms up like twin scythes that wouldn't cut. Like this I reaped the dew and rubbed it on my face, my neck, my thighs. My skin quickened and I shuddered. The droplets on my flesh misted up and into the air and I felt my blood coursing through me.

When I returned inside, Arabella was already in the kitchen. It was darker than in the yard, the only light coming from a lantern hanging above the butcher block, but I made out her starched linen skirt and favourite green bodice. She was stooped over Fanny, the small one, who held a tight fistful of her skirt with one hand, two fingers of her other hand in her mouth. Fanny stared at me warily, one half of her hair combed out like a tuft of bush, some of her eyelashes still tangled from sleep. Arabella was braiding the other half of her head.

"Be a helping hand to your auntie today, you hear?" said Arabella as I entered.

Fanny's eyes remained on me, glaring, as though she hadn't quite decided that I wasn't an apparition.

I went to the pantry shelves and my hands sought out the jars of hominy, sugar, and lard.

"What say you we do the washing by the stream, Fanny?" I said, glancing back over my shoulder to her.

Her eyes widened, but she said nothing. Arabella snorted gently and shifted around to do the bushy side of Fanny's head. Fanny stared resolutely at me, and her grip remained on the fistful of skirt, and it lifted as Arabella moved, as though it were taken by a bout of wind.

"Ain't fully wake yet, are you, honey?" murmured Arabella.

"Course, you could keep sleeping, like a normal child, 'stead of rising like the dead . . . but that ain't your way, is it, sweetie?"

"You going into town?" I asked, pausing to prod at the basket of berries on the table.

"Mm-hmm," she hummed.

"Good," I said simply. And I meant it. We would be a week late on the news if we didn't send it in by Sunday.

"Anything in particular I should know?" she asked.

"No. Well. Nothing you likely don't already know. Circe said they kidnapped Gabriel before going over to Simeon. Tortured him."

"Mm-hmm. Heard that. Poor child."

"And Simeon reported that the old woman seemed to turn one of them, the Indian, to her favour, right before . . ." I trailed off, remembering that night, as if I had borne witness to it all.

"Curious."

I thought to warn her of the old woman's demand for pears. Of her callous sneer. But I held my tongue. It wouldn't matter, anyhow. Everyone bent to Arabella's will.

Instead I simply nodded, and balanced the berry basket in my already laden arms, preparing to step out back again.

"I wanna do the fire," blurted Fanny, her voice raspy.

"Not today, honey, you too young still," said Arabella.

She was pulling the final strands into Fanny's second plait, and Fanny, with her hair now tight to her head, and her big eyes, looked like a little billy goat.

"I can brush your hair," countered Fanny, still staring warily at me.

I saw Arabella's smirk as the child unclasped her fist from the skirt and opened her hand, presumably awaiting the comb.

I tried to match her bovine glare.

"You need it," she assured me.

We were at the stream when the clouds began to roll over like a great, dark otherworld tumbling above the earth, and I prayed, for a moment, that what we heard was a clap of thunder.

Fanny and I had spent the morning together. The older children, Lewis and Chloe, were gone to one of the pre–Emancipation Day working bees, but she was too young still to go with them. Velora was too old to watch her, and Tom was mowing for the neighbourhood. On days such as these, she fell with me.

Fanny was insistent on her participation in all forms of labour that she witnessed. If she was to simply play and entertain herself, she would have to be tricked into it. There was no reasoning with her. She had the fervour of Arabella, if not the eloquence, and had much to say of her own physical prowess and stamina. But once she was in the task itself, it became clear that regardless of how proficient she was, her true goal was social. Down at the stream, she pushed the hem of a skirt against the washboard vigourously for about a minute, before sighing and flicking the suds on her hand into the water. She watched the froth swirl around her ankles and then float off, until it was torn asunder by a nearby log, half out of the water. She put a hand on her hip and gazed at the bushes on the other side of the stream.

"Fan, this skirt still needs those strong hands of yours," I chided.

She released another long sigh, and shook her head as though there were sorrows on her mind that she could not even begin to express.

I tried not to smirk.

"I'm never gonna be old," she said, still looking out across the water. "Every day comes, and I still ain't old." She looked down at her feet. "Auntie says I was a baby once, and they had to send me 'cross the river like baby Moses."

I had heard the tale.

She sighed a third time, as if this report of the passage of time were terribly insufficient in assuaging her current doubt.

"Wanna know a secret?" she asked, her brows lifting with excitement, her misery evaporating.

"Sure."

She leaned in toward me, both hands on her hips.

"Miss Walker has a baby."

She whispered, despite us being quite alone, and drew out the word *baby*, real slow. Her breath was hot and sour.

I knew—I had already been approached in the search for an interim schoolteacher—but I could see this was particularly sensational for Fanny, and so I feigned surprise, nodding slowly.

"It kicks her already, from inside her stomach," she mused,

standing straight now and nodding earnestly. "It's a kicking baby."

I hummed in affirmation and nodded, before coming to an idea.

"Fanny honey, do me a favour. Take my knife," I said, fishing it from my satchel. "And very carefully, see that young black birch up a little way? Yes, that one. Go to it, and from one of the little branches, cut yourself a chewing stick. Sound good, honey?"

Her eyes were wide and she smiled in a crazed way as she examined the knife in her hands. She began to draw it from the leather sheath.

"No, you keep that on it till you ready to use it, hear?"

Her smile disappeared and she nodded vigourously.

"And once you made your cut, put it back in the sheath, understand?"

I mimed the action slowly to be sure she understood.

"Yes, Sinda."

"And Fanny—just remember: yesterday I wouldn't have let you use that. That's only 'cause you older."

A hint of her smile returned, and then she turned and was off, prancing out onto the bank and toward the birch tree. I shifted my seat on the rock so that I could see her while I worked.

She meandered up to the tree, skipping until she stopped abruptly to sit and examine her foot, bringing it startlingly close to her face. She looked up at me but I lowered my head to the washboard and pretended not to notice her. She could take her time—this was perhaps my best chance to get the washing done.

She withdrew the knife from the sheath and prodded the bottom of her foot like it was her school slate tablet. My stomach clenched, and I nearly called out to her, but I restrained myself. The blade wasn't terribly sharp, after all, but I looked around to be sure no one else would witness this, for such a sight would not go over well with Velora or Arabella. But Arabella was gone to town, of course, and Velora considered herself too old to walk about the savannah. We were down the gentle slope from our lane and the meadow. Around us was this shallow valley: the stream, gurgling over rounded stones on its way down to the swamp; the stooping oaks, heavy with age; some smaller trees, like the birch; the long grass and the chittering birds.

This was when I noticed the cloud, rolling in slow from the southwest.

Fanny took some time gallivanting about the tree, pausing to draw the knife and shout at it. I let her play, and pushed hurriedly through the task of washing and wringing cloth. By the time her muddied feet splashed into the stream again, I was nearly done.

She brandished her branch at me.

"Very good, Fan. Let me see that. And the knife too."

I stripped the bark for her and handed it back. "Now, sit and chew!"

Fanny obliged, gnawing studiously on her stick.

That was when we heard the gunshot.

I looked to the cloud, but it was passing us, and I knew, before the sound had finished clamouring, that it was not thunder. It was not far from us. No farther than the main road. Fanny's eyes were wide, the stick clenched in her teeth.

Then there was another. And another. Then two more.

I put the washboard and the remaining clothes in the basket and reached to her.

"Fanny. Take my hand now. We gonna walk slow up to the house. Don't make a sound."

There were no more shots, but as we skirted the meadow and neared our yard, we heard shouting from the lane, very close. I recognized the voice of Yarrow, the dog master. His booming yell, then a howl. I considered waiting in the savannah, but I felt exposed outside, and I did not want to turn my back to whatever ruckus was ahead of us and find myself running in the open bush. At least indoors I could barricade, keep Fanny safe. We tiptoed through the yard, up the side of the house, and slowly around the porch. I could guess, from the words I discerned in Yarrow's wail, what had happened before I saw it.

Three constables, all but one atop horses. Their backs were to us, and they struggled to still the beasts, prancing and snorting with panic. One of the horses had blood running down the knee. They faced the main road, blockaded by Yarrow, his hair wet on his forehead where his hat had been, his portly figure heaving with breath. On one side of him was Tom, standing nearly as tall as the horses, holding his scythe, the blade of it curving up at his feet, his own hat casting his eyes in shade. On Yarrow's other side was Saison, his cane in one hand, the other holding Yarrow's shoulder as the bigger man rollicked in grief.

Around all of them were three dogs, dead and dying on the freshly cut grass.

Yarrow was moaning and muttering. "Sons o' bitches," he was saying, again and again. His one hand was atop his head, and I realized that I had never seen Yarrow without his hat. His other hand he held strangely rigid, four fingers pointed to the ground. I looked past him and could see more dogs, many more. They were quiet, but all crouched and bristling. On some, I could see their bared teeth, even from where I stood. My grip on Fanny's hand tightened.

"Fanny, you get in the house."

"No thank you."

"Fanny, I ain't asking—get!"

"*No!*"

I looked up and saw one of the constables glance at us, and Tom raised his head, though his eyes were still obscured beneath his cap.

I picked Fanny up and she shrieked, clawing at my neck like a little beast. I carried her to the front door and threw her inside and shut it. I heard her scream again, felt her pull against the door, but I held it firm without much effort. I would go in with her, but when she calmed. And I could not shake the need to bear witness to whatever was coming to pass here.

"John, my hand," said one of the constables.

I recognized him—the young one from the other night. He clutched one hand with the other, and I saw his whole back quivering. A bite; a bad one by the looks of it.

John, I presume, cleared his throat.

"Now, boys, we don't want any more trouble. We're sorry for your dogs, but if they attack on public property, I or any other man—"

"They're doing what you couldn't do, dammit!"

Yarrow spat as he yelled.

"Where was you yesterday, huh?"

"Now, calm down—"

"*Where was you yesterday!*"

The dogs yipped behind Yarrow and he thrust his hand down again in that rigid manner, silencing them. I even heard a whimper.

"Now, that's enough of that!" the older constable, John, shouted as he drew his pistol, pointing it skyward. His horse shuffled nervously.

I saw Tom take a small step forward, as if readying for a stroke with the scythe. My heart quickened. Would this be what pushed him to violence? He was large enough that even a bullet would not stop his blow. And that blade. I shuddered thinking of how deeply it would cleave flesh. Such a wound would not be healed.

Saison let go of Yarrow and waved both hands above his head, shouting pleadingly and walking forward to the horsemen.

Shit, I thought. If only Arabella were here.

As this was happening, a small figure, a gnome, crept from beside the house to the body of the nearest dog, which was at the edge of the lane, between me and the constables. I had noticed it but didn't look because the action of the men was so big and loud, and I figured the small being was a figment of my imagination, a trick of the midday sun. But as Saison waved, I saw, from the corner of my eye, the dog raise her head up to the gnome—a last, dying look. It was the dog who had followed me the day before. The black fur of her neck wet with blood. And the gnome, I could see, wore a small blue frock and two tight braids on the back of its head.

"Fanny!"

I heard the terrible shriek in my throat as though it were coming from some faraway place.

I heard my own feet clatter on the porch and then thump in the grass, and then I was there, the dog blinking weakly, Fanny strangely calm in my arms. I was expecting her to fight, but she was soft, and her calm astounded me. I looked her over, and felt her, to see if she was hurt, but nothing. Her eyes were serene and sad.

"She was a nice dog," she said.

I looked out to the men. They were bigger than they had seemed from the porch, and staring at us. As if this hot grass of the lane was a stage I had unwittingly thrust myself upon, and they, the actors, were dumbfounded at an insolent intrusion from the audience.

It would have been comical if not for the dying dogs, and the live ones. And the primed pistol. And the scythe.

I began to back away slowly, with Fanny in my arms.

"Hi, Daddy," she said.

"Hey, baby girl," said Tom.

They all still stared.

"Get on in the house, now," he said.

"Yes, Daddy," she piped sweetly.

I could have strangled her, but continued stepping away, toward the backyard.

"Look," said Yarrow, reentering the scene, "you come back unannounced, they will again be on the prowl. And then I shan't call them off."

He clucked his tongue and pointed eastward. "Home," he said.

The pack of dogs behind him trotted off past houses and into the bush. Yarrow shook his head and followed them. Saison put his hand on Tom's shoulder and ushered him toward his porch. From there, they stood and watched.

I rounded the back of our house and heard the constables mutter curses. Then the sound of hoof steps as they rode off first down the lane and then eastward, on the main road. Then there was quiet.

Arabella returned shortly thereafter, and by the time she arrived at the house, she had of course heard the news of the day. All the working bees had been interrupted to investigate the shooting, and thereafter to help Yarrow cart off the dead dogs and bury them on his land. By that time, Circe and Deacon had chicken, or some type of bird, roasting, by the smells of it, and folk had begun to congregate in the tavern yard. I heard the whine of a fiddle, a trembling tambourine, and the hum of singing voices. The choir of sin, as Velora called it. There would be surreptitious servings of dandelion wine, I wagered. And sure enough, by and by I could hear snippets of Yarrow's drunken bellow.

Fanny was sleeping in my cot. She had insisted that if she was to have a nap, she would very much like to try my cot. I hadn't fought her; I was too eager to have her incapacitated. The clothes were still down by the stream. Normally I would have gone to fetch them, but after the events of the day I wouldn't dare leave that child alone again. Instead, I sat at the desk of the study and tried to write.

To my surprise, I found my pen moving well. I didn't know the old crone's story, but as I wrote I began to question how much I needed to know of that. I knew enough of the bounty hunters' movements through town, and then the farm. I had been close enough to see, in frightening detail, how the events of that night now threatened to push Dunmore into the abyss. No, the old woman I didn't know, but what was she to the story anyway? An old slave woman, tired of running, who'd had the mettle to pick up a gun.

Arabella found me reading over my own words. She stayed at the house while I went to get the laundry. When I returned, I began hanging clothes. It was late for drying, but I had hope: the days were still long, and the yard took the afternoon sun. Arabella came out and picked up a bedsheet from the basket. She shook it out of its tight twist and extended one corner to me. She had changed into a loose frock, and this made her look more real, more human. I noticed, as if for the first time since knowing her, the droop of her shoulders and breasts. She smiled wearily at me.

"I'm sorry about Fanny," I said. "It was foolish of me to let her out of my sight. I hope you and Tom will forgive me."

Arabella nodded. "She's slippery, that one," she said.

"I should have locked both doors."

"Good thing you didn't! Then she would have broken the window."

We chuckled.

"Don't worry about Tom," she went on. "Besides, he and Yarrow are busy boasting about how she saved the day from more bloodshed. Descended like a cherub from heaven."

I sniffed and shook my head. Cherub my arse.

We worked silently for a moment, listening to the sounds of gathering at the tavern, and the buzzing of the meadow.

"Sinda," Arabella began, "I'm sorry to say you'll have to return."

I didn't understand, and leaned around the shirt I was hanging to look at her.

"To the jail," she said.

"What are you talking about?"

"The old woman. She wouldn't talk to me."

This made no sense. Was she joking? I couldn't tell. She looked at me frankly enough, but I could discern a hint of a smile around her lips.

"Very funny," I said, resuming my task.

"I suppose it is!" she chortled. "In an unexpected way, yes. But still quite true, I'm afraid."

I whipped back around to look at her. "She wouldn't speak to *you*? You, Arabella Brimmer?"

"Not a word," she said, shaking her head. "Well, word enough to chide me for failing to bring a gift."

I could not believe my ears.

"Pears?" I asked in nearly a whisper.

"Yes!" She laughed, her head back, and then stood, regarding the sky with a lingering smile, as if she were unexpectedly struck by its beauty. "I don't even think anyone grows pears anymore," she mused.

I was confounded. This news was rewriting the order of my world.

"She asked for you too," she said.

"No."

"Yes, ma'am—said she wouldn't speak a word more if not to you."

"How . . ." I trailed off, still failing to imagine this as truth. What had I missed? What did she want with me?

Ah look, how your spirit yearns to know.

I shook myself out of my bewilderment.

"It doesn't matter, Arabella—I've figured it. Wrote a piece already. We don't need her. We have a decent story without her testimony."

Arabella smiled warmly—condescendingly again, I thought, and I felt myself begin to bristle.

"That's wonderful, Sinda; we can send it off soon as you're happy with it. But the woman's story we must have. It ain't just about the paper, sugar. It's about the case to come. It's about the money we can raise, and the men we can galvanize to action. It's about making a change in this country. A change in both countries, even."

I huffed and continued hanging clothes.

"Sinda, you know what the abolitionists need. They do not live what we live!"

Her voice struck an urgent pitch. She was in full churchwoman swing now.

"A man can only act on what he sees. And our lives will only ever be a story that they can glimpse through *your* ink, *your* words!"

She paused to survey me. I didn't meet her gaze. She took a step closer, speaking softer now. "A tale that reminds them, in brutal detail, of the injustice we suffer, and of their duty to intervene."

"And what if that's not her story?"

"Come now, Sinda. The woman must have been what—eighty years a slave? You know what that means."

I glared at her a moment, before responding.

"I think I've told you, before coming to Dunmore, I lived my whole life in my father's house."

She smiled gently and nodded.

"And have I told you, to this day, I do not know what he endured, or even where?"

I looked straight at her, and her eyes grew even softer, more comforting.

"I'm sorry, sugar, that silence can be hard."

"Sorrow or not, some people don't want to speak of their suffering. And I am not the one to deny them that choice."

She looked at me solemnly, for a long time. The frog calls began to pipe up from the swamp, and there was in the distance a chorus of laughter from the tavern. Arabella's eyes were full and attentive to my every detail, and I felt naked before her. Then, a smile.

"But would you deny them a chance to tell their story on their own terms?" she asked.

"No, that's another—"

"So you'll go, then!"

"What?"

"I'll prepare your fruit," she quipped, still smiling, and bustled off.

"But Arabella—"

"Don't worry, dear," she said, waving a hand back at me. "If there are pears in this backwater, I'll find them! Mind Fanny, please!"

She was gone and onto the lane, leaving me, a light wind wrapping a damp sheet on the line around me like a shroud.

"Shit," I muttered under my breath.

Chapter IV

Pears were nowhere to be found. But Mrs. Tatton supplied Arabella with a generous portion of mulberry, plum, currant, and raspberry—as well as a full jar of jam, famous at the picnic to come. Additionally, Circe contributed a cloth full of biscuits, a quarter of a round of cheese, and some of that leftover ham. I brought it all with me, and at the courthouse I suffered the turnkey's ramblings as he inspected the basket.

And then, there she was again, as though I had never left, seated with her legs out in the hay, and grinning at me.

"Now, look what you've brought me this fine day, James," she said.

The turnkey chuckled. "Yes and with a proper feast too. You ladies fancy a picnic to celebrate the day?"

"Oh, I don't know about all that. I'm not British, you know, James."

"Hogwash! Come on to the pen, it's lovely out."

I looked between the two of them, chatting like old friends. James opened the cell door, and the old woman extended a hand toward him. He helped her up and she brushed off her frock, grunted, and trotted out of the cell behind him. I stood, confounded for a moment. The woman waved a hand at me, beckoning me to follow. A guard, dressed like a constable, walked slowly down the hall toward us.

She turned back to me again. "Bring the stool," she said, pointing at the small milking stool outside the cell.

"Oh, and dear James," she said, and he turned to her. She gestured with her head at the guard who moved down the hall toward us.

"Mind your post, lad!" James shouted. "I'll handle this lot."

He was at the end of the hall, his hand on a large door. The other guard nodded and returned, just as eerily as he had come, to the darkness.

I bent to take up the stool, looking cautiously at the old woman and the turnkey. Her charm had, somehow, in that moment, expanded to something far more powerful. Did she have designs to rope me into some plan of escape? I would have to watch her closely.

James guided us to the outdoor courtyard, what the prisoners called the pen. It was a square of unkempt grass and high, cut-stone walls, over which we could hear the movement in the streets of Chatham.

James left us there with a jug of water, and we settled in the crook of a wall. I offered the old woman the stool, but she waved it away, and with her back against the wall she crouched and extended her hands to me, as if in prayer.

"Pour me some water, girl," she said.

I sat on the stool and took up the jug, tipping it over her

hands. She caught the stream and rubbed her palms, fingers, and face for a long moment. When she looked up at me, droplets hung from her eyelashes.

"Next visit, soap, yes?"

I nodded, feeling, begrudgingly, a pang of pity for the old woman. Shame, perhaps, at having been so ready to abandon her. And beneath all that, a firm and resolute feeling in my gut that recoiled from me before I could name it.

"So," she began, crossing her legs and pulling the basket to her, "no pears, no pears. . . . No Frenchmen anymore, then?"

"Hardly, I suppose," I said, realizing the connection. I suddenly remembered reading, somewhere in Frost's library, that Detroit and its surroundings had once—a lifetime ago—been quite French, and that many of that tongue were orchard masters of apple, yes, but also pear.

"A fine plum will do," she said, and took a full bite of the blood-dark fruit and then hummed with pleasure.

She chewed and slurped, blinking her eyes comically at me. The green innards of the fruit shimmered in her hand like light.

"Thank you, girl," she said, bowing her head.

"Now," she proclaimed, still chewing, "while I gorge, a tale. One from you, yes?"

I nodded and took a breath. The night before I had prepared as much as I could for this trading of tales, though the fear of my own ineptitude made my heart flutter.

"Don't be shy, now," she mumbled through the plum. "My mouth may be full but you have my ears."

This unrelenting heat has reminded me of a summer some ten years ago. I was still in Spancel Narrows then, and it was the orchard keeper Victoria Younger who brought the idea forth. At first mention, the men groaned like dogs.

"You want a what?" said Paul, one foot up on a cedar timber, leaning on the handle of his bucksaw, which was clamped in the cut, halfway through the log.

The timber jutted proudly up and out of the woods where the men had felled and limbed it. They were at work on the long, part-time task of the corduroy road, which was by then almost finished. The road was in its second summer of construction; the men had built it over the bumpy footpath that began where the proper road ended abruptly, in uptown Spancel Narrows. They wouldn't finish that day, but they were damn near it. Already the quarter was singing their praises, for where the footpath had been a narrow and muddy affair, the levelled logs drained well and provided stable footing for men and mules alike.

I looked between them and the cluster of houses above us. Twenty or thirty more logs would bring the road to the flat point where people sometimes gathered to picnic and light a fire. But now, before even this latest scheme was completed, Victoria was asking for more.

"I want for us to rent a steamboat for Emancipation Day," she said again, speaking with as much gusto as annoyance.

Paul had stopped his rhythmic push-pull behind the saw to

gulp a tin of the cider Mary and I had carefully shuffled down in several jugs in the hold of a cart. The other men too had emerged from the bush to drink, still holding or leaning on hewing axes and cant hooks. Junior, my brother, lay in crooked relaxation, cradled in a thick coil of ship rope with his hat over his eyes. It was Sunday work, after all, done on our own time, which meant that a measure of idle chat and gossip were accepted portions of the bargain.

Paul was a stout and ruddy man who worked at the mill in town; thusly he could supply some tools and expertise to lumber work. In the summer he always seemed to overdress; a constant stream of sweat flooded from his pate and the lids of his eyes. The sweat ran diligently around his cheeks, pooling sometimes on his bumptious lips. Likely for this reason he was often in the habit of smothering his face in his kerchief with a disturbing vigour.

"Hell," said Paul, responding to Victoria but speaking to everyone, "what you want to go to sea for right when we all but finish Queen Victoria's highway?"

He thrust his open hand toward the road, the green wood neatly cut and embedded in a path that curled around the steep wooded rise. Folk chuckled cruelly at that. Cruelly, because the corduroy road had also been Victoria's idea. And it was a good idea. For years, folk had been damaging wares and spraining ankles trucking loads up the steep footpath from town. The Negro quarter of Spancel coveted the privacy of the woods and the slope, but had never failed to begrudge the troubles that the journey here entailed. Many would have simply continued indefinitely killing themselves on their daily way up and down. But Victoria persistently summoned one and all, Sunday after Sunday, until "the highway" was built, and the people of the quarter could trot proudly to town.

"Tell you what," said Stephen Ayre as he topped his tin with cider, "the day they let a whole bunch of niggers take a steamboat out on the lake"—he paused to gulp greedily and then smacked his lips—"be the day that steamboat mysteriously sink!"

Folk laughed again, but nervously this time. The Ayres were still a new family in Spancel Narrows, and as such Stephen didn't rightly have his talk-back privilege. Victoria glared at him with her stony eyes until he withered and began to whistle nervously, and the men looked down and away and began to chirp and mutter.

Don't look too square, Stephen; you might not have another child.

She giving you the overseer eyes, shit.

I stood close to my friend Mary, and we glanced knowingly at each other before sipping long and slow from our tins, so as not to reveal our smiles. I relished the tart and cool flavour of the cider and glimpsed the curve of my nose in the amber liquid.

"Well I think it's about time we celebrate the day," said Victoria, finally, her hands tucked in her starched apron. "I've discussed with McCullough and we need twenty dollars to rent the steamboat. We have a month to put the money together. I've given him a five-dollar deposit already, so any who have the means to contribute, you bring the money to me before the twenty-fifth of this month."

And with that she turned and walked back up the hill to roll dough, as was her custom in the evenings.

Mary and I stayed awhile with the men until they were bored with their own chat and went back to work, invigourated by the cider and the smells of their suppers that began to waft from the cabins all along the slope.

We lugged the cart of jugs and tins sticky with the remains of the juice back up to Victoria's shanty.

When Victoria first arrived to Spancel Narrows, she worked as a washerwoman for five years. During that time she would go in the early mornings to prune and multiply old half-wild apples in the forest of Samuel Frost's land until they grew to produce several different colours of fruit that were as sweet as they were tart. For these fruit, as well as for her apple butter and pie, she was famous not only in the quarter but in all of Spancel. Victoria knew how to *plan*. Despite what anyone might joke about, the idea of renting a steamboat for celebration was irresistibly intriguing—and if anyone could make it happen it was Victoria. Even those who had been on a steamboat had never done so in leisure. Some of the men might have stepped aboard as stevedores, lugging grain or lumber, or feeding wood to the boilers and dripping sweat from the intolerable heat. But to board a steamboat in leisure, and just sit on the water in the warmth of midsummer, not having to do anything but eat? That was a thought that brought an incurable smile to the lips.

And so, despite the gibes, everyone worked to make Victoria's plan happen.

The women passed a quilt from house to house to share the labour of stitching, and when it was finished we sold it for five dollars at the town market. Old man Henson and several others joined the road crew that worked Sundays, breaking stones in order to put money in the pot. Daddy put aside a couple of dollars from his month's salary. No one had money sitting around, but a month was enough time to conjure.

And food—well, that was easy. The Ayres mixed a batch of their strawberry cordial they were always boasting about. Mother dug up an early crop of potatoes and plucked a few choice ears of corn and Daddy brought home a sack of hog bones from the butcher wagon and we cooked a big batch of soup. Junior brought in a turkey, three partridges, a brace of pigeons, and several snipes, which he gave to Hestia to brine and smoke. Hestia herself sacrificed no fewer than three melons from her patch. And Victoria Younger went to work with her oven, her fruit, and her piecrusts. Other folk fished, baked bread, stewed greens, pickled pig feet, and gathered wild berries and plums. Someone even secured a small cask of brandy, but Victoria found that out and had them sell it and put the money toward the rental.

The ship captain, McCullough, gave up our reservation to the mayor a week prior, and could only say after the fact that he wasn't liable to deny the man rental when it was the mayor himself who'd loaned the money to buy the boat in the first place. So we went the following Sunday—not the actual date, but in truth the postponement and the lingering possibility that our reservation would be further disregarded lent a thrilling fervour to our preparations.

The day came to pass, and it was splendid; Victoria didn't even have to say so. She just sat back and smiled with her eyes and watched, her stillness broken only by an occasional frown and a quick chiding anytime a young 'un would get too rowdy. As we left harbour Flynn played on his banjo, Phyllis was on the fiddle, and old Jack struck a clacking rhythm on the bones. And once we were out of sight of the town we danced and hollered. The youngsters pulled the old folk up to dance and one of the newcomers shed tears because, as he said, the last time he capered it was in fetters at the pleasure of his master. I brought my mother up to do a jig and when she got tired I danced with Junior, then Mary. She and I twirled and glanced at the boys in the maroon reflections of each other's eyes. Then I myself got tired and dizzy and had to sit on the bench to settle my belly. When we were halfway to the end of the peninsula and all we could see was fierce blue water melting into sky on one side and the shore of quiet, listing jack pines on the other, the boat slowed to the gentle lap of the waves.

We feasted. There was delight to be had. Pigeon pie, boned turkey in jelly, broiled shad, a saddle of mutton, plum pudding, jellies, stews, soups. We ate until we were full and when we saw the extravagance that was left we ate some more out of embarrassment of having brought so much.

As we drifted along, I noticed some children had begun to clump by the gunwale at the stern of the boat, where they jostled and hollered. I rose from my recline against my mother's legs and wandered to them, away from the grown-folk chatter. I found Mary and stood by her with a hand on her shoulder. She looked out to where the children were pointing and waving. There were two canoes that were paddling up along the shore. There were men in each canoe and they were Indians, I could tell by the grey flicker of birch bark on their vessels. Little Susan hollered to them to come up and help with all the grub. One of the men hollered back, asking what we were having, and Susan and the children shouted over each other, counting off the dishes of our feast. By this time, a number of the women and men had come up behind us, peering curiously out at the water. The Indian in the canoe shouted to ask if we would trade for some fish, and he hoisted a large sturgeon. It was grey and scaled like a dragon and the children screeched and laughed. They continued to draw nearer, taking a curve away from shore to approach us. Daddy appeared at the gunwale and bellowed a few words that I did not understand, but that I took to be their language. The men in the canoes chattered back in a chorus that sounded as much like words as it did laughter. I left Mary and wended my way to my father, sneaking a hand in the crook of his arm. I looked at the movement of his throat as he spoke words I had no knowledge of. He adjusted his arm, putting it around my shoulders without looking at me. More words spilled out of his mouth, round and strange. The children watching tried to echo the sounds, interjecting boisterously. A young boy, Billy, emerged at the edge of the gunwale with his arms full of a coil of rope that he thrust over the edge. The rope thrummed against the hull of the boat as it fell, and the end of it hit the water softly and grew dark and graceful. Billy's mother scolded him. The Indians laughed; they were by then only a stone's throw distant, and they had stopped paddling to talk with Daddy. Their paddles, held firm in the water, drew curling ripples as they drifted.

On the deck behind us I heard a heavy stomping of feet, and I looked back to see McCullough bustling down from the pilot-house. His eyes were wild and he cut through our gathering like a knife. He reached the gunwale and cussed as he looked over it. He took the rope in his hands and brought it back up in a few powerful pulls. Billy's mother apologized to him, and folk sweet-talked him, telling him there wasn't no harm, and wouldn't he have some pie. He didn't respond but wrapped the rope, wet and dripping, around his shoulder and walked back to the pilothouse. Daddy spoke again to the men in the canoes, and they laughed. Billy laughed too, and loudly, but his mother cut it short with a fierce tug on his ear. We felt the rumble of the boiler below, and a gentle jolt as the paddle wheel behind us slapped the water and began to turn. The Indians and the shore fell away slowly, and we waved to them before they were out of sight behind the churning paddle wheel. The steamboat had begun its wide turn to the periwinkle blue of the water.

Folk spoke above the churning, and above the gentle brush of wind against us as we went back to the picnic spread at the main deck. Billy's mother led him by the ear. He knew not to squeal.

Some had developed another appetite by then and spooned another round of food into their bowls. I went back to Mother and stretched my legs out on the deck, leaning my head on her knees and nearly dozing in the gentle forward pushing of the boat. Mother tugged at my hair and began to braid it. I closed my eyes but could still see the light of the sun and I felt its warmth. My belly was straining with soup and salty smoked meat, and my mouth was still sweet from the pie. I settled in and just listened to the voices.

"Good Lord, I'm fit to bust."

"I say, this blue remind me of where I was born."

"Where was you born, Jack?"

"Peggy, pass me that pie, there's still debauchery to be had there."

"West Indies, just outside a town named Rosso."

"What! How come you never told anybody, Jack? Thought you was a thoroughbred American like the rest of us."

"No, I's a Frenchman."

There was a bout of laughter and snorts.

"When I got to New Orleans as a boy, I didn't even speak English."

"And before that? Where your mama come from?"

"My mama came from that very island. Had blacks there afore whites. That's all I know."

"Never heard of that before. You smuggled that brandy in, Jack?"

"Is true what I telling you."

"My mammy came from Africa soil. I know my mammy's story."

"Susan, don't stand on that railing like that!"

"I'm going with the Indians, Mama!"

"My mammy was the daughter of the chief of a tribe who lived on a great river called Charee. This I know to be true. My people had a wealth of ivory tusks. We were so wealthy that one day a band of Portuguese stole all that ivory and stole some people along with it. That's why when my Mama got here she never did accept slavery. She knew she was above it."

"Charley, go easy on them currants, boy."

"I'm telling you, I would hear her talking to the massa, telling him he was nothing, not a damn thing. Telling him that back in Africa soil she would have ten times the wealth he have. And y'all wonder how I learned to talk."

"How 'bout you, Dred? How'd you get to talk Indian?"

This, from Victoria, made me start and open my eyes slightly.

Daddy was leaning his back against the railing, picking apart a walnut. He smiled, or grimaced; I could discern the sly curve in the white wool of his beard.

In the silence, Charley Russet interjected. I knew it was because he was sweet for me, even though he was younger and smaller, neither of which was likely to change, as I was turning out to be a tall girl and Charley seemed to take after his short father, Paul.

Charley grunted, strutting like a little rooster to Victoria. "You ain't know?"

He gesticulated this more than he spoke it, his mouth stuffed with currants, tunic open to the sun like a little vagrant. He chewed urgently and swallowed.

"Everyone know Dred talk Indian."

He coughed and patted his paunch.

"*Everyone* know," he continued, pursing his purple lips in dramatic pause, glutting off the attention given to a storyteller who at least pretends to know what he is talking about.

"He took scalps of them paddy rollers and everything, ain't it so, Daddy?"

"Boy, shut your currant-thiefin' mouth 'fore you hurt yourself," said Henson, his spoon deep in a half melon perched in the crook of his thighs. "Where this boy learn to talk like that?"

"Where you think?" said Hestia, and everyone laughed. (Henson and Charley were practically inseparable.)

"But what of it?" said Phyllis, nursing her newborn boy, not yet named, beneath the shade of the pilothouse. "What of it, Dred? How did you come to talk Indian?"

Daddy squinted in the sun a moment, chewing his walnut. "Hell," he said, "you know I's so old, when I come up they didn't hardly have white folks. Just wild animals, Indians, and obeah worship."

People moaned and chuckled nervously, but Daddy wasn't one to fill an awkward silence.

"Well, I heard," said Phyllis, still nursing her babe, "that you and Henson came up through the church like the rest of us."

Henson smiled, shaking his head, and took a large scoop of melon in his mouth, chewing irreverently.

"That ain't the case," said Daddy. "I'd seen Henson once or twice down south, but I came up my own way."

"Mm-hm!" piped up Henson. "Fact, first I saw Dred this side of the border was down in Toronto, some twenty-odd years ago.

Before Junior and Sinda was born, right? That's right. We found ourselves pressed into a carriage, against our will, mind you, by none other than Mackenzie King and his lackeys. They were drumming up rebellion, ain't that right, Dred? Remember? Bade us take courage from the States and cast off *the shackles* of Great Britain."

Here folk rumbled with an orchestra of moans and kissed teeth.

"Oh yes," Henson went on, "and if I do recollect when the man said shackles, Dred here started to snort. I looked at him, biting my tongue, but I couldn't hardly help but laugh neither. And then once we started, oh Lord, there was no stopping! We was free men then, just hooting at the most ridiculous thing we heard in centuries! Oh, we was hooting—made those white boys good and nettled, their faces looking like this." Henson contorted his face like a gargoyle, and jerked his head side to side, so that all could see and laugh, till he himself broke out in laughter, slapping his knee.

"Oh, soon as they looked the other way, though, we made fast out that carriage and into the woods. Ain't it so, Dred?"

Daddy nodded, back to chewing on the walnut.

"Well," said Victoria, "for those of us too meek to make our own way, I am grateful that the church brought us out of darkness. Besides, I would sooner go back to slavery than to heathenry."

Whatever chuckles and smiles that had still been lingering from Henson's antics were cut short at this pronouncement. There were some amens, and moans of affirmation. I looked to

Victoria, confused. Her hands were crossed and she was nodding slightly and looking resolutely at the boat deck. I knew that despite responding to Henson, her interjection was directed at Daddy. I felt anger rising in my gut—what right did she have to that stern look? And had anyone even noticed? They must have, for there was, despite the murmurs, a lull, uncharacteristic of the Spancel crowd. Daddy said nothing—he was dissecting another walnut with his knife, and his face was back to its faint grin that could equally be a grimace. I looked to Mary, but her eyes were fawning on Victoria, and I realized that what I saw as cruelty, Mary saw as a necessary, pious charisma. Hestia I found sitting in the shade of the pilothouse, raising an expectant eyebrow at Henson. My mother put a hand on my shoulder, but she was silent as well, and I felt the silence heavy on my own lips, and my anger grew feeble and withered, until it could only be described as loneliness. Henson finally chimed in:

"Oh, don't even mention that, girl, ain't none of us going back to nothing."

"I'm just saying, chains or no, my spirit free."

"Amen."

This time, a firm chorus of amens echoed through the group.

Victoria had not missed a beat. It was as if she had been waiting at the ready for a response. And with that staunch sentiment, the people found their voice, and the deck was in motion again, animated now by a bout of slave tales. How *ill* or *well* used you could be by your master. How you carried on at nightfall and evaded patrol. The great working bees in the barns of Maryland and Virginia. The lash, the hundreds and hundreds of lashes.

The way flesh cracks open to the whip. The way a pummelling from a paddle bored with auger holes will swell up a body to twice its normal size. Memories of men and women half-buried like fence posts and whipped to their core.

Memories too of the free camps of the swamps and the underlands of the backwoods. Tales of the scrupulous studies, and of the very dreams that made way for escape. The caves in which you hid. The friendly coloured folk, whites, and Indians who helped along the route. The dastardly meddlers who shot your back as you ran, and the constables who arrested you at Baton Rouge and Louisville; Baltimore and Pittsburgh; Cincinnati and Buffalo, even. Yes, even there, at the cusp of your freedom. And thenceforth the peddling doughfaces who raised money for starving fugitives of which ne'er a one fugitive had seen a cent!

And as they spoke, folk would rub the scars they could reach at their ribs, and at pieces of lead still nestled near the bones behind their knees and under their shoulder blades.

This was usually the stuff of nighttime storytelling, and here, in the open sea, where the sun pierced every veil, folk were aquiver with the newness of stories told in the light. It could be that under that glorious sky, these stories emerged as a commemoration to mark the immense victory of our existence there. The only other times such talk emerged in the light of day was at the portent of an unspeakable break in the ground between us. It was talk to skirt such a rifting, a rifting too vast to bridge. I've often wondered if it's the same in all promised lands; there are green pastures, and then there are chasms. In our case I suppose it was because the land, though it may have been promised, was not truly ours. Not ours at all. We were merely tenants of a more temperate lord than we were used to. Having suffered the terror of bondage, the rule of a temperate lord may feel like sovereignty, even if it isn't. And not a one could deny the suffering that we shared. So we reminded each other, again and again. Tales of our suffering made one feel that anything after that surely must be freedom.

But this is my father speaking through me, of course. Or rather, something like this is what I imagine he would say, if he had the words.

Chapter V

The old woman chuckled as I finished speaking. She nodded too, sitting on the grass with her back against the west wall, which was now lit up with the morning sun.

"So that," she said, "is how peddlers of British freedom celebrate."

I nodded and smiled, despite myself. She squinted at me, her eyes grey as the stone of the wall behind her.

"Questions, many questions . . ." she mused, raising her eyebrow at me, "but a question first, before we fall too deep: What changed in your spirit?"

I didn't understand.

"Come now," she huffed. "When you last left here you were like a slave fleeing the whip! What changed? A new appetite for lashing?"

I bit my tongue hard at a rebuttal, and instead calmly reached into my satchel and pulled out a folded newspaper.

"Simply this," I said, and tossed it on the grass in front of her. She glanced at it and snuffed.

"It's the county paper," I said. "Reprinted from somewhere south. It reads 'assassination' on the front there, in big letters. It's about you and the bounty man."

She hummed like a barred owl.

"You write that?" she muttered.

"I'm not so sensational," I said, meeting her eyes. She almost looked disappointed.

"I write for another paper," I continued. "A coloured paper. We'll publish the story this week, in different terms than the one before you, no doubt. But we'd very much like to hear that story from your own mouth. So I brought you fruit, and a tale."

The old woman nodded and patted her knees.

"I have much to tell you, girl. In good time. Your tale was good."

She looked ahead, squinting, and she raised a finger, bobbing it in the air. "But now, another question: you said you were lonely that day."

She looked at me, cocking her head so pointedly that I doubted she held real curiosity. She was playing. At what, I didn't know.

"On the water," she prompted.

I looked at her stonily for a moment more, before sighing in resignation.

"I felt I was in some way bound, or marked by . . . by my father's past, and yet I didn't even know what that past was."

"Oh," she cooed sagely, and then fixed her eyes on me again. "And did you ask him?"

"If you knew him," I said, "you would know how much use that would be."

"Did you fear what he would say? Perhaps he lived something so terrible, you were afraid to hear of it?" she prodded.

I had no response, and finally she hushed. Her words, though, remained in the quiet between us. We heard a man cussing a mule on the other side of the pen wall, and the old woman chuckled.

"I asked him," I said to her. "'I can't now,' he would say, or 'I reckon I won't say much more,' not minding that he hadn't said anything at all. And I grew tired of eking his memories out of him."

She hummed irritatingly. "Well, no matter," she said. "Why talk about what you know of him? Tell me what you know of yourself."

I hadn't come to speak about myself, and I feared another wasted trip. I felt irritation descend heavily on my brow like a stone.

The old woman saw this and laughed. "Ooh, you have a wonderful rage brewing in you, girl."

"What I know about myself," I began, straining to curtail my grimace, and she nodded, humming.

"I am a woman of little patience," I said. She continued the infernal humming as I spoke, and this only served to stoke my ire.

"But I am your ally already," I went on solemnly, and this seemed to silence her noises, if only for a moment. "I was even before we met. Believe me, if Simeon hadn't called the sheriff I would have secreted you far enough north that no law would have found you."

The old woman looked at me, squinting. The sun was now in her eyes, making them gleam. She seemed perfectly comfortable. I continued: "But Simeon did call, and so here we are. I will bring you fruit, if you desire. I will listen to your story. But that is the extent of the comfort I can provide you."

"I don't seek comfort from you, girl," snapped the old woman, jutting her head into the shade between us. She glared at me darkly before continuing.

"Or anyone, for that matter," she said, and leaned back, closing her eyes against the sun. "A tale for a tale. Very well. Where I was born, you have asked to know . . . well—that's something else. Let's begin like this: there was a village once, at the wayside of a vast swamp that was full-full with beasts, bulrush, wild rice, and trees."

The old woman was a teller indeed; she spoke with motion in her hands. Her voice rose like a sudden gust of wind, and fell quiet like the shuffle of leaves. She lingered in silence between words.

"The people of the village knew what too few know now: that home is a changing thing, and no home will be so forever. But they contented themselves with a place for a while. And after a while, they would move on.

"One day, a man and a woman came to this village in a large canoe, filled with many wondrous things. Goods of great trade value. The two offered the village the goods in exchange for sanctuary. They were strangers, appearing like spirits on the water. And since they were strangers, the elders of the village thought for three days and three nights over what to do. One elder believed that the couple was a gift to reward the people of the village for choosing a good place. Another believed they were a curse, sent by a trickster god, and that whatever they gave the village would be ripped back again, tenfold. A third elder, after listening and watching for quite some time, went into the swamp to think real hard on what should be done. This third elder came back, and said what she had come to: that both elders before her had spoken some truth. The couple was a gift indeed; they were strong with the flame of life, and they would work hard and birth children. On the other hand, the canoe filled with wondrous things—that was a trick. A trick to make the eyes forget what they had already seen.

"You see, those winters ago, the land had plenty—plenty that the people knew how to receive. Those days the pigeons numbered so many, when they flew they cast the land in a fluttering darkness, blocking out the sun for a day and the moon for a night. To eat, one needed only shoot an arrow to the sky. The fish numbered so many they made the river hum, and one could walk across their backs and not fall in the water. The rice grew lush in the marsh and the fruits of the forest hung heavy on the boughs. The third elder knew this, knew that the village wanted for no canoe full with wondrous things. And so she said to accept the man and the woman, and to burn the canoe, and bury the things as gifts to the ancestors. And the people agreed with the third elder. They gave the man and woman refuge in the village, and the third elder took them into her clan. And by and by the two had many children, and played no small part in the fortune of that village."

The woman paused and breathed long, looking at me with a scrutiny that made me grimace. But I held her gaze. And finally, she spoke:

"And do you know who that woman was, who arrived at the swamp with a man and a canoe?"

"I would suppose it was you."

"And you would be right. And what, would you suppose, is my clan?"

The old woman grinned silently, with her head tilted back against the stone wall. She was now bathed in sun to her neck, and her head shone like a torch flame above her body.

"I haven't a clue," I said, looking squarely at her. "Am I to believe that this swamp in your tale is the very same swamp where Dunmore now moors?" I asked.

She did not respond, but grinned wider. I saw the dark spotted purple of her gums.

"An elaborate story," I said, more to myself than to her.

"What you believe," she replied sharply, "is none of my concern. You're not at Sunday service, girl. This is a tale for a tale. And it's your turn."

I looked on her a moment longer and wondered—really wondered—if there exists a greater nuisance than the whims of old people.

"I met with Emma last night, and she gave me your text," I said.

"Good!" she exclaimed. "And were you tempted?" Her eyes narrowed and glinted in the sunlight.

"I didn't read it, if that's what you're asking," I said. "Though I did note the name and the date, which I must admit has me curious. So I brought another text, to make good on our barter. This text I found back up in Spancel Narrows, in the study of the man who taught me to read."

I paused and glanced at the old woman. She leaned her head forward and blinked expectantly. So I continued.

"Frost was his name. He lived alone on an estate overlooking the water, east of Spancel and adjacent to the Negro quarter on its south side. There were rumours of why he wasn't married; rumours which, despite his wealth, made him a natural ally. And though he suffered, whether for the rumours, or for his proximity to us, he was indeed a friend. We knew this because Frost would never neglect to make a toast when we visited, passing around crystal glasses of sherry to whoever would drink, and his eyes behind his spectacles would well with tears.

"One day I was arranging a forgotten corner of his study, perched on a ladder with a silk kerchief about my mouth and nose to shield from the dust. There were mostly bills of sale to be put in the fireplace, and old surveys that I saved from flames, for they interested me a great deal more than they did Frost. But that day there was also a document I was not expecting to see. It was a thick sheaf of papers, and were it not for the leather jacket that enfolded them I might have lumped them into the coals with the old receipts. But I paused, and read. It seemed to be a journal with a woman's name at the top, and the writing was hard to decipher; quickly scribed, perhaps. The words were strangely familiar, like a story I had heard from one of the old-timers, yet I couldn't think of who it might be. I skimmed through the pages and saw a break in the script; a different name titled the page, and the words spoke in a different voice, though the handwriting remained the same. A few pages further there was yet another name, and as I continued I saw another, and another. As I pored over the pages, I realized what I held between my fingers: a compilation of fugitive stories, nearly half a century old."

The old woman hummed, her eyes now closed against the sun, and I waited a moment, noticing my fingertips rubbing on the cool leather of the sleeve in my satchel.

"I hollered for Frost, and he came to join me at the base of the ladder. He inspected the papers, squinting behind his delicate spectacles, and I saw his confusion slowly dissipate and reveal his most essential face: that of wonder. He told me the document must have been his father's, brought with him from the Maritimes, years ago. His father, a reverend and abolitionist, had helped in an effort to transcribe the narratives of the Negro British loyalists from the 1812 war. Many of them had been enslaved in the hinterland of Virginia, and the elder Reverend Frost was enlisted by an American in Washington. The goal, I gathered, was to record the fugitive stories and cast shame on their erstwhile masters. Frost didn't know whether the document had ever been published. I suspect it hadn't. There are so many that have not.

"He bade me take the papers when he saw my interest in them. As chance would have it, I left Spancel Narrows the very next night, and only when I was out on the open water did I realize I had the papers in my pack. And though I've kept them with me all this time I've never really read any of it."

"Why not?"

I shifted my eyes quickly to look at the old woman, who,

apart from this utterance, remained with her eyes closed, in perfect repose. I shrugged. "Sick of slave tales, I suppose," I said.

She snorted at that, giving no explanation, and I could feel the shame souring my cheek. Freeborn children had no right to be sick of slave tales. We were doomed to them. Beholden. Being an adult didn't change this, it seemed.

"Tell me their names, then," she said.

"The names. Well, yes. Here is the narrative of Louise Joachim, sixteen years a slave; Pollydore Limbo, thirty-eight years—a short one, that; Atwell and Allick Bailey, twenty-two years, quite long; Chiron Stock, thirty-one years, for several pages; Basel Veney—"

The old woman had begun chuckling wickedly, and I was trying to ignore her. "That one," she said.

"Basel Veney?"

"No."

"Chiron Stock?"

She nodded slowly, a smug grin on her sunlit face.

"Very well."

The Narrative of Chiron Stock

⚺

THIRTY-ONE YEARS A SLAVE

The winter of my birth, I was placed under the care of a slave named Monk. I'd sleep on his chest, and to keep me fed he'd take me up from our hammock to the sheep pen and nudge over a lamb and have me suckle ewe milk straight from the teat. That spring, Monk made a cradleboard to fit a saddle and I would spend hours strapped atop a gentle old draft horse named Hadrian as he and Monk loosed the soil for tobacco that first season after tragedy struck the Ruttles of the Piedmont.

I recollect falling asleep to the roll and hiccup of Hadrian's ploughing stride and the musk of his sweating haunch.

My father was Apollo, and him I've heard much about. Monk told me he came to Virginia fresh from Africa soil, and he must've learned to ride over there, 'cause he wasn't on the farm but for a few months the first time he saw a proper running horse. Monk told me he never would forget the day. All the hands out in the field suckering tobacco and Apollo ducked out of sight of the overseer and went right to the stable and started whispering to the beast. The horse was a hot-blooded, storm-grey Appaloosa, property of a visiting military man.

Soon enough the overseer saw he had a slave missing and set off in a panic. He found Apollo in the stable; horse and man, eyes closed, head-to-head. Well, that overseer started to holler and cuss and yell for the hands to bind this blackie fast for him to break a hickory rod over his head. But Apollo didn't wait for that. He leapt on the back of the horse, knocked down the overseer, and hightailed it straight down the path and then west into the woods. Monk told me so himself. Watched the whole thing from the field, pretending not to notice with the rest of the slaves as the overseer ran like they never seen him run to alert the men in the house, and then the house started to get loud with cussing, shouting, and carrying on. And within moments nearly all the white men on the property were saddled and armed, and headed out.

They tried to catch him, but wasn't no horse that could keep step with that Appaloosa, especially with a man riding like a daemon. Monk said he never would forget the sight of my pappy crouched up tight and disappearing into the mane, and the sound of that horse's hooves knocking the ground. Old man Ruttle pulled Monk out the field to help track him, seeing as Monk was more skilled than most mountain men, having lived among the Mingo for a spell of his youth. And Monk told me he tried to track my pappy. Followed the galloping hoof steps until they slowed and went for days into thick woods, up toward the Blue Ridge. Ruttle had the bloodhounds on the trail too, but somewhere up those mountains, the horse tracks got lost. Next thing you know, one of the dogs got took by a panther. They didn't see it. But they heard it. The half yip as fangs closed over the throat. The rest of the dogs barking all confused, skittering in circles on a precipice. The whole thing was such a mystery that those men got real shook up in them mountains and thought, though they didn't say, that my pappy dealt in a powerful type of wickedness. Ruttle put a bounty on him, but to no avail; he was clear gone, leaving the old man to pay heavily for that horse, fine beast that it was, and to swallow the loss of Apollo himself, a young, stout bondsman worth probably a thousand dollars. No one would admit so much, but many folk had something of a feeling that Apollo laid a curse upon that house that wasn't lifted for many years.

Monk told me my mama was a real quiet, beautiful woman named Fortuna, who wore her hair in a long braid. Said she was strong and sombre as her belly grew, and as the months crept by everybody was wondering, though they knew better than to talk about it—wondering whether Apollo would be back for her.

Monk recalled the night—the air was cool and fresh with vernal smells, and he slept deep and well. He had just got back from being rented out on a military excursion over the Blue Ridge, so he was dead tired. While usually not even a snake could pass under the barn without him knowing, this night, a Shawnee war party had done set fire to the house before Monk woke up. This was most unexpected, as raids so near the coast had diminished since the start of the Independence War.

Anyhow, when Monk did rise to the sound of mayhem, and come up out the barn to protect the house, he didn't get two steps before he took an arrow clean through his leg. Then those

Shawnee warriors butted him into the ground, and left him to do their business in the house. Good old Monk lay in the grass till he worked up the spunk to break off the arrowhead and pull out the shaft, whereupon he wrapped his wound real tight and made his way in the dark, crawling and hopping the five miles to the Tillotson house, where my mammy had gone to birth me.

In the time it took for Monk to reach there, and for the Tillotsons to round up the militia and make it to the Ruttles' house, it was already morning. The slaves that were there had taken old man Ruttle down from where the Indians had hung him up by the leg in the barn and pressed embers from his burnt-up house deep into him. He was half-naked, all raw with burns, and weeping over his two eldest sons, who lay bled out on the hay, and over his wife and youngest sons, who had been taken by the band.

Old man Ruttle swears he saw my father among them.

"I saw that darkie," he said, "sittin' on that damn spotted horse."

Ruttle lost still another thing that day, for though I was born healthy and hollering, my young mother, Fortuna, passed away that morning at the Tillotson house.

Given the ruin he found himself in, old Ruttle felt compelled to sell off a host of slaves to a travelling coffle, so as to build his life anew. I would have been sold too, but the coffle would not take a newborn without a mother. By then, there was only one Negro woman left at the Ruttle house. She was a cook named Sybil, and seeing as she was awfully spiteful in nature, Monk took it upon himself to be my mammy. Monk said I was lucky he could even do as much—what with all the trouble my pappy done caused, he was afraid old man Ruttle was liable to take me down to the river and drown me like a cat. But Monk said I shouldn't be wasted and he would care for me. And Monk's word was probably the only one to which Ruttle would have paid any mind.

See, Monk and old man Ruttle had had their scuffles in their early days, and Ruttle had on two occasions threatened him with the cowhide. But as Monk would say: a man shan't take what he needn't take. On both those occasions Monk simply up and left to the woods; the first time for the entire summer, and the second for the entire winter.

According to Monk, despite his temper, old man Ruttle was far from the worst buckra out there, for he had a heart. Monk would abide him, said he, but he would not abide the lash. Retreating to the woods was a security, for as he would proudly tell me, ne'er a man can sell a nigger who can just as soon go six months in the bush with only a knife and the clothes on his back. No, Monk wouldn't be for sale but at the whim of his own choosing, and his greatest gift in raising me was to ensure that I would have the privilege of that very same choice.

I have memories that were not made with my eyes. Sometimes, even now, in the dark, I will feel lowbush branches on my feet and legs, and hear the calls of night beasts, and the echo of the Rappahannock River rushing, like a great breath. As a child, soon as I was old enough to know not to cry out, I would go with Monk from the barn and into the woods behind, holding his hand. Once below the trees Monk would slow, and move in utter silence, as if in a dream. Sometimes, in that dark, I would dream indeed as we walked and awake the next morning in my hammock with no memory of being returned there. But most nights I recollect better than the days, which I spent with the horses and the slaves in the field, stealing naps when I could in the stable. I recollect the night in the forest when Monk spoke softly, "Now follow me, in silence, if you can." He rested his forehead on mine for a long moment, and then he released my own small hand. I grasped for him, but he was gone as a shadow folds into the dark and I was alone with the whimper of my own breath, and the crawling insects, and the hoot of the owls. I stood in terror for some time before managing to find my way back to the barn, where at least I could see by lantern light sifting through the boards.

It was some days before I worked up the courage to follow Monk into the night. This time, I went quick, trying to keep my eye on his cloak as he went under the trees. But no matter how fast I ran, he would always evade me. I would walk blindly and find my hands on trees, stones, and moss. I went on clear nights, when the moon cast a light like a pale flame. Then I would follow him farther, until I tripped, or looked away at some sound or other amongst the ferns. When I looked back he would be gone. I went in daylight too, alone, studying hard at the ground, and at the trees, and I felt I was a child amongst giants. Sometimes I would find Monk's snares with a rabbit or squirrel dead or dying in the cordage, and I would take those back to the barn in triumph to skin and clean them, and we slaves would add the meat to our dinner. But at night, no matter how fast I followed

Monk, there was no keeping step. It was months of fruitless chase before I stopped trying, and I would merely go and sit in some peaceful place. A certain night, one of weak starlight and no moon, I went walking. Near to the farm, I passed, by the sounds of it, a bear rooting up an old stump, feasting on the grubs, and if she noticed me she didn't let on. I gave her a wide berth, and when I could no longer hear her, I found a half-fallen tree that I knew well, and sat on it. There were above and about me the flap and swoop of bats on the hunt, and I heard also the slow crawl of a salamander in the ferns. I swung my legs from my perch to keep the gallinippers off my feet and wore my sleeping blanket as a cloak. A moth landed on my brow, and I was not afraid, for it was a gentle creature and I knew the sound and flutter of its wings. And then, maybe a furlong distant, I heard beyond other sounds footfalls that were no beast. I came down from my spot and walked, staying off the leaves, finding the quiet ground of roots and stones. Slowly as a creeping vine I went.

I found Monk through a break in the woods, his hands in the rushing water of the Rappahannock. I could see him now, for where starlight dies below the trees, it grows on the water. He pulled up a small basket and it streamed with water, the river trying to pull it back. He tossed it onto a rock and it shook, and wriggled, still dripping. I watched silently, and he turned to me.

"Good," he said simply. And then he tossed me a short branch of hickory. "Now, this is your blade. Cut me down."

I smiled, thinking it good fun, and ran at him. But he lunged and plucked the stick from my hands. I ran at him again and he swooped, and passed the stick twice over my neck, hard. I went at him a third time, but he drove my breath from me and bound me up in his arms. I felt like a mouse in a snake's grip, and I cried out. He released me, and we sat and dipped our feet in the water, until I was keen to try again.

"This time," said he, "I am you." And he picked up the stick, and knelt, so that I, standing, looked down on him.

I understood, and grabbed at the stick, but I could not wrest it from his hand.

"Use both hands, like so," said Monk, and he placed both my hands over his own that held the stick and showed me to bend the wrist quickly toward his neck.

"Now take it," said he, and the wood came easily from his grip.

I laughed and brandished my prize at him. He moved like a flash and it was in his hands again.

"Most men," said he, "hold their weapon far." He held the stick out toward me, showing me. "They know that it is feared, and they forget that a weapon is wielded by whoever will use it well and quick."

I snatched it from him, at speed.

"Good," he said and lunged at me. I dodged him, and he made a show of landing in the sand. I pounced on his back, and we rolled and wrestled until we laughed.

This art took me far longer to master than moving in the dark. I was a young man before I could trounce him, and even then it was only once or twice.

Once I was seasoned to the dark, I would accompany Monk

on his night walks. His trapline ran a wide circuit, and we brought back all manner of fish and game to the Ruttle slaves. The longest of these journeys, by far, was not a hunt, however, but further, to a place that most would say only exists in legend, and I might have agreed had I not been there myself, more than once now. This first time was when I was still a boy, though old enough to recall. Old enough too to work the long harvest day, and in turn, old enough to question the strange condition that is bondage. I believe I had asked Monk if it was true there were places a Negro would be his own master and do as he pleased. I don't think he answered me—we were by the river setting traps, and I recall only the sounds of the night, and the smell of the water as it eddied and misted amongst the large rocks of the bank.

The journey was his answer to me. The place is called the underlands, a Negro village of warriors who raid the plantations of the Piedmont and even as far as the low country of the Chesapeake Bay. They are led by a man called King Cullin, who came many years ago to a place where the mountain bade him dig. All who reside there are masters of the forest and the night, and their dwellings are impossible to find, for the village, it is said, is below the earth itself.

That evening, I recollect sleeping, as was our habit, a two-hour stretch at sundown, and then rising under cover of dark and walking. I had long given up asking Monk to travel by horse. He would only laugh when I asked, and by then I understood why. Travelling the road by foot, one could hear a horse a league away, leaving ample time to take a loop through the woods and remain unseen. We had only once, in the early days, come close to a band of patrollers, led by a pair of keen-nosed dogs. When we heard the howls on our tail, Monk had me climb high up a great old pine, and I listened as he dispatched the dogs one by one with swift blows through the skull with his blade. The men came following, but without the dogs, they were lost. I watched them wander around for nearly an hour thereafter, their torches casting weak orbs of light about them in the heavy dark. But that was only once. We listened closely to the road and kept a cutting of spruce pine to rub the scent from our feet and legs, as this will throw off all but the keenest of hounds.

The route was long as a deep sleep. Monk bade me note our direction always, by sky, and wind, and land. There were markers of our path too: the trackway, where it split and cut south, the ruins of an old stone cross on a ridgetop, a gnarled catawba tree whose trunk grew in a crescent around the great bear stars when one stood facing north. The night stretched on as if it would never end. I recall walking, Monk before me, and before him a meadow break in the forest and the setting moon bright behind a swath of clouds. All of a sudden he stopped and extended a hand back toward me, instructing me to halt. There was a deadly quiet in that moment, and Monk slowly stooped until he was on all fours.

"Kneel," he whispered back to me, and I obeyed.

And then, the trees beside us creaked and boughs drooped to the ground and there were two men, one on either side of us. They were long and lean, nearly naked, their skin covered with dry clay, which gave their flesh the semblance of stone. They took us down through the earth, and into the underlands. There, we walked through hallways of dark, earthen walls, and came to a great vaulted room that I could see from the light cast by a hearth of embers. There were drums in this room, and men and women painted with clays of different hues and wearing strange assortments of clothing. Cloaks of bear fur and gentlemen top hats, buckskin and fine cotton shirts. There was food. Monk himself had brought a crop of yams and a brace of rabbits that he gave to the old women tending the hearth.

We passed through another room, quieter, but with more light, cast from a live flame on a torch. There were shelves cut out of the walls full with jars, and on the ceiling were wreaths of dry herbs hanging low enough to brush Monk's head. There was a man lain on the ground, his hand tremoring on the earth. He looked as though he was as weary as all the world, and moaning. There were others around him, someone seated by his head, holding his ears; another with an old bent back, puffing on a pipe and billowing out a thick, sweet smoke; two children silent, their hands on the man's arm.

We were ushered through to a cavern wherein we could see the moonlight from a crack in the ceiling, and it shone on the centre of a large pool of slowly flowing water. There we bathed. The water was fresh and sweet, and the cavern was peaceful with its soft sound and its enclosure, and I was overcome by a powerful sense of relief. Everything I had known to that point, everything Monk had taught me, was to be guarded and watchful to the open world. Here, I was deep in layers of stone and earth, and for a moment, I had never felt more safe. The walls danced with the waves of the moonlight on the water, and then the feeling was gone and my mind strayed to the sight of the moaning man, and it made my stomach churn.

"He is wounded," said Monk to me, reading my thoughts.

"How came he?" I asked.

"The war to break the chains," said Monk, his head near the dark surface of the pool, his voice clear as a bell, though he only whispered. "It is the longest war. When you wish to serve on the front of that battle—*if* you wish . . . it can be now if you choose. I can leave you here. You know enough to be of use."

"I go where you go," I said quickly, dreading the idea of being without him.

He nodded solemnly.

And then, as I looked around again at the shimmering walls of stone and earth: "But why shan't we stay, Monk?"

He reclined and closed his eyes. I was perched on a rock, and cupped water on my legs and arms, slowly cleansing myself.

"Do you know, I had a boy once, like you," he said, opening his eyes. They were full and sad as I had never seen them.

I shook my head. I had never really considered Monk's life before me.

"I lost him," said he, "too young; to this very war, I lost him." And his voice became broken, like a gorge cutting deep into the world.

There was, for some long breaths, only the sound of the trickling water and the drums echoing through the halls, as if from the earth itself.

"At the Ruttle house," Monk went on, "strange as it may be,

I have got some measure of security. Even now, we will be absent for as long as it suits us, and nothing will come of it. And that is a thing most could never even dream of."

He looked back to me solemnly.

"As long as you are in my care," he said to me, "I will not lose you."

We rested in the underlands as the day broke, and slept well and deeply in the cool, quiet dark. The next night we journeyed again, back to the Ruttle house. I still recollect the glare that old man Ruttle gave us when he saw us in the field the next afternoon. But Monk was right; nothing ever came of it.

So it was that I was raised Chiron Ruttle, and but for naming me after the centaur of Greek legend, old man Ruttle never indicated that he knew or cared who sired me, and neither did anyone else, save for Monk, who first told me the story when I was old enough to keep hushed about such things. And by the time I was grown, my affinity for horses was of use enough that I was allowed to ride, and was even rented out on several occasions to drive cattle all along the frontier where we had settled. By that time, no one had either memory or reason to remind old Ruttle that wouldn't his young horse nigger be the pup of that Apollo who rode off one day on the colonel's prized Appaloosa? No, that was an all but forgotten tale by my time. A legend of the old days. The days when Negroes from Africa soil knew how to speak spells to a horse and turn it into a panther, and a wealthy white man's family could be lost in a hapless night of fire and unsettled fury.

As fate would have it, that youngest Ruttle boy, Alexander, was not forever lost. He came back one day, grown and strong, like a great bird returning to roost. His story I only learned the full of when I was a man.

He told me of that night when he was taken. Said he recalled the very cake he had eaten, and his warm, soft bed. Those were the glory days; despite the rumpus caused by my pappy's escape, old Ruttle had served well in the militias of the revolutionary war, the farm was flourishing, and he was set to join the ranks of men of importance in Washington. Alexander woke up that night in the dark, thinking that hell itself had opened right up and let all the daemons loose. Such violence can't be understood by a child. He knew of Indians, but only insofar as he knew they were strange, in the way that beasts of the forest were strange to him. But he had never seen anything like this. Never seen anyone attack a slumbering family with purpose. How was he to know what drove such ferocity? He knew nothing then of the Indian villages massacred in the Ohio valley. He knew nothing of what a blood rage will drive a man to do. He was a child of six years whose mother had shielded his eyes from even the suffering of the slaves who shared his very roof.

The warriors cut down his elder brothers with swift blows

to the spine that leave the body to twitch. They bound his screaming mother. He rushed to his father, who had been clubbed un-
conscious, and they took him and his younger brother, who
followed him, wailing. They bound them and strapped them
and their mother each to a horse, and rode into the dark. The
next day they put all three in neck halters and had them walk
barefoot in the bush. The following day, they walked through a
river, and Alexander's mother grabbed his young brother and
launched herself into the deepest part of the flowing water, and
screamed for Alexander to join her. He tried but got held fast by
the man who rode with him.

They traded Alexander to a Chippewa band for a brace of
rifles that same autumn, and his new masters paddled him to
their village on the outskirts of Fort Detroit.

Alexander said he had a hate and a shame he thought would
eat him up. The hate of a young boy wishing he'd died fighting
for his family, for his race. But love knows to find a home in the
body, no matter how unnatural one's circumstance. Slavery is
unnatural indeed, but the bonds of love that emerge, even as a
slave, are no less strange and powerful than between free men.
And the Indian brand of slavery, though in some cases it is brutal, still it is not so hard. That said, I have met a Negro woman
enslaved by the great Mohawk chief Joseph Brant. Though she
speaks very highly of him, her treatment by his wife matches
that of the cruel southern mistresses, and she bears the scars of
her ill use to this day. But to speak in general terms, once taken
in by the Indian, a slave is family. He may try and run, and he
will be caught, but not punished as most white masters will do,

ofttimes whipping runaways near to death. As Alexander told me: when he ran from his new family he was caught gently. He recalled wailing in sorrow and being consoled by his new mother, who sung to him until he fell asleep.

Especially under these circumstances, vengeance and all that come with it are things that can be forgotten, or nudged out of place by comforts, and thrills, and by and by, belonging. One will remember pain every now and again—the gurgling scream of a mother before she drowns. But a young boy does learn to take comfort in the things around him. Alexander, young as he was, took comfort little by little in the taste of a corn stew, how it quenched his hunger more fully than the bread of Virginia. He took comfort, by and by, in the strange sounds of a language not his own. The horror and excitement as he began to understand the songs of his new kinfolk. The smell of his cedar bough bedding began to soothe him as he cried himself to sleep many a night. He took comfort in the play of his new brothers and cousins, and the thrill of paddling a canoe, and of spearing a fish. The celebration at the sound of his laughter, and the power from holding on to the fish bucking on his spear end. The first time he raised his voice in the yell of a song. The hate faded even more the first time he fell in love, and when he woke up one morning next to his lover with a smile from a dream of being a grandfather, and his children's children in that dream were Indian.

And so it was, by the time he was fully a man and his people were called to war, he thought nothing of taking the tomahawk and cutting down a whole horde of white men. He donned war paint and celebrated Indian victory. He mourned Indian loss.

And at the crushing loss of the Battle of Fallen Timbers, he saw his brothers die, bled out from lead shot and the bayonets of the Americans. Those same brothers who brought him into the world of the living. His grief was so fierce that he went to the burial ground and lay in the dirt and would not raise himself up. But his kinfolk lifted him up. When they gave up the land around Detroit they ensured that Alexander would have a home there, and a farm for his family. Since the Americans were there to stay, he would serve as the tribe's interlocutor with American men. He would live like them, dress like them, again. Such was his battle now.

So it was that after all of that hardship, and comfort, and war, and forgetting—about twenty winters of it—Alexander came back to his birth family. We were in Kentucky then. Old man Ruttle had brought me, Monk, and a bunch of other slaves. I recollect the evening. It was after a day of felling hardwood and hauling it with the draft horses. That evening I was tired but enjoying my task of driving the cattle in from pasture. I rode swiftly atop a dun-coloured Chickasaw mare of good blood. She was sturdy and fast, and could turn like you wouldn't believe. I would lean off to one side to balance her as she flew in her agile way to flank the herd. I was agile too. I was a stout young man nearing my prime.

Just as I was getting the last of the beasts in the gate, I heard the trot of horses coming down the lane.

It wasn't unusual to have visitors, but I dismounted; I knew well enough to dismount in the presence of a white man. I looked and saw horses; one with a rider, and the other a packhorse. The rider slowed his horse to a walk and nodded to me. He was dressed in a peculiar mix of travelling clothes: a felt hat, buckskin tunic, and military-style breeches. He looked both solemn and ill at ease.

"Evening, sir," I told him. "Is the master expecting you?"

"No," he said. "Is this the Ruttle house?"

His way of speaking was strange. Slow and drawn out. I had never heard a white man speak slow like that.

"Yes, sir," I told him.

He pondered this for a moment, chewing on something, as if he wasn't sure he had asked the right question.

"Shall I escort you in, sir?" I asked.

He nodded and we walked in silence; he on his horse and I on the ground, leading mine. I showed him the house and alerted old man Ruttle that he had a visitor. Then I went back outside to stable the horses.

By the time I had come back in the house, old man Ruttle was holding the man by the shoulders and had started to weep and groan like a beast. The younger man embraced him and held his head against his shoulder. He was now much bigger than his father. He was handsome and stoic as he held the old man through sobs. Monk was in the living room too, and discreetly regarded the reunion with tears in his eyes. Old man Ruttle called for an extra place to be set at the table, and for spirits. When the two took seat, Monk approached and shook the young man's hand.

I fetched a quarter cask of corn whiskey, and then went to the kitchen to eat some pork and johnnycakes, quietly, along with the cooks, old Sybil and Luella, who were also silent. We all huddled by the crack in the door and listened.

The old man had regained composure and was yammering about the early days in Kentucky. Around the time Alexander had been took, men were bringing back tales of the land of plenty on the other side of the Blue Ridge. Rolling hills full of grass so lush it would make a man's cattle and horses grow stronger than one could imagine. A land full of buffalo that never knew a gun, and water aplenty. How once he lost his family, the land was nothing but sorrow to him. And so, after about ten years, he mustered up to sell the farm, pack up his property, and join a mountain caravan. It was a dangerous journey, for the mountains are known to eat men. But there was safety in numbers, and we had Monk and me to scout and hunt for us. We had too the glorious promise of frontier freedom around the bend, so said the old man.

I began to get restless. The old man's story was familiar to me. Sybil and Luella began to get tired of it too. They shifted, rolled their eyes, and muttered. I had finished my johnnycake and was gnawing on a string of gristle. I recall thinking perhaps the old man was afraid to be silent and listen. Afraid to know this full-grown son who sat before him. This strange, silent man who was also somehow his boy.

By and by, the old man began to speak of the frontier skirmishes. Here, my interest piqued, for I knew what he might tell next.

He had worked himself up to a loud bellow, so his voice was not much muted through the hall and the kitchen doors.

"And who in all the world was interpreting for the savages, I ask ye," he said.

He did not wait for a reply.

"That blackie Apollo!" said he.

I cringed in the pause that followed. I imagined the old man's mad eyes, quivering in his way. And it struck me that this was his moment. The moment in which the old man placed all hope. There was a culprit, after all—a villain—for whatever horror had come to pass. And that villain could be named, and damned.

"Ah," said a soft voice, which I knew must be Alexander's. "Poor devil," said he.

I stopped chewing on my gristle and looked at Sybil and Lu-ella, who now clutched each other, eyes to the door as if they could see through wood.

"Poor devil?" said the old man, and I heard the spittle flare on his lips. "Poor devil!" said he again.

"Perhaps," said Alexander, "perhaps he didn't have a choice but to join them."

There was no answer. The silence this time was frightful, and the air seemed to thicken with each tick of the grandfather clock. I thought to start making noise, because a quiet like this could only be conspicuous. Servants were meant to be unseen at times, but not silent—not listening.

"Stay here," said the old man. "Stay here with us. I'm getting old, son. The curse is lifted now, but I'm getting old."

There was another long silence. I heard a light scampering in the corner and then saw a mouse scurry from behind a sack of flour to a cranny in the wall. It nosed the air before disappearing. I steeled myself—for what, I didn't know. The silence mounted unbearably, so that I felt if I even released my breath I would be heard.

Strange how time amongst a people changes a man. Not only how Alexander looked, for without knowing him, if one were to tell me he had Indian blood, I would not doubt it. But more haunting than that was his comfort in silence. It wasn't normal for a white man to let so much silence into a room. If a man disagreed, he should tell you so. If he did not, he would commiserate. Hell, if he didn't mean to tell you what he thought, he would lie. But to sit in equivocal silence was, I would wager, the most unfamiliar thing old Ruttle could have encountered at that table.

"I can't stay," said Alexander finally. "I've been granted land near Detroit by my clan. It's good land, and I farm it. I work also for government and private businessmen as an interpreter, and I don't wish to give up those contracts."

"Which government?" asked the old man.

"Does it matter?" said Alexander.

"Yes, it matter, boy! What they done to you up there? And what clan you talking about? What clan? Boy, you looking at your clan right here!"

We heard a thumping, and I knew it to be the old man pounding himself on the chest, as he was fond of doing.

"I brought you a bale of fine furs," said Alexander.

The old man had no response.

"Coat beaver, mink, and fox," he went on.

"I'm no fur trader, boy," said the old man, and his voice began to crack.

"You need not trade the furs," said Alexander, "though if you do take them to a merchant you should accept no less than a thousand pounds sterling, for they're worth at least that."

I could barely contain the whistle that began to escape my lips. Sybil and Luella rollicked silently on their chairs. Pounds sterling had not been in full use for many years, but we knew they were worth more than thrice an American dollar, which meant that Alexander's furs were the value of four healthy slaves, maybe more. And none of us had imagined furs could be worth more than flesh.

"I know that it is not your custom," Alexander went on, "but I have learnt to exchange gifts with my kin."

We heard the old man snort. "And I suppose I am to respond in kind?" said he, and there was a further, aching silence.

"What can I give, woeful farmer that I am?"

I held my breath and heard my blood pump.

"Give me that young horseman and the mare he rides upon," said Alexander. "I could use a pair like that."

A silence followed. Sybil and Luella looked straight at me, though I kept my gaze on the dark nook where the mouse had disappeared. I was back in the caverns of the underlands, where I was first faced with the possibility of a life elsewhere. I was Monk's boy still, and I could flee if I chose, return when this man was gone, and carry on my life here. But there was some strange and fateful tenor to Alexander's return that called to me.

I looked at the old woman. Her eyes were closed and her head was still leaned against the stone wall of the pen.

"Why do you stop?" she asked without opening her eyes.

"I didn't know if you were awake," I said.

She huffed and flicked her hand at me. "I been talking to you the whole time," she muttered.

"Talking? I thought that to be the sounds old women make in their sleep," I said.

"Read the damn writ," she said. "This brings back old memories."

This made my heart quicken, and I looked over my shoulder to the thick doorway leading from the courthouse into the pen. I feared the turnkey would come fetch us at any moment.

"He done forgot about us," said the old woman, settling her head back against the stone wall. "Keep reading."

There was a subtle urgency in her voice that I hadn't heard before. I picked up the sheaf of papers and continued to read.

Bidding Monk farewell was the hardest part. I knew it would be, and when the moment came, I saw it would be equally hard for him.

He had raised me in every sense of the word. The smell of him is in my bones.

"I may see you again," he said to me.

He grasped my hand and I grasped it back, tight.

"But if I don't."

Monk breathed deeply and clasped the back of my neck in his other hand. I closed my eyes and we touched our heads together.

"You'd do good to recollect," said he, and I heard the smile on his lips. "You needn't take anything from no buckra that I wouldn't take."

"I will, Monk. I will not forget."

He stepped back and looked at me a long moment before nodding and smiling, finally.

Alexander and I took a long route back, riding two weeks to Albany, where he attended to business before making the trip to Buffalo. There, we boarded a schooner to Detroit. We passed most of this journey in silence. Alexander was a fair and sober man, but peculiar. He was never fully comfortable in the English language, nor was he fully endeared to its speakers. Indeed it did not take long for me to understand that it was his Indian brethren and not Alexander himself that insisted he rejoin the white race.

The Detroit that I came to know was a place with a current of change as strong as the water that flowed in the river beyond its shores. This change, for me, took some getting used to. There were not only purebred Americans, but old Britishers, French orchard masters, half-breed traders, Indians and Negroes of every description. There, I saw an Indian woman who was a powerful merchant and master over several servants who were Indian, Negro, white, and every mix in between. The order of affairs here could be most strange. It was not a predictable frontier place such as I was used to.

Alexander had been given a choice piece of land on a river north of Detroit. When the two of us arrived, there was only a wigwam that we shared. The rest of his village had relocated to lands to the northeast in the Indian territory of the Saint Clair lake. His kin would come in canoes with supplies of wild rice, corn, fish, meat, and all of our necessaries, as well as bales of peltry, which we would take to port in Detroit. That first summer as we toiled together on the land, we would hear the call of his clan as they poled up the river to meet us. I recollect one of those times, I glanced up at Alexander; his tawny face was wet with sweat, and I saw a rare glimpse of joy in the widening of his eyes.

We cleared fifteen acres of old forest, and hired a Detroit teamster to take the wood to mill in town. We built a frame house and stable for the animals, and harvested nearly one hundred bushels of potatoes that we stored in a dug-out root cellar lined with birch bark. That fall, the fall of 1796, Alexander's wife came to join us with their two young boys. She was a kindly Indian woman named Lizette, not from Alexander's kinfolk, but from a people farther north. The family moved into the house and I stayed in the wigwam. That winter the snow fell heavily, and I only made it to town on two occasions. Mostly I recall hewing wood, snaring animals, and looking past my fire to the gently shuffling bulrush of my dwelling as it moved in the wind. I missed Monk terribly.

Alexander must have noticed my melancholy, because one day, early the following spring, he came back from an appointment at the fort commissary. With him was a Negro woman.

"This is Anne," was all he said, and he walked away.

Anne and I looked at each other, knowing right well what was expected of us. I have not felt so afraid since my first time facing beasts in the dark wilderness of Virginia. Before me was no beast, but a woman, stout and shapely, with eyes that seemed as full and beautiful as river water.

As to my fear, let me speak plain: I did not think myself a handsome man. My brow was thick, as were my features. My skin was dark and marked with the pox I'd survived as a boy, and I had lost several teeth from suffering a hard fall off a horse. In addition, I was not a man who had often been distracted by women.

After about a week of avoiding her with downcast gazes and mumbling, I found myself beside her one evening as I washed my face and hands by the river shore before supper. She was washing clothes and linens.

My heart beat full and I dried my hands on my shirt and took a deep breath. "I would have you know," I told her, "that you have no cause for fear in me."

"I know," said she, glancing up from the tub. Her voice was jovial.

"What I mean to say," I went on, "is that I'm not a man of hard passion. And Alexander is a very reasonable man."

She stopped her washing to look at me plainly. There was the purling of the water over rocks. I waited a moment for her response before gathering that I hadn't said anything yet to respond to. I liked her plainness.

"If you would not be my wife, there is no harm in it," said I. "I would simply speak to Alexander, and we would arrange...."

At this I trailed off, because I could not bring myself to say the words. What choice was I offering the woman? The choice to be sold into the dark unknown, where ill use and bondage was the only certainty?

She interrupted the silence of my thoughts.

"But I do want a husband, and children," she said, maintaining my gaze. "Besides," she added, "you seem a man of good stock."

She regarded me for a moment more before she chuckled and returned to her washing. I became aware of my face, and my chest, which had frozen solid, and I cleared my throat to bring movement again into my body. I opened my mouth to reply, but I had no words. A winter, nay, three seasons with the silence of Alexander and the bush itself had me forget how to speak. I simply nodded to her and retreated into the dark of the woods. I was too timid to join the house.

That evening Anne came to my wigwam with a hunk of pemmican and two baked potatoes.

"Take them from my hands, Negro, they hot."

I took them, and Anne looked at me from across the firelight of my hut with an amused wrinkle on her lips.

The following week was carnival in town. Catholic customs were still strange to me, and the notion of a masquerade after sundown with a horde of strangers did not appeal.

"I told the mistress I'm Catholic," Anne had said to me the Sunday before.

I had lit a fire in my hut and was removing my moccasins, eager to rid myself of the cold sting of melted snow.

"Are you, then?" I asked her.

She regarded me with her penetrating smile that seemed to always make my face flush and itch.

"I asked that you be my escort on the night before Lent," said she.

So it was that we donned masks and paraded the streets of Detroit for Mardi Gras. It was frightening and strange to walk freely in a town at night. With all the disguises we could not know who was who, and it took me some time to remember that my skin was also secret behind a mask. Mirth was the prevailing spirit, and Anne gripped my arm tightly for most of the evening, and pressed her face to my shoulder, and I felt that perhaps I would not pass my life in solitude after all.

She stayed with me in the wigwam after that.

Strange as our circumstance was, I grew to love her dearly. And Anne maintained that I was a man of good stock. By and by, she bore a son and then a daughter: Samuel and Stella. Anne and I were never married, but both the children were baptized at Saint Anne's in Detroit. Samuel was the first, and when it came time to record his name, I told the priest that the surname should be Stock. Alexander was godparent to my boy, and at my declaration his face did not betray even a hint of malcontent. Perhaps he did not know, but more likely he did not care that I had shuffled off the name of my master.

By the time Samuel was born, Alexander had already two boys and three girls. The lads were raised in the manner of the upper class of Detroit. They were meant to carry on Alexander's position and become noblemen of the skin trade. It was the title in their heritage, and they took to it like bloodhounds to the hunt.

Though I was ever fair and temperate with them, they grew to scorn me. The first time I truly reckoned this was late one evening after my family had gone to bed in our cabin. We were long since out of the wigwam, and by then my children were old enough to work, and Alexander's boys were home from the college. I heard a rustling in the dark outside and went to see if it was some beast come to dig up our root cellar. I came onto our small porch and listened to the night. By then I could tell it was no beast, but a man. The breath was short and soft, but still audible amongst the sound of wild things. I stepped off the porch and heard a swift pound of footsteps come from behind the cabin, whereupon I turned to see a dark form run headlong toward me. In an instant I leaned to the side and brought my knee into his middle, and heard the air leave him and felt him fold in two. Another form pounced up from a bush with a yell and grasped both my wrists. I pulled him to me, ramming hard with the top of my head. The hands on my wrists released and the form fell away from me with a grunt. I took the hair of the first attacker and kicked his legs out, letting him fall hard to a stump on the ground before us.

I'm not a large man, but Monk certainly was, and fast besides. Since I learned to hold my ground with him, ne'er a man has been able to throw me.

As soon as I had heard the yell from the bush I recognized the two lads, but I figured to punish them by making as though I did not know them in the dark. I looked on them, their bodies heaving with breath on the ground. The younger boy, whom I had rammed, moaned. I heard the blood in his nose.

"You mustn't come up on me so, lads," I said.

"Chiron," said the elder, still in the dirt, "the day will come when we will best you."

"It may," said I, "and then what a shame you will bear of having thumped an old man."

"Well, you best not do anything wrong," spoke the elder again, turning to lay flat on his back, and gasping through his words. "For then you shan't strike back."

I regarded them silently in the dark, before helping them up. The elder's back had been bruised on the stump, and I had to nearly carry him back to his family before I went in to join mine.

Anne and Stella slept soundly as I kissed them on their cheeks. My boy, Samuel, awoke and nestled his head to me. He was ever a gentle boy, and I knew the horses would take to him.

I caressed the tight coils of his hair until he slept, and tears crept from my eyes.

Alexander's lads bore an affliction I had seen amongst a certain portion of slave masters from Virginia to Canada. Men who fear their own impotence, and seek to dispel it by beating the slaves over whom they act as lord. Indeed, I have seen men lashed beyond all sense. Men whipped to their very core. Such things are beyond punishment. In these cases a master whips not to punish, but to chase some daemon from his own sight. But the daemon will not flee, and so the master whips, and whips, and does not let up.

Alexander was not a man who whipped to chase daemons. The old man Ruttle neither, despite his temper. But these lads had the mark of cruelty in their eyes. This I knew without ever having seen them touch a lash.

Even now, speaking of them, I feel the heat of rage come up in my bones. But I must speak of them. Such is my circumstance as a man who has been a slave. I cannot tell you properly of my life as it is—as it was—without telling you of the life of my masters.

Alexander died quickly in the spring of 1807 from a bad case of consumption. The doctor who came to treat him said we were to keep distant, and so I never had the chance to speak with him before his death. He had told me years earlier that it was in his will that when he died I was to get my freedom. So the eldest boy confirmed when he returned from the funeral in Detroit. I asked him what was to be of Anne and our children. He told me they were to carry on at the farm. I could not believe him and asked to see Alexander's will. Though I could not read, I would find a man who could, for it shouldn't be. What freedom is possible while a man's family is still in bondage? The eldest boy said if I was so bold as to call him a liar he would transfer the punishment for that offence onto my family. I tell you, that moment birthed the terrible rage I still carry.

I could not stay at the farm for fear of coming to blows with the new masters and incurring any misfortune for my Anne and the young ones. It pained me terribly to leave them, but I had to put out. I knew a number of men amongst the black militia at Detroit, and I found work immediately with them. Soon thereafter, I enlisted a friend to pen a letter. These, if I do not mistake myself, were my words exactly:

Young Masters,

I write with respect for your recently deceased father whom I served without a day of faltering these eleven years. Please give my greetings to your dear mother and sisters. If they enquire, I am in good health, and doing very well. I sit on a mount and hold a rifle, to keep the good citizens of Detroit safe at night.

Your humble servant,
Chiron Stock

One night, in my new appointment, I had an encounter that roused the spark of boldness in me. I was patrolling near the shore of the Detroit River, and I heard a bullfrog call that wasn't no bullfrog at all.

I drew my rifle from the sheath and dismounted and crouched behind a stump, scouring the trees in the direction of the call. The horse I rode, Sampson, was a strong beast but not smart. He snuffed at me and bent to chomp around his bit, on the riverside grasses. I looked into the bush, but all I saw was the dark sway of willows. I was near the river by the southern outskirts, and I could hear the lap of water on the shore.

"This is Officer Stock of the Detroit militia!" said I to the willows. "Show yourself," I muttered, more to the barrel of my rifle than to anything else, for by this time I had been in enough skirmishes to tell that a man that would neither present himself nor flee was ready for a fight.

A voice came from the trees: "I heard tell of your new appointment, Chiron," it said. The words were muffled by the bush and the breeze from the river, but it seemed to me the speaker was smiling.

I lowered my rifle, listening close to the dark under the swaying willows.

"Who goes there?" I asked.

"An old associate," said the voice.

And with that, a figure in full buckskin stepped from behind the curtain of willow limbs, arms outstretched in surrender. As he came nearer I saw and recognized the shape of his dark face, struggling to keep a frown.

"Well, I'll be," said I, and rose and walked on toward him, picking up Sampson's bridle and ignoring the stubborn tug.

I met the man under the dark of the swaying willow branches. We regarded one another a moment there, under weak starlight.

"It's damn good to see you, my brother," I said, and we embraced.

His name was John, and his is a spirit very dear to my own. He was an Indian I had met at a Three Fires Council one evening on a green isthmus of Walpole Island. I had often accompanied Alexander on business and was quite used to blending into the background and tending to the horses if there were any. However, on this occasion, the moment I arrived John greeted me and throughout that council conferred with me, translating where I did not understand, muttering his own thoughts on the discussion, and posing questions to me in a hushed tone. I didn't have much to say, but I recall thinking for the first time that perhaps I did have a stake of my own in the political tumult in which I found myself.

Since then, John and I had met a handful of times, and each time we grew closer. Our last meeting was at a gathering on Alexander's land not long before his illness, and on that occasion our wives and children were present. His wife was a Negro woman, and free. We watched the youngest of our little ones sniff each other like bear cubs and then play on the grass until they cried and slept. We heaped them together on a moose hide by the fire while we and their mothers spoke and laughed for hours. There's a special bond between men who see their family find comfort in their time together. And all the more when one man ain't master over the other.

I am sure we both thought of this as we embraced under that great willow.

"Well," said John, whispering through his grin, "am I under arrest?"

I chuckled, my hand on his shoulder. "That all depend," I told him. "You wouldn't happen to be a marauding Indian, would you?"

"Not I, sir!" he said to me in the British parlance, raising his chin in a show of pride. "How shameless of you to ask."

Funny to hear him speak like that. He was the only Indian I knew who spoke English a far sight better than most white men. I laughed again.

"What you doing here?" I whispered to him.

He looked at me real solemn for a moment.

"Some folk from across the straits need a bit of help," he said.

A devilish smile came upon him, and upon me. My company, the Detroit militia, was known to harbour and employ runaways from the slave estates of Upper Canada. American disdain for our British neighbours on the other side of the straits meant that once the runaways reached this shore there wasn't a damn thing their masters dared do about it.

I had seen a wealthy British man stumble through the streets of Detroit, stripped of his wig, cursing, not able to fend off the American mob that chased him with flailing mops and rags dipped in hot pine tar. He survived all right, though I would say his dignity remained tarnished long after his burns had healed. Since then, British men had become increasingly scarce in the streets of Detroit.

This animosity was good for us. Though it ached my heart that my wife and children remained in cruel bondage on this American soil where other men's families rejoiced in freedom, still it was good. For white men, nation had meaning enough to harass, cudgel, and even kill each other. But we slaves, Negro and Indian alike, quietly celebrated each escape; it mattered not whence they fled. We knew that the land of one man's freedom would always be the land of another's bondage. Our nation was not bound by a shoreline. Our nation was in our very flesh.

Chapter VI

I stopped reading the narrative again. My mouth was sore from speaking, and the sun above the pen now bathed us both in a warmth that had begun to draw sweat in running beads from my neck, down and under my frock. I put the sheaf of papers away in their sleeve and I fanned it in front of my face for a breeze.

The old woman was unfazed by the heat. She had come more alive as I read on. Her grunts and gestures had filled my pauses. She'd nodded vigourously at certain moments. At others, she hooted and hummed in recognition, wagging her finger at me and smiling. I tried to ignore her, but little by little I began to notice my nostrils flare with mirth at her antics, and more than once a smirk began to press behind my lips.

"You seem to enjoy this tale much better than my own," I said to her in between fanning myself.

The old woman responded, but whether to me or to the narrative itself, I couldn't tell: "Oh, but yes, this brings memories. Memories indeed. How happy I was."

She chortled, shaking her head and patting the ground. Here, I could not help but to smile curiously. I noticed the jug of water on the ground, and I filled the two cups.

"What do you mean?"

"You don't know?"

I shook my head, feeling too hot to suffer what felt like a riddle coming on. I gulped the water. It was warm and sulphurous, but quenching. The old woman's eyes stayed locked on me with a narrow glare.

"Are you playing dumb with me, girl?"

And then—perhaps it was the sun, so oppressive in that pen that the possibility of bantering, or even thinking of it, was nauseating—I spoke without thinking.

"You're the Negro woman in this text, aren't you? The one married to Chiron's Indian friend John?"

"I am indeed," she said, nodding. And then, with a raised eyebrow and a half smile: "And how did you know that, Lensinda Martin?"

I opened my mouth to speak but faltered, for the truth was, I had no idea how I knew. No idea if I knew, or if this was some trick the old woman was playing. All of a sudden I felt awash as though a cool breeze ran over me, quickening my skin, though the sun still beat down heavy. My head was dizzy and it was as though my whole mind went into my skin, and I was taut and tingling all over.

The old woman's voice was far, as though in another room. I saw her shrug. "Maybe you're smarter than you look," I heard her say, and I felt my mouth shut in its familiar scowl.

She looked up at me as if expecting a retort, but I was still out of sorts.

"While you find your tongue," she said, "have another story. Have you heard the underside of this tale you've just read me?"

The underside of the tale? I shook my head no. My mind whirled between belief and doubt, failing to distinguish one from the other.

"No?" she asked, pursing her lips. "Have you ever heard of a man, name Matthew Tillings?"

I considered the name and felt my brows crease. I shook my head, befuddled. It was familiar but I couldn't place it, and these questions were confounding me even further.

"No?" she trilled, her gaze incredulous. "Well, I guess that doesn't matter, no, but the tale you must have."

She was speaking so quickly, losing me in a labyrinth of words, and there was something I needed to say, but I couldn't grasp it.

"Wait," I said, trying to quiet her with a wave of my hand. "Just wait." My voice was cracked and bare. "I don't believe you."

She looked at me blankly from her patch of dry grass, and after a moment placed a hand gently on my knee. I looked at it, her skin wrinkled and gleaming as a prune, her knuckles crooked at the joints. Her touch nearly made me squirm and brought my mind back into my head, and I felt the heat of the sun again, and took a long breath.

"I think you mean," she said, "you don't believe yourself."

Before I could think of how to respond, she pressed into my knee and rose up on her feet.

She dusted herself off, picked up the basket of food, and

walked the few steps to the south wall of the pen, which rose high and dark. The sun was high above it, and while the west wall where we had been sitting was now bare to the light, the south wall cast a thin shadow at its feet. I followed with the stool and my satchel, and then went back and fetched the water. My knees found the grass at the base of the south wall, and I was dizzy with heat and portent.

"Like this," said the old woman, with her back against the wall and her hands spread against it.

"See how the stone is still cool."

I sat on the grass and laid my back and head against the wall and felt the cool dark mass of rock tug the heat from me. The old woman came in front of me and put a hand on my forehead, and it was wet with the sulphury water and cooling. Droplets ran over my eyelids, and I closed them until the dizziness passed. When I opened them, she was seated on the stool beside me, looking at me with flashing eyes.

"Come, a story! Look how I am alive with memories."

"I think I'll have some of that first," I said, pointing weakly to the basket at her feet.

She pushed it toward me. I unveiled the napkin and took a biscuit, some cheese, and a spoonful of jam. My stomach snarled loudly before the food reached it, and the old woman snickered at the sound. I didn't pay her mind, savouring each bite with my eyes closed. I heard her sift through the basket, and for a moment there was only the loud whine of the cicadas, and the quiet smacking of lips. I looked at her; she was staring at the court-house walls and plucking crumbs of biscuit from her lap.

"How could that be?" I said, gesturing at the space between her and my bag with Chiron's narrative poking out of it.

She smiled slightly and made a delicate fluttering sound in her chest, her eyes passing over me with a long, unsparing look. I closed my eyes as another twinge of dizziness arose, milder now.

"We do not have all the time we should like, girl."

She spoke softly now, and I opened one eye a crease to glimpse her through the shuddering tracery of my eyelashes. She was less disorienting like that, as blurred form and voice.

"Listen, and I will take us back to that moment in the straits, a lifetime ago."

My boy was no more than twelve at the time. He and his father came home before they were meant to. My shamefaced husband would only give me half-truths and quick answers, but my boy— there was a story whirling in his eyes, though he did not want to speak. So I grasped him by the shoulders and told him: Boy, I will tether you to my body and you will never leave my sight again if you don't tell me every bit of what's come to pass. Then he spoke. And I remember to this day, though perhaps he himself does not. You will see when you have children; you recall when they were in danger sometimes better than they themselves.

They had paddled, he told me, harder than he ever had, with more weight than he knew the canoe could take. He had ached to rest, he said, but on that night there was no rest to be had. He paddled with vigour until he reached the threshold of his strength and then there was no more strength to be had; only pain, only shoulders wet with screaming heat, begging him to stop and rest. And still he pushed his chest forward, digging stroke after stroke in the river. Once, he glanced back at the dark shapes in the swollen boat belly, bearing low with weight so just the lip of it came up over the water. The river was black and vast like the earth and wild with the shimmer of starlight. Everywhere shimmered and rollicked with current—everywhere but the black boat belly. He lost his rhythm and felt the boat lurch and the river surged and gurgled, threatening to push them under. My husband, in the stern, gasped with the effort to right their course, and the sound of his breath made my son afraid, though he knew he couldn't indulge in fear any more than he could indulge in pain. So he set himself to the dark, pulsing river, ready to swallow him, and he made his body work—dig and cut through the water—and he made his mind remember.

It had been a green river the day before. The two travelled light and the boat skimmed the water as they set off. This was the first time I allowed my husband to bring him alone—and without his sister too; she never forgave me for that.

When they beached there were many boats already there, and men dotting a trail up to the grandest house my boy had ever seen. In front of this house there was a maze of flowers and bushes that grew strange and sparse. Before that was a wide lawn on which the throng of men gathered and greeted one another. There was a woodpile that stood as tall as him, and next to it a man blew into a smoking nest of cedar wisps and cattail until flames fluttered in his hands like the wings of a wounded bird.

My son stretched his arms and waved off mosquitoes as he took in the land around him. Off some way, there was a cluster of cabins flanked by a large patch of corn and a massive barn. And all around, a meadow drifted on like the sea. He had never seen a plain so vast. It only gave way to the forest in the far distance, where the trees looked small. There, by the trees, was a group of men making their way toward the house. Near to them was a herd of grazing cattle. He turned slow, and followed the plain to where it drooped to meet the shore and the straits, and an island that swallowed the sun in a flood of red and deep violet.

As he looked back around, he saw among the cabins a young girl looking right at him. She was about his size and she stared keenly from behind one of the porches. He stared back, and just when he was beginning to think she was made from wood and not real flesh, she ducked back behind the porch. He looked up at his father a few paces away, speaking with another man, practicing his Indian tongue. My boy looked back to the porch and the girl was there, spying on him again. This time she let out a little shriek that he could hear despite the chatter of men, and she ducked away once more. He kept his eyes on the spot, and waited stock-still until she slowly raised her eyes from behind the wood, and when she saw him staring, she thrust her head back down a third time. The moment she did so he dashed as quickly as he could, darting around the strange gardens, picking up speed until he dove into the corn.

He made his way through the corn with stealth, until he could see the cabin in front of which the girl sat. He crept out of the field and ran lightly to it. He touched the back of the cabin and his hands came away sticky with pitch. He went carefully to the end of the wall and peered around it to look at the girl. She was looking at the area he had just left. Her head moved side to side, trying to find him in the dusk and the smoke and the slowly milling men. She was very pretty, he noticed. He stared a moment too long and she saw him out of the corner of her eye and she screeched and jumped to face him.

"How'd you get there?" she yelled.

He tried not to flinch, and instead put up a foot against a log of the cabin wall.

"I'm a hunter," he said. "I move like a fox."

"Is that so?" she said, and she strutted in the way of young girls ready for hips that haven't grown yet.

"So it's you that's eating all our chickens then, huh, Mr. Fox?" said she, circling him. "Massa Tillings sure will be happy I caught you, then. He'll give you a real good lickin' too."

Said he, "I don't know who Massa Tillings is, but it don't matter, 'cause can't nobody catch me."

She stopped real quick to face him and cocked her head to one side. "What you mean, you don't know? You don't know who it is that bought you?"

He blinked a few times, and looked from side to side—some of the men from the fields had begun to pass them by, and he saw that they were Negroes. My boy hadn't a clue what that girl was talking about. One of the men looked over at him and winked, leaning on his axe as he walked. He hadn't yet seen many Negro men, and so he looked hard at the man's back.

"Hey! I asked you a question!" The girl pushed out each word with movements of her head, and she stepped up to him with her arms crossed. He took a step back and bumped into the wall of the cabin, and his hand clung to the pitch.

"No one bought me," he said. He pointed with his head to the group of men gathering in front of the fire. "I paddled here with my pa."

"What!" she said. "I thought there was only Indians there!"

She leapt over to her post behind the porch, and he joined her. He was proud to show his father, handsome and well muscled as he was.

"I only see Indians," she said, as if she were saddened.

"Aye, he an Indian," said my boy. "I'm an Indian too."

The girl took a step away from him and was solemn for the first time as she eyed him up and down. He glanced down at himself—he was shirtless and still warm from his paddling, and he wore simple buckskin breeches and moccasins. He thrust out his chest, to show her that he was not ashamed.

"Well . . . I suppose you is dressed as an Indian," she muttered, eyeing his lower half. "Maybe you is."

She looked back on his face and hair—his woolly locks that grew curling tightly toward the sky.

"But you sure is a nigger too."

They stared solemnly at each other. The girl started to strut again, pausing only to swipe away the mosquitoes.

"Tell me, Foxy: Why is all these Indians coming to the farm?"

He squinted to recall my and his father's words.

"It's for the reason of, uh, getting gifts," he said.

"Getting gifts? Who's getting gifts? Massa Tillings?"

"No," he told her. "The Indians getting gifts."

"From who?"

"From your massa," he said. "Guns and all the things a man needs to hunt."

"Why would Massa Tillings give gifts to a bunch o' Indians?"

"Because he's afraid of other white men across the river, and so he gives us gifts in case they ever try to fight him."

"What! You lying. Massa Tillings couldn't be afraid of no one."

"No it's true, see," he told her. "Else he wouldn't give us gifts . . . he knows we good fighters, and we make it our business to hunt down white men who go where they ain't supposed to go."

The girl had been creeping closer to him, and without warning she stepped all her weight right on his foot. He tried to step away, but she caught his other heel with her ankle and pushed it outward in a quick thrust until he couldn't stretch no more, bringing his rump tumbling to the dirt.

"Ha ha! What a fighter you are!" she told him.

He tried to spring up as quickly as he had fallen and push the girl, but she twirled out of his reach. He was hot with anger and wished nothing more than to do something to her to make her feel a fool. But he couldn't think of anything, so he cursed her with his Indian tongue and walked away toward the fields behind the big house.

"Oh, come back here, Foxy!"

He began to run, and she gave chase. He grit his teeth and smiled, because he thought himself swifter than most men, and surely this girl. In the open field he cut a swath through the meadow grass and the wind blew a low whistle in his ears. He slowed to glance back at his trail and, to his horror, the girl was gaining on him. She held her skirt in one hand and her legs pumped underneath with long bounds. As he turned back around to the field, he saw a tree.

He dashed toward it. It seemed to him magnificent all alone in the field. He ran, and leapt, and caught the first branch.

She yelled behind him to stop, but he just grinned and pulled himself up and up. He looked back to see the girl slow and look around in despair. He climbed higher.

"Come down!" she said to him in a low, pleading voice.

He looked to her, because something had changed; she wasn't yelling now, and he heard a fear in her voice that made him feel grand. He pretended not to hear and climbed higher, gripping the bark with his feet like a bear. When he looked down again the girl looked small. His eyes drifted to the base of the tree and his body jolted with terror. There, where the roots should have been, was a woman, bare-backed, with her hands reaching up and her face pressed against the bark. He nearly lost his grip and had to scramble to hang on. A thorn from a branch pierced the flesh of his hand and he yelped with the pain, but dared not let go. The tree must have been haunted and this woman was its vengeful spirit.

He looked at the girl, who was now bent low in the long

grass, looking back between the big house and the tree, and gesturing fiercely at him to come down. The change in her made him even more afraid now, and all of a sudden he noticed the darkness—the sun had gone behind the island on the river and clouds were everywhere. Shadows moved along the tree line and a cold wind brought a howl of voices and the smell of smoke from the other side of the big house. I know he wanted nothing more than to get down and leave, but he did not have the will. Slowly, he took his hand from the thorn, and gasped as the blood left him. The spirit beneath him moaned. His blood had landed on her face, and with eyes closed she opened her mouth and tasted it with a white tongue. The girl in the grass started to whisper to him but he was seized by fear, and he could not make out her words.

The flesh on this tree woman was swollen and lumped. Her arms, still reaching up the trunk, bent as if she would clamber up toward him. He heard the clink of iron. She coughed heavily and was still. He felt the pounding of his heart against the tree and only then could he hear what the girl whispered to him.

"Foxy. We ain't supposed to be here. Get down, Foxy! They're coming for us. Come down!"

The tree woman coughed again and spat; her body shivered and she made a most terrible, deep-chested moan.

There were footsteps in the grass. He heard them, yet still could not move. It was as if the tree bound him to it. The blood from his hand went in a crevice in the bark and was swallowed. He dared not reach higher for fear of falling; he dared not go down for fear of something worse. He thought to call out to his father, but his father was far and out of sight on the other side of the big house. In the direction of the house he saw what he had heard: a dark form, a shade stalking through the field toward them. The girl had stopped whispering and he could not see her in the grass. The shade came closer, and the footsteps grew heavier. He tried to fold himself into the wood. The shade spoke, as if to the girl.

It waded through the grass and the darkness, muttering. It kicked a patch of grass. There was silence but for the ragged breathing of the tree woman. Suddenly, heavy steps and a yell— the girl.

He heard the rip of cloth. Another yell from the girl was muffled, and then cut. The breathing of the tree woman grew stronger and stronger until the shade seemed to notice, and there was silence. Then, the woman loosed a scream that must've reached the heavens. It was shrill and piercing, and then she took another breath and the scream was full like a warrior's, and then a third breath and it was a wail that echoed against the big house and died.

My son closed his eyes and clutched the tree. The shade mumbled curses and shuffled away from the girl toward the tree woman and struck her. She made no more sound. The girl got up off the ground and ran toward the cabins.

The shapes of men began to appear near the house. My son heard the galloping of a horse, and the sound of iron again, and as he opened his eyes and looked down he saw the shade begin to drag the woman away through the grass. A man on horse-back came near and dismounted.

"Take her to the stables," said the man. He wore a long linen shirt and a hat, and his voice was like the grating of wood.

"Yes, sir."

"And for goodness' sake, shut her up. If the wench keened any louder the whole of creation would hear her."

"I don't know what possessed her," said the shade, as he lifted the woman's limp body and put her on the saddle of the horse as if she weighed nothing.

The man snorted and put his hands on his hips and gazed at the base of the tree where the woman had been. His eyes trav-elled up the trunk until they reached the boy, who stared down at him like a raccoon. He could make out the whites of the old man's eyes, and the wrinkles of his face. Without moving his head, the man reached his hand toward the shade, who was mounting the horse, and spoke.

"Hand me your lash," said he.

"What's that, Matthew? Why, sir?"

"Give it to me and get to the stables before I flog you myself."

The shade tossed a bundle to Matthew and rode off. Mat-thew was looking at the ground, and he began to step slowly toward the base of the tree.

"My boy," said he, rubbing his eyes in weariness. "Jacobs may have been too witless to see you, but you are not invisible to me."

The man fiddled with the bundle in his hand, and my son did not stir.

"Whose child are you?" said Matthew, his voice turning hard. Still my son did not move.

Then Matthew lunged and there was a sound that broke the air and my son felt fire across his back for the first time. The lash ripped his body from the tree, and he fell the long way to the ground.

He tried to move but the earth had clanged his bones, and as he lay on the grass it was as though he were stuck in mud. With great effort he raised his head and saw Matthew reach his hand back, as if to the end of the world, but right then, there was a sound, a movement that Matthew seemed to feel. It made him wince as it passed him, and then it hit the tree with a deep tremor. Matthew's eyes broadened. His hand remained behind him, his eyes locked on the tree. My boy turned his head slowly, and saw something that made him smile. Lodged midway in the trunk of the tree, and quivering as if with fury: his father's tomahawk.

Matthew looked toward the house to see my husband and three other men striding toward him. He opened his arms.

"My lads," said he, "there's no cause for commotion. It's merely one of my rascal Negro boys."

My husband did not stop as he passed Matthew.

He went to my son, who got up, slowly, given strength by the presence of his father.

He told me he would never forget the dumb blinking in the white man's face as he looked between him and his father, and the understanding finally came to the man. He had not whipped a slave of his, but the son of the people whose allyship he sought to win.

Back at the fire, my husband showed my son to where their pack lay on the ground. My boy pulled out his mat and sat on it, exhausted. His father unrolled his own, which held their belongings, and he sat next to his son, offering him a piece of smoked fish I'd packed for them. The chatter of the men soothed him, and the fire warmed his face. He bit into the fish, savouring the taste of the fat, the brine, and the smoke.

"What happened, son?"

My husband chewed a poultice for the boy's back. The flesh was wealed and tender, but not broken. My son told him what had come to pass, and my husband listened as he applied the poultice, shaking his head ever so slightly. The boy observed over his shoulder, noting his father's face shifting slowly out of solemn thought into a weary smile.

"You know she will beat me for this, don't you."

He meant me, and he was right for thinking so.

My son smiled and felt eased, until he saw the shade approach the fire, trailed by a number of Negroes carrying heavy loads. For the first time, he saw the shade's face in the light of the flame. It was paler than he imagined. The shade snapped his fingers, pointing to his left and right, directing the men behind him, each of whom carried barrels and large bundles.

The shade spoke to the Indians, listing the gifts they were to receive. My husband translated for our tribe. Others spoke in their tongues. There was tobacco, West India rum, and British wool blankets the first night. The guns were to come the next day.

The men around the fire spoke late into that night. War was brewing, and men always have much to say about war.

My son knew this was a meeting of importance, and he tried to hold attention. All the great war chiefs were there. There was the Shawnee man called the Panther and the Wyandot called Roundhead, and others too who were of legend to him. And though he tried to remain awake, sleep began to pull. He fought it, but his new blanket was soft and warm beneath him. Finally, slowly, he lay on his side and glanced up at a cloud passing over the moon. Sparks chased up toward it. His eyes closed and were too heavy to open. The voice of the Panther drifted over him and he saw a star arc from behind the moonlit cloud. The darkness swallowed it quickly.

When he lurched awake, it took him several breaths to recall where he was. The night was black and the men around him were asleep. He lay on his wool blanket and his deerskin covered him. He removed it and sat up, breathing heavy. The fire was a full mound of quietly flaming embers. His father was gone. He felt a pang between his hips and got up to piss. Carefully, he stepped through slumbering men. His hands tested the dark before him. He relieved himself in a bush with small berries.

There, he saw a dark form coming from the direction of the

cabins. It was his father—he knew from the way he stalked—
and my son called out quietly. His father came to him quickly
and silently. The two knelt and pressed their knuckles into
the grass.

"What were you doing, Pa?" he asked him.

"I found the father of the young girl you met. He is also the
brother of the woman you saw at the tree," whispered my husband.

My boy was puzzled, and rubbed sleep from his eyes.

"Tonight we will steal them away," said my husband, and my
son's heart began to pound.

"But Pa," he said, "if we leave tonight, they will know we
took them. There are men awake, and everyone else will stay
for at least another day, and they will know."

"Yes," said my husband, "and yet, there will not be another
chance."

My boy did not understand, and so his father explained.

"The man who lashed you is used to being feared, yes. He
would think that anyone who meant to free his slaves would
fear being known. And that thought is a weakness."

My son nodded.

"Walk without sound," whispered my husband, "roll our
things in your blanket, and meet me by the boat."

It was easy, he told me, to walk without sound on the trimmed
grass. He gathered their things and descended the hill. At the
beach he saw three forms around the boat. He came closer and
made out his father, a Negro man carrying the woman of the
tree, and the young girl. The girl was crying.

"No, Papa, no. I ain't going," she said. "Massa Tillings said—"

"Hush, child, hush!"

My boy loaded the pack in the boat. He heard his father speak:

"While on the water, the girl must be still or we will drown."

My son looked back and glanced upon the girl. She was looking at him with malice.

"Yes," came the reply. "I will bind her to me."

The Negro man picked up the woman of the tree and placed her in the boat. She groaned gently. My son shifted the blanket beneath her to centre her weight. Her face was swollen and ugly. She reached and put her hand on his. He couldn't help but draw back in fear. His father handed him a paddle.

They dragged the boat into the river and he lifted himself in, and steadied the craft while the Negro man stepped in, holding the girl. My husband pushed off and they were in the straits. The current rushed against them strong, shimmering with starlight. He paddled as hard as he could.

And so they brought them to Detroit into the care of Chiron. All this my boy told me, and as he did I felt a panic and a rage come upon me. I could have killed my husband. He had put everything in danger. My child, our home. Everything.

Do you recall my tale of the man and the woman in the boat full of wondrous things? The swamp, and the people who took them in? That was our story. We had come fleeing, and against all odds these people gave us refuge. We accepted their aid, their food, their protection. Through years of humble work we had earned our place there. It was our home. And then my husband, in a fit of madness, risked everything. The gifts the tribe was to receive were no small matter. They were arms when war was coming. And my husband saw fit to steal a whole family of slaves from under the nose of the man providing the very means to our survival. If our village did not receive those gifts, not only my family, but all the families could have been scattered to the winds.

I did not sleep for the two nights it took for the other men to return. And when they did, I looked with shock on the guns, and the powder. Nothing was missing, and the people were untroubled. It seemed, despite my fears, that Tillings's slaves were of less value to him than his allies.

This made it easier to forget my anger. It is easy to forgive in the quiet before war. Easy too to forgive a lover.

Does your body ache for children? Mine did, even then, when I had several already.

And so, once forgiven, he gave me our last child. I recall looking by the light of the shifting embers and the stars peeking in from the opening at the roof of our hut. My family, tight and slumbering, the tug of his fingers at my heel. I remove the little one, deep in dream world, from his chest, and hear the change of his breathing, slow, quiet.

I clamber on him and pull the bearskin up; his eyes alive like the embers; our bodies limb-to-limb, belly on belly, hand on hand, pressing for a light sweat. Slow. Slow enough we hear night sounds of owls and wind, and the calling of frogs. The snores of the children too. Our breaths get long together, our chests full . . . we clutch hard as if to test how much flesh can bear . . . my teeth at the scar on his head.

I move on him heavy like stone on earth, till knees sting, and his skin hot like the sun inside him, and I press, and press, until the sun inside me too, and it rack us and send us through sky, and sky, and water, and land. Darkness. And breath. Breath, and skin. Arms in hands, clutching firm, precious skin, and chest on chest, lips tasting wet salt, and air. The shuffle of embers. The snore of a child. And we both smile, I know, though it's too black to see.

Our love was always in the black of night. And he, the stars between my arms.

Chapter VII

The old woman's voice had become distant as she spoke, and she gazed up at the high reaches of the wall.

"I must admit," I said, and smiled when she glanced at me, "I wasn't expecting the tale to take that particular turn."

She gave an owlish hum that grew in her belly, slowly evolving into a girlish laugh, so strange and full of mirth that I could not help but join in.

"So, John, your husband—was that his real name?" I asked, once we had quieted. And it struck me, as soon as I said it, that I still did not know her name.

She raised her brow at me and sighed heavily. "Names mean so little to me," she said.

"Come now!" I chided. "A lover such as that must have had a name you whispered in the dark."

I was poking fun at her, but she did not pick up the jest.

"Names can be bought," she said somberly, "and changed. Stolen too, mind you. Which is perhaps why you ask—perhaps why you still do not believe, yes? I *am* that woman in Chiron's text. How did he say? A Negro woman, and free?"

She paused to smile at me, and then her eyes drifted around

the prison walls, and she snorted as if to laugh at the irony that the passage of time had imbued in those words.

"But you ask of a *real* name," she went on. "His was a changed name already, true. And we took new names in that village. Long names, full of meaning. But when I met him, his name was John. And that, simple and empty as it was, was always good enough. He filled it with his spirit."

She sat silently for a moment, staring at her hands in the folds of her skirt. When she continued to speak, her voice was quiet and full of feeling.

"It was good I forgave him when I did," she said, still looking down at her hands. "He never did see our last child, that I named Jeannie, for him. He came back from hunting with a bad trouble in the chest. All the men from that trip fell sick. I did not let the children touch him. But I touched him. I stayed with him, trying to calm the blood in his throat. And still he took every effort to wake, and smile. His whispers grew weak. 'Tell them I die happy,' he said. And I know he meant the children. 'Tell them to speak to me, even in the earth. Even in the rain.'"

The wind dipped down into the pen, ruffling our clothes, and the old woman chuckled and upturned her hands to the air.

"Isn't that right, night lover?" she said, looking up, and I became aware of the tears in my eyes.

She yawned and, noticing me, gave a tired smile. She leaned off the stool and found a spot on the ground once more, where she stretched out her legs, rested her head against the stone wall, and closed her eyes.

"Now that we've summoned him," she murmured after a

long pause, "let us hear his voice. You have the text from Emma, yes?"

"I have it," I said, sifting through my satchel. My fingers touched on the folded parcel of papers.

"Well then," she chimed, her eyes still closed. "Read to me now, girl. It is a journal written by my husband. It tells of how we met. Only by cunning have I kept it with me. I have had it read to me only once since his death."

She opened her eyes and looked at me frankly.

I pulled the papers out of my bag. I unfolded them delicately, and looked over the words. There were some small rips and blotches, and the script was tight and elegant.

The old woman huffed impatiently. "Come!" she said, waving her hand as if to beckon me. "Break open my heart for me, girl."

The Journal of Jean Baptiste Bâby,
dit Patterson, Montreal, 1795

⟶

There are happenings I do not even whisper of. But I must hear them somehow, if only by the scratch of ink on paper. The difference, after all, between an act of war and an act of murder is, I imagine, a question of documentation.

In the house of a merchant, even a slave woman has tools as well as materials at her disposal. Lengths of babiche leather, black spruce wattape from the packs of engagés, returned from their long trade voyages to the high country. Pieces of wood salvaged from casks of brandy and boxes of apples. A large tin tub with which to soften the wood, secret under the clouded water of soaking potatoes.

The Merchant liked fresh eggs, and had a hutch built that boasted far more comfort than most slave barracks in the city. I went into it one frigid morning in the New Year. The hens were huddled together, pecking at their morning grist in the mounds of hay. They clucked angrily at me. I crouched for a moment at the threshold of the hutch. And then I saw, balanced carefully where the roost met the wall, two wooden frames bound taut and webbed with leather. Their form looked stiff and elegant, like the wings of a large bird. Their function I could guess, though I spoke nothing of it, despite my tremulous curiosity. They were meant, I wagered, to tread atop deep snow.

I couldn't fathom how she had the time, let alone the knowledge to make such things. Her days began and ended in the dark. Kneading bread, her lithe form rolling into the dough. Lighting the hearth. Boiling tea. First a secret brew for herself— I asked her once what it was and she only smiled. Every day she served breakfast and then bundled herself in her coat and favourite Indian shawl, and headed to market. She brought back live fowl and sheep that she killed in the back, in front of the hutch. She liked to do so herself, despite the protest of Geneviève. She saved the blood in stoneware, and the hides, which she knelt upon to do the washing in the midmorning.

How do I know such details? Two things. For one, my role required an eye for detail. At a glance I could say with near certainty if five hogshead of high wine were missing from a shipment of eighty. I could recognize true English wool weave with the touch of a finger. I could hear quiet steps at night that were not the dozing treading of feet on their way to a chamber pot.

The second thing. I loved her, from the first moment, though love as a bondsman can necessitate strange action. In her presence, my senses were sharp and my body truly alive. Not even on my best hunts have I experienced such an acute awareness in my being. Every fibre of me was drawn to her.

The first I heard of her was from the Merchant's brother, in writing:

I hear it is quite fashionable in the north to avail yourself of a Negress to tend the house. We have no need of another wench. Take her; a gift to us both. She was rescued from a band in the mountains. She has no kin now, and she is seasoned.

Three months later she arrived with a shipment, direct from the Antilles.

I fetched her at the docks office. She was small. Smaller than I imagined, and she held her meagre belongings to her tightly. And she was dark indeed. With eyes that glimmered dark and fiery as embers. She wouldn't speak to me at first, but not out of coy apprehension. No, it was more piercing than that. She nodded curtly when I identified myself. I walked with her to the house and showed her to her quarters. I acquainted her with the kitchen and with Geneviève, with whom she was to share her duties. Geneviève was a kindly pânis woman, intent to see the good in life, and in her lot. She worked hard, and was a devout Catholic. Her faith did not bother the Merchant but did the mistress, who was ever hard on her. Geneviève had been abandoned by no less than three white men who had promised marriage and then promptly left. Her shortcomings showed in the lines of her face, but not in her heart. She greeted the new woman warmly, and set about fussing and chattering about market gossip, and the fine company blankets she had put aside for her.

The new woman caught me staring at her hands, so small and wiry, and her eyes burned into me. I could feel the heat of them on the dark flush of my face. There was a tingling over the cicatrix that ran from my brow into my hair.

When I presented her to the Merchant and mistress at supper the mistress cooed over her.

"You are such a small, pretty thing," said the mistress. "What are we to call you?"

"Cash," said the woman, with a squared jaw, and my heart quivered at the sound of her voice, deep and sharp.

My own quarters were adjacent to the kitchen, and so I heard her sing to herself beneath the thunder of Geneviève's snoring. I did not understand the words of her songs, but I understood that they spoke of a different, warmer place. A place where people danced as they worked. As I fell asleep to the melody, my dreams became hers, or so I imagined. I would dream a long journey south. Perhaps to Vermont, where slavery is abolished. Or further. On a ship, borne by southern currents and wind. To a mountain somewhere that is balmy and green. I have seen paintings of that part of the world, and read of it. I thought often of it when I was a child, thinking of what fate might have befallen my own brother, who was sent there. In my visions it was a place lush with bounty and adventure. It was good to dream something different. My own dreams of homeland surge into me sometimes at the smell of smoke, and I recall flashes of snow soaked dark with blood, before I shake the memory from my head.

In a corner of the cellar one day, I found flour and seed on the ground in the shape of a circle cut with a cross. This in front of dried herbs and bits of cloth and tallow fashioned into candles, and dark markings of blood. It frightened me. Of this I never spoke to the Merchant. But I did speak to her. Warned her that even rumours of witchcraft could lead to a hanging, or worse. But she only regarded me with her unerring gaze, her eyes that pierced like fangs. And I loved her all the more.

One autumn day, I saw her put her hand on her belly after coming back from market, and I knew. I have never asked her about her dealings or about the nature of the conception. I never wanted to know. The mistress had her suspicions; one could tell by the cold way she regarded Cash once her belly began to show mere months after she had arrived. Lucky for us all, the mistress herself was already with child, so it did not take long for her to bathe herself in ignorance and return to her soft, doting ways. She gave birth to a healthy girl child they named Stéphanie.

Cash grew swollen beneath her frock, and she became more terse and fiery in her quiet way, but did not let up on any of her chores. She consigned herself to her lot. We all learned to do so. The winter was long and brutal, as it always was. By March, the countryside was still deep with snow.

And then, one morning in late March I awoke to a knocking. I rose from my pallet, thinking it some vagrant or thief rattling at the chicken hutch. I took my cudgel with me. The night was calm and frigid, and the glow before dawn began to light the land gently. A soft snow was falling. I opened the back door silently and peered out past the ribbed icicles onto the lot. The knocking had stopped and as I surveyed the land I saw the source of the sound. A woodpecker, larger than I had ever seen, looked back at me from his perch on the nook of the great maple outside. He was as large as a crow, his red crown barely visible in the half darkness. After a moment he swooped away like a hooded shadow, and I was left standing in the back threshold, looking at the lot. I knew not the meaning of the vision, so I listened. Listened first to the almost silent falling of snow. Then I listened to the house.

And it struck me with a panic. I crept to the kitchen and heard the grunting snores of Geneviève. Only Geneviève. I knew, yet I opened the door to be certain.

Geneviève lay on the floor, rollicking in her heavy breath. Cash was gone. I gripped my cudgel and refrained from striking the nearest thing to me. The cicatrix above my eye began to throb, and I felt my breath grow shallow. I wouldn't wait until morning to betray her. I went straight up the stairs to awaken the Merchant.

I knocked and heard his grunt in reply.

"It appears Cash deserted in the night," I said from behind the door.

Silence, for a few moments. Then: "What the devil are you saying, man?"

"Cash has fled, sir," I said, louder this time.

There was silence again, and I imagined him blinking with confusion and sleep. I wager that it had truly never occurred to him that her every action, every diligence, every hour of labour had been bent not on a sense of servitude to him, but on this moment of flight.

I heard him curse, and the sound of his feet on the floor,

stumbling in the dark. The door unlatched, and he squinted at me, buttoning his nightgown.

"What in God's name is the wench thinking?" he sputtered, half smiling with excitement at the prospect of a hunt. He shuffled over to his wardrobe. The mistress was asleep, breathing gently beneath a pile of linen and wool. The child too, in the cradle next to the bed.

"We are not likely to find her, sir," I told him as he pulled up his breeches. "The snow falls heavy."

"We shall find her!" he said loudly, and the mistress snorted awake.

He glanced at her and kept speaking, winking at me as he worked his buckle.

"What with all the engagés have told me of your hunting prowess!"

There was no time to argue with this man. It was true I could hunt. I could stay in silence until beasts moved across my path. I could often see the routes that animals take through the underbrush, and pitch a deadfall or set a snare. I could stalk a doe over the mountain and shoot her at a fair distance. But a hunter knows his limits. Many times I had lost a trail, never to recover it. What if I fell astray on her tracks, unable to interpret the calls of animals and the markings of human passage through the trees? I could not hazard going amiss. There were men who could read the forest far better than I.

It made no difference that she was near to her time. She was as constant as the sun. She had not slowed in her errands, nor

faltered in her strength. With a few hours of headway and supplies from the kitchen, she could be anywhere on the island, or
beyond.

"What's all this?" mumbled the mistress, still obscured beneath the folds.

"I suggest that we call for a tracker," I said. "Someone who
might be able to find her . . . expeditiously."

"No one," muttered the Merchant, buttoning his coat. "There
is no one."

"Perhaps . . ." I feigned pondering. "Perhaps Monsieur Lepin."

Lepin, or as he was known colloquially, the Wolf, was the
stuff of folktales. Once, in his younger days on a run to the
upper country, a brash engagé by the name of Beniteau tried to
swindle him. Beniteau led a mutiny. He whispered to his compatriots that they did not need a leader, or at least did not need
one who took more of the earnings than the rest of them. One
morning he awoke the Wolf with a primed musket, while the
others packed the bateau. They left him with naught but his
clothes and the skinning knife he kept sheathed in his moccasin. That was enough. The Wolf simply turned the forest against
them. Stalked them. Ran like a deer through woods to catch
them at their camps. Called dark witches to sit on their chests
while they slept. Summoned bears to raid their cache and de-
vour their pemmican. Eventually, crazed with visions of daemons and the haunting dark of the forest, they went mad and
drowned themselves in the river. The Wolf paddled the eight-
man canoe himself into Montreal. Nowadays, he had retired

from running pelts. But he had country-born children, scores of them through all the river routes from here to Athabasca. He provided for them by bringing goods and provisions every spring. He mostly made his money by taking wealthy white men and their boys into the bush to learn how to hunt. They marvelled at his proximity to the wild. He was as much of a curiosity as the savages themselves.

I gave the Merchant a description of Cash's clothes, for he would not remember as I could. A blue kersey jacket and petticoat. Perfect for disguising her swollen belly. And the cotton cap with yellow strings. Which would obscure her face. Her Indian shawl, of course. With this he went to post an advertisement in the *Gazette*.

I went to find the Wolf.

He resided in a small cabin on orchard land nearly a league north of the port. It took me half the day to reach him; the two draft horses, Tybalt and Benvolio, struggled through the still-deep snow on the sledge paths. We were flanked by the ever-reaching forest. The pine boughs heavy with icy cargo formed a canopy that nearly blocked out the light of day. I thought of Cash in her home-fashioned shoes, the peril of the drowning depths of snow in untrodden wilderness, and I drove the horses hard. They frothed at the mouth and sweat to keep my pace.

The Merchant had given me a signed note of the promise of reward. Twenty dollars. Four times the usual for runaways. She was an exceptional slave. Moreover, she was two slaves in one body.

I found the Wolf crouching by the firepit in front of his cabin, smoking a hide. I hailed him and propositioned him with the case at hand.

He considered, lifting his bushy grey brows wearily and puffing on his pipe as he prodded the hide. Finally he stood and stretched his legs and nodded to me.

"Tell your merchant to forget the *Gazette*. Save his money," he said, before turning and trudging up to his cabin.

"I will bring her before the week is out," he called to me from over his shoulder. It was a Wednesday.

I nodded and was on my way. I lost myself in memory on the ride back to town.

It was an engagé who took me to Montreal all those years ago. Rescued me along with my brother off the riverbank deep in the upper country, I was told. The man had found us silent and black-eyed, nestled in the crook of a tree like raccoons. My village was cold black ash behind us. The engagé tempted us down with hardtack. I don't recall that. I don't even recall my brother's name. But I do recall his face, and his grip about my shoulders. I recall being seated atop a bundle of furs and the two of us feeling like birds flying over water. I recall falling asleep to the chants of the paddlers and the rough hand of the engagé petting me like a dog. I remember the man's voice and the way his moustache curled brusquely over his mouth, making it seem he had no lips at all. *Doucement ti pânis, doucement*, he would say.

He sold us to his employer in Montreal for four hundred livres. The employer's name was Bâby. They shipped my brother, who was bigger and stronger than I, to an associate in Martinique. I might have gone with him, but it was Mistress Bâby who insisted that I be kept, and promised that she would care for me. She cropped my long hair and when I cried she nestled me in her bosom, and I would hush. She taught me French and English, and arithmetic. I learned Chippewa from fellow slaves in the quarter, and some Mohawk here and there. The latter sounded like my own language, Ouendat, which had left my tongue, it seemed, as soon as my brother was gone, though my ear could still pick it up. I'd heard it on a few occasions, but I never disclosed my origin to any of those countrymen—whether for shame or for sadness, I couldn't say.

If I had a tribe it was that of the young slave boys of the quarter. Mistress Bâby took me with her to market and church. I think she yearned for a child, and though I may have yearned for a mother, the veil of family was thin. I always suspected that to her I was little more than a creature she could show off. Her interest in me was most acute when she summoned me to count out money at market, or to recite a passage as I poured wine for her visiting friends—my service was a trick and amusement more than anything. As soon as I was done with my house chores, I ran to the streets to seek out my compatriots. When Bâby fell ill and died suddenly, I was already a young man, and it was Mistress Bâby's brother-in-law who sold me to the Merchant.

The Merchant was a dark-featured, handsome man, perhaps ten years my senior. Were it not for his beard, which he kept full and well groomed, his Indian blood would have been more apparent. Indeed he was a mongrel, as a drunken fellow merchant once proclaimed at a dinner. At that gibe, the Merchant smiled and slowly dabbed at his moustache.

"If only your sword was as sharp as your tongue," was all he said, staring at the fool with his hard, dark eyes.

The drunk reddened and blustered. It was not a challenge, but a threatening reminder. The Merchant rarely travelled without his sabre, a navy cutlass given him by his father, and his speed with it was known. One did not become the most successful smuggler in Lower Canada without handling a blade well.

He was a petty merchant, and he did enough official business with the North West Company to cover his tracks. His father was an English naval officer who settled as a businessman in Montreal. Not aristocratic, but with enough ambition to secure himself a position of wealth in the new British territory. The Merchant's mother was French, half-Abenaki, and as such the Merchant was godfather to many Indians, both on the island and to the east, to whom he would send gifts every year. This kinship served as both his benefit and his detriment. He was often denied invitation to the halls of the great merchants and military officers stationed in Montreal. But what he lost in unearned privilege he made up for in undeclared business. More than once he was publicly accused of smuggling. His accusers knew it. Everyone *knew*, as it were. Not because they had proof, but because they would do no differently if they were so positioned.

He did smuggle, of course. Sending a man on the deliveries

in order to alibi himself was, among other reasons, why he had me.

Under the cover of nightfall, I would depart from the stable and take the old portage pathways with the loaded cart or sledge hauled by Tybalt and Benvolio. If anyone of import were to inquire I would show them my papers from the Merchant.

My pânis is transporting a small shipment of gifts to my relatives in such-and-such locale. Inquiries may be addressed to Charles Patterson of Montreal, offices on Notre Dame, opposite the Seminary.

Uniformed men would accept that if they valued their station, for they knew what clout was wielded by the downtown merchants. For anyone without a uniform bold enough to waylay me, I had a brace of flintlock pistols tucked into my sash, and if that was ever insufficient, I kept my club at my feet. Fencing was a gentleman's sport, but we slaves would fight with cudgels from the time we were boys. An old West Indian Negro named Hermes taught us. He was grey, but robust and tall with broad shoulders, one of which bore a brand of the fleur-de-lis. We boys would run from church on Sundays, to the stables of Hermes's master. There in the hay, we pretended to sing and dance while we learned to wield a stave. Hermes showed us to hold our cudgels as both shield and spear, as deadly as any blade. What we failed to parry, our bodies learned to repel. A man's full-force blow became nothing to me. To any cudgeller, a broken finger or bruised rib gave us no pause in a fight. We hid our injuries stoically, dedicated to the secrecy of our art. I assumed the mantle from Hermes in his later years. It was I who oversaw the band of slave boys eager to forget pain. Hermes gifted me the hefty ash club that I carried on my journeys. It could pass as a thick gentleman's cane. The first time I used it in front of the Merchant, I broke the hands of two robbers wielding bayonet tips—deserted soldiers, by the looks of it—and sent them packing into the bush whimpering in pain. We were on our way to the Merchant's Abenaki family, south of the Saint Lawrence. He looked on me slyly for a moment, first with suspicion, then with something resembling pride. Since that time, I have conducted many business expeditions alone.

On such a trip one autumn, I was taking the cart to Bout-de-l'Île with several hogshead of West India rum. The Merchant's relations at Montreal's western tip were to sell the tax-free spirits to the people of the town. The Merchant owned a large plot there, where one of his godchildren raised a family and farmed oats.

I donned my beaver wool cloak and departed in the dead of night. The cloak was a fine thing, and since bandits are far more likely to attack poor men, it was my first layer of protection. I travelled without incident, having only stopped on a few occasions to clear fallen brush from the path. Sometimes I would descend and walk by the cart, for warmth. I plucked needles of fir boughs as they passed overhead and chewed them until they turned sour and broken in my mouth.

About a league out from Bout-de-l'Île, as the sun was rising, I heard a group, not far from the cart path. I couldn't make out the words. The language was Odawa, perhaps. By the sounds, I wagered it was a small group of men breaking camp by the shore of the river. They were four, it seemed, as I pulled closer.

Two canoes, overturned on the shore grasses, a fire, and a pânis woman tethered to a tree with a halter around her neck. My own neck constricted at the sight. I regarded them impassively as I came near, and I clucked to calm the horses.

One circled through the forest to cut off my path. The three others approached the cart directly, chattering amongst themselves.

The circling one emerged on the path a few paces ahead and waved his hands, spooking the horses. He held firm to stop them and they whinnied and came to a halt.

I greeted him cautiously, keeping my eyes on him, while still paying mind to his companions, who slowly approached my flank.

He was a fierce-eyed rascal, a good deal shorter than I, and lean. He had tall moccasins and skunk garters, a moose-skin coat with a large copper medallion fashioned as a brooch, and a stovepipe hat with three hawk feathers, blotched with red. One for each scalp. Such was the claim of that decoration.

"Bou-jou," he said, imitating my voice, and he chuckled.

"What do you want?" I asked, irritated by his brashness.

I saw in his eyes the envy. He was lean indeed, underneath that fine moose jacket. Likely hungry if his party were coming in so late in the season. He called to his companions, one of whom had moved to the back of the cart and had begun lifting the hides that covered the cargo there. I did not understand Odawa well, but I gathered the meaning. Skinning me like a hare. He continued muttering as he held Tybalt's halter and stroked the horse's long nose.

In one motion, I stood on the cart and drew my flintlock pistol from my sash and cocked the hammer, levelling it at his chest. There was silence. Snow fell gently and I feared the wetness of it would dampen my piece to misfire, but with my eyes I dared him to give me cause to test this possibility. They had a slave woman that would fetch good money, and risking their lives in robbing me was not a good gamble. But one never knew for certain what a man would do. I saw from the corner of my eye his companion on my flank brandished a tomahawk, and I drew the other pistol toward him, priming it in the same movement.

The Indian in the stovepipe sneered and spoke.

"Sauvage francisé."

He said the words slowly, enunciated well enough to tell me that he had practiced that phrase before.

"Bête sauvage," I uttered back to him in a heartbeat. It stunned him for a moment, and it nearly stunned me, though I hoped not to show it. I hadn't practiced those words, though I had heard them many times. And it surprised me how easily they left my mouth.

He recovered from his momentary shock and nodded with a wicked smile, boldly turning his back to me. He walked lazily through the trees toward his camp and the others followed him.

I sat and clucked to Tybalt and Benvolio and we pressed onward. I released the hammers of the pistols slowly before stowing them back in my sash.

I had tried to tell Cash. But such a thing cannot be told, most of all to a woman whose eyes burn like embers. Captivity is learnt with time.

One does not simply run from Montreal. First was the problem of escaping the city. The city never closed its eyes. Even at the quietest night, there peered a restless woman from a Saint Paul window, eager to talk to her father the printer, or her brother-in-law the port administrator. Or soldiers, teetering from a tavern, looking to prove their dedication to maintaining the order of the Crown. Perhaps a day labourer, rising early to their patron's fields, hungry to turn a runaway in for some scrap of wealth or reward. Even other slaves were especially keen to ascend beyond their lot by reporting their fleeing fellow men. One was always seen. And if the seeing eyes did not know to whom one belonged, they knew how to find out in short order.

Once a friend of mine, a young ratcatcher named Titus, courted a damsel—I don't recall her name, though I had courted her once myself. She was the daughter of a farmer named Brazeau, and Titus was the slave to the notary Du Charmel. They had been catching each other's gazes for quite some time, until he got up the courage to give a bouquet of yarrow to the girl as she packed up her market stand at dusk. She smiled like the coy creature that she was. It was only once, but once was enough.

"We are not white men," I told Titus, and he cursed me, but I did not let up. "Gentlemanly courtship does not become us, man. We are forbidden. Go to them in ways that are forbidden, and for God's sake, not in daylight."

As we heard tell later, a jealous young Irishman, indentured to the smithy, had witnessed the exchange and told the young woman's brother. The girl's family admonished her, putting a terrible fear in her such that when Titus approached her at market the following week, she made such a racket as to be sure he never made so bold again.

Yes, there were always eyes on a slave. The only hope of deserting the city with a moment of leeway was under cover of complete disguise during a heavy snow or rain. This much was possible, as Cash had managed, but once on the land, the danger multiplied tenfold. Only the most experienced hunter could go through the forest and survive. And if one could not go undetected, either by the trackers behind or the people through whose territory one passed, it was a sure return to bondage. Men, villages, came to the island for one reason: trade. And I knew of precious few who were averse to trade in human flesh.

Was it cruelty? Perhaps. Many might say so if they are not the ones who would rather forget. And moreover, many consider a slave's own position enviable. They saw only the comforts. Then again, for some men as myself, with good luck in masters, perhaps bondage was enviable.

To go by land was therefore impossible. To go by water, unthinkable. It was as if the waters themselves would bring you back. I went up the mountain north of the port once. I had just returned from Detroit and the voyage was so fruitful that the Merchant rewarded me with a week of rest. I was tired, but it was yet summer and I took to the bush with a bag of provisions. Atop the mountain I climbed a great maple and perched and watched the island move. Then I understood. The city was small and meek, nestled in the encroaching woods, but it had a power that cut through wilderness. That day I understood that a city like this closes distances that were once unfathomable. I could not see the river to the north, but I could feel it behind me, ferrying boats full of goods and men. To the south and west I could see the river flow steadily. The waters brought boats, creeping and minuscule, from all directions. Revolving into the port. I could see coils of smoke from Sault-au-Récollet and Bout-de-l'Île. And another village was being erected to the east. There was newly cleared land farmed on the smaller islands on the river. The pull of the port was hungry and bountiful all at once.

When I was a child there was a pânis woman—she was Fox, I believe—named Marie Quarris. She belonged to a starch-maker named Jarret de Liveaudière. She was strong and had a voice that could not be silenced. The sound of her voice ringing out in rebellion became a fixture of Saint Paul. *Ne me touches pas avec tes mains sales! Maudite français!* Wealthy folk would redden and remark on the impropriety of housing such a way-ward and willful woman. But some of us slaves would smile—laugh, even, if we could—and pray for her continued mettle. She was the bane of her mistress. And one day, she took beads and sifting cloths and knives from the attic of her masters. And she was gone.

The Indians with whom she offered to trade the goods laughed, I imagine, just as that Odawa man had laughed. Perhaps she presumed they would take pity on her. An Indian, like them. They laughed, I am sure of it. Sauvage francisé. They were on their way to the port already. Nothing could be easier than to bring a wayward outagamie back to her master. They would be rewarded with coin, as well as the goods she carried; one can only carry so much on one's back. And likely they would secure a future trusting buyer for their efforts. They returned her to Liveaudière without a tongue. We all knew she would not have submitted to her capture in silence. Her masters recoiled at her swollen, bleeding mouth, yet their concern did not last; they renamed her Echo. And there were no more willful shouts that rang in the corridor of Saint Paul Street.

One day, a farmer by the name of Guertain taunted her in the market. She walked away as if she did not hear him, and sometime later returned and bashed in his skull with a cobblestone. People yelled and fled and she remained until they came and put her in long irons. She was hanged the following week.

All these thoughts and memories haunted me in the long hours after Cash fled. I would have never imagined myself aiding in the capture of a runaway, yet I could not stand idle and deny what I knew to be true. Escape was a fantasy that would be swiftly broken with unimaginable suffering or worse. I prayed that she was unharmed, despite the unlikelihood of that possibility growing with each passing moment. I prayed that the Wolf would reach her before anyone else.

It was late in the evening on April third, five days from the time I rode to see the Wolf. I was in the study with the Merchant when we heard the knock at the door. I went to it and opened it.

The Wolf was squinting, his eyes downcast; between us and all around him fell thick, slow, flakes of wet snow. Behind him Cash stood shakily, huddled in a company blanket. I ushered them into the living room, where they could warm themselves by the fire. All rushed to attend to her and the Merchant raged, threatening lashes while the mistress protested and called Geneviève to bring hot water. The Merchant lost heart in his threats when he saw what a pitiful state Cash was in. She lay on the rug, bloody and blue-lipped, and did not speak. The Wolf sat by the fire and brooded. His wool head wrapping and his brows dripped from the wet of melted snow.

The Wolf had tracked her across the river, he told us. Found her at the lodge of a Mohawk woman he knew. Cash was barely clinging to life after giving birth, and the children had not survived.

"Children?" exclaimed the mistress.

"Yes," said the Wolf distantly. "Des jumeaux."

"Two little ones, how terrible," mused the mistress, fitfully dabbing Cash's brow with a cotton rag.

They had burned the stillborn children, the ground being heathen and too frozen for burial. When Cash was well enough to travel the Wolf loaded her on his sledge. *T'es bien brave, Negresse*, was what he said to her as he pulled her in the early dawn of the forest. She had lunged and tried to flee, and he waited until she exhausted herself, nearly drowning in the depth of the snow, her homespun snowshoes long gone. He went to her and lifted her spent body, loading her again on the sledge, and continued on.

I prepared dry clothes for her and carried her to the kitchen quarters, where Geneviève had already put on a bone broth to simmer. I laid Cash down on her pallet and left while Geneviève helped her to change. She was so weak. Late that night, I heard her coughing painfully. I rose from my bed and went carefully to the kitchen. I stirred fir needles into the broth and took a bowl of it to her, where she lay curled next to Geneviève's heavily breathing form. She sat up slowly and looked at me. It was near-total dark, but the embers from the hearth lit her wet eyes. Neither of us said a word. I heard her breathing soothe as I spooned her the broth. And my heart tore at the knowledge that I had been perhaps the principal instrument in her capture. I thought to tell her but I could not bring myself to say the words. Not yet. But I vowed that one day, I would.

Chapter VIII

I finished reading and lowered the sheaf of papers, gently re-folding them. They were sharp and broken at the creases. The old woman lay as if asleep, in the crook where the wall met the grass. A black ant crawled up the ruck of her head wrap toward her eyes. I leaned across and swiped it to the ground before it reached her face. When I took my seat again her eyes were open and on me. I looked away and sighed, realizing I felt unstifled for the first time that day. The shade now fell over the entire courtyard. It must have been late afternoon. I heard yells and hoof falls from over the stone walls. It was near time I departed, or else I risked missing a ride back to Dunmore that evening.

"So, Cash, is it?" I asked.

She nodded and smiled.

"And this husband of yours," I prompted. "Did he tell you of his betrayal?"

She nodded.

"Did you forgive him for this as well?" I asked.

"Ah, we forgive lovers too many things, do we not?" she said and sighed ruefully. "I understood him. He feared losing me, he feared for me, he feared telling me of his fear. There is, in that condition, so much fear that becomes you. He read me the journal once, and I cursed him, but not enough for me to forget my love. He promised to write me another. But I didn't want another. I wanted the truth. Yes, I raged. But I could not deny that I understood him, and so could not leave him for it. And he was a lover, not only in the silence and the dark."

"So I've heard."

She cackled and reached over and grasped at the fabric of my frock. I giggled and looked for a moment on her fingers tugging a fold of the faded green cotton. There was a thread loose that brushed up against a wrinkle on top of her hand. As her hand shifted I saw that it was no wrinkle but a scar, the depth of it white like a bone. She lifted her hand and my gaze drifted to the papers between my own fingers, and my smile faded as I pondered the text I had just read.

"I'm sorry for your children," I said.

She hummed curiously. "Perhaps you would not be," she began slowly, with a wicked smile, "if I told you their names."

I scowled, but she continued abruptly: "But first, let me pick up where my husband left off."

"Their names?"

She kissed her teeth and shifted her legs, contemplating.

"What were their names?"

"Ah, but you know what I think of names. Better a story, yes?"

———

There is a haunted deep spot in the waters not far from here, you know. Begat of the love between a Negro woman and an Indian man.

The two were slaves who decided one day that they would cast off their shackles for a time. So the woman, who had once worked hard and diligently, took it upon herself to become powerfully unruly, such that their master, a merchant, began to question her value to him.

One day, the merchant received a letter from an old acquaintance who lived many hundreds of leagues upriver, inquiring for the sale of a Negro woman and offering for her an impressive sum of peltry. In those days, a Negro woman was the most rare and valuable cargo that could be had in the north.

The merchant was moved by the promise of coin, and given that the woman had become willful, he took the inquiry to be a circumstance of fate and without delay arranged for the packing of a bateau—a big old canoe.

He sent the bateau with a crew of twelve, including his most trusted bondsman, the Indian. He packed it full with goods from England, and of course, the Negro woman.

The problem was, that bateau never reached its destination. Not that spring, in the month it should have taken to arrive, nor that summer, when the merchant expected his return shipment. So the merchant wrote his associate, and he waited. He received no answer. He wrote other businessmen and acquaintances, and the news he got was that his associate had been dead for two years. Lo and behold, every letter the merchant had received from the man appeared to have been forged. He asked all the runners who came into town, but none seemed to know anything about the disappeared bateau.

And finally, another slave he held in his household came to him in tears one day. She told him that the Negro woman had loved the Indian man. The slave said that she had overheard the two of them talking. The Negro woman had said she couldn't bear being sold from her lover. She would sooner wait till the bateau was in the depths of the sea, far from land, and then she would light a barrel of gunpowder and blow the boat to smithereens.

A tragic tale, no?

Another story:

There was once a man, a hunter, who raised dogs. One day this man undertook the bold task of taming a she-wolf to breed with his pack of dogs. The wolf was grey as smoke and supple. She didn't grow to be large, and so one could have mistaken her for a dog were she not so silent in her movements. One day, this man went hunting with three of his best hounds, including the she-wolf. He followed them as they coursed a stag down a ravine. He tried to keep up but grew tired with the speed of the dogs. Soon he could not even hear their howls, but he did not fear. He was an accomplished tracker, and so he slowed to a walk and followed the tracks through the leaf cover. By and by he came upon the two other hounds, dead on the ground. The she-wolf had torn their throats out and gone her own way into the woods, never to return.

Cash smiled, squinting at me from her seat against the wall beside me.

"There you have it," she said.

She seemed to be becoming part of the masonry of that stone wall. She found such easy recline in its corner.

"Two tales!" she exclaimed abruptly. "Which one is true?"

I contemplated.

"I believe them both," I said, grinning slightly, before leaning in and whispering, "But I have always had an affinity with she wolves."

She cackled and grasped my hand, patting it. Her skin felt cool and callused against mine.

I looked on it, so small and benign, and allowed the difficult question to rise to my lips.

"The crew of twelve?"

She hummed and nodded soberly, withdrawing her hand. "Those deaths weigh heavy on my heart. I made them quick as I could one night, with a strong dose of a most potent poison. Those who did not expire forthwith, we finished quickly with the pistols."

The air, it seemed, grew dark around her as the metaphor of the tale melted away, and my heart fluttered with the thought of the brutal resolution in such a night of killings.

The crack of a teamster's whip made me jolt, and the rollick of wheels and hoof steps on the other side of the wall set my heart pounding. I recalled again the dilemma I would be in when it came time to leave these walls. I had no watch, but wagered that if I didn't leave immediately it would certainly be too late to catch a ride to Dunmore, and I would have an uneasy night ahead. I looked to the sky, now cast with the purple stripes of sunset, and I noticed all of a sudden that the crickets had struck up their chorus. Cash, beside me, was looking up as well, but her eyes were closed and her hands curled one around the other. I shuddered off my agitation, and placed my hand on hers, looking softly at her. I could not judge a crime done to liberate oneself from slavery, not even one so grave. Cash met my gaze and smiled weakly and grasped my hand back, firm.

"I have not forgotten—you've left me with an unfinished tale," I said.

She raised her eyebrows coyly at me.

"The names of those children who perished," I said. "Your children."

"Ah . . ."

She released me and eyed me hungrily, folding her hands again and placing her chin on them.

"But it's your turn," she began. "Tell me a story."

"Good God, woman, you're insatiable. What do you want?"

"To know you."

"You know where I'm from, my profession—"

"Where you're from—girl, that too would only be a name. Tell me a story, so I know who you are."

She paused, her eyes meandering over me, her mouth pursing primly.

"I for one would like to hear the tale of how is it a girl such as you travels from the far reaches of the upper country, and alone too, it is said."

I was quelled for a moment, trying to think of who might have told her of my journey. They were a meddlesome bunch in free country. Just as quick to gossip as to lionize.

"That," I said, "is a tale I would not speak too loudly in these walls. When you are released, perhaps."

She huffed sullenly and lay down on the grass.

"My hanging will come quick, I think," she declared, with something like relief in her voice.

"Is that your wish?" I asked, taken aback.

"Yes," she said. "I have seen old women die slowly, their mouths full of muck, and I want none of it."

I did not know how to take this. So I offered her a small distraction. "Well, what I can say . . . the tale you ask for concerns"—I drew my words out and smiled as I saw her perk up in anticipation—"well it concerns a ship that preys on the lumber vessels of the inland seas, and a pirate who speaks to mermen and trees."

She chuckled. "Sounds like a lover," she said.

I pursed my lips, and she raised her eyebrows at me.

"I have no lovers to speak of," I said curtly.

She snorted and closed her eyes. "I'd wager," she said, feigning a weary sigh, "there are men and women in these towns who would do many things to lie with a high yellow woman whose skin is uncut by the lash."

This would have irritated me had it not been so true.

"Here," I said, smiling, as an idea, a memory came to me.

⸺⸺

The first time I ran away, I went far. I was a young girl then, propelled by a rebellion I can't recall. I climbed up the escarpment and into the rocky ground of the pines. I saw a cave with the crumbling skins of rattlesnakes, and when I sat down to rest, vultures began to circle me. I picked myself up and trudged along. Finally, I came to a meadow, where I found myself face-to-face with a she-wolf who looked on me from behind the rent body of a ram. Her blood-soaked jaw enticed me.

I was lost and thirsty. I walked slowly toward the wolf and reached for the carcass. She growled and took my hand in her mouth roughly. Her teeth were blunt and wet. I refrained from crying out, and instead lay in a sort of stubborn, tired defiance, looking up at her from the prickly aster of the meadow floor, my hand still held in her jaws. At this she released me, and returned to tearing at the flank.

I joined her and went slowly, moving my hands according to her growls. Seeing her eat awoke such a hunger in me I felt there would be nothing more satiating in the world. I found the heart of the ram through an opening in its throat, and pulled at it until it came out, clinging to ropes of red flesh. I gnawed it for blood, which was warm and frightfully thick. Some clotted in my teeth. I did not need much to feel full. Then the wolf left and I followed her for the remainder of the day as she went up the ridge, stopping once at a creek to drink. I sipped greedily too, before scrambling after her, up the rise. Finally, we came to her den, which was the hollow of a massive hemlock, fallen an age ago and rotted out into a tunnel on the forest floor. The inside was flecked with fur and slivers of light. The sun disappeared quickly into the land. The she-wolf went to a brood of tumbling pups, who yipped and greeted her with prodding snouts before coming to me. She vomited gently, a steaming red soup held together with her bile, which the pups fell on. She attended to them as they feasted, and licked up their urine and excrement. I sat in amazement and exhaustion, leaning on one end of the hollow, until we all fell asleep.

Many years later, I walked to that hollow with a boy one Sunday. I told him the story of the wolf as we approached, and watched with a smile as he crawled in on all fours, looking back at me from around his stout rump. He howled and I laughed, and pushed him, and straddled him. We undressed in the cramped hollow, and I took him into me and rollicked atop him till he whimpered, and still I did not let up.

Cash nodded as I finished my yarn.

"How's that for a lover?" I said with a smile.

She guffawed.

"Oh, you," she said, quieting her laughter.

"It's late," I muttered, looking back at her.

"It is," she replied, and she raised her head to the sky. "But tell me, Lensinda Martin," she said, raising herself to sitting. "Before you leave, would you like to hear one more?"

It was time I departed, I knew it was, but I could not quite bring myself to say so. The last omnibus would be gone soon. I would have no means to return to Dunmore that night, and would have to wander the streets and keep my knife close at hand, but I could not leave.

I glanced up at the sky. There was still the ebbing light of dusk, and the old woman's eyes were still full of story, and we might never have this time again.

You will never have this time again.

I nodded, and Cash coughed ceremoniously before beginning.

See here. A moth has flown into my throat, and there is an old voice on my tongue. This is a tale I recall from my childhood, from the green mountain of my birth. I recall skin of elders in firelight, shining like tar. I recall a fruit in my hand, hard as the bark of a tree, but soft inside, like sweet churned butter.

In the old savannah in Africa soil, two young men went to hunt.

In the walls of the city that was their home one was a prince who slept on a bed of fine peltry, and the other was a slave who lay on a straw mat. But in the old savannah, under the ancient trees, the two were as close as brothers.

Together they tracked herds of buffalo and flocks of river fowl. They bathed in rivers and lit fires at night to roast their kills. One would tell a story until the other would sleep, and while one slept, the other would sit watch with spear and knife.

One night while the prince was standing guard, listening to the creaks and calls of the savannah, he felt such a sense of peace that he decided to lie against the wide tree where they had made camp, so that he could better see the stars. So he crouched and reclined against the soft skin of the tree, and looked up to a canopy of stars that bathed the savannah in a gentle glow.

The whole grassland was his cradle; a chorus of animals sang for him.

To better hear the song, he closed his eyes for a moment. And indeed, the sound grew and came alive in his spirit. He opened his eyes, and the stars were even more beautiful than they had been before.

"What a sense of peace," he thought to himself, and he closed his eyes for a moment more.

His friend the slave turned in his dream.

And then the world turned upside down.

The slave and the prince awoke to the weight of many men on their chests, hands on their throats.

Whose hands?

Night walkers who had seen the fire and crept to them.

The men struggled. They were strong from their roaming and they writhed in the dust; they kicked like horses. They were pinned by hands, hands, and more hands.

Whose hands?

Slavers who saw the fire, their feet cut by grasses, their captives bound in a line in front of the moon.

When the young men were held so tightly they could scarcely breathe, the prince warned his captors that it would be a grave mistake to take them. The slavers paid him no mind, but the prince did not let up.

"Our clothing may be simple," he said, "but we are the sons of the King. Take us, and you will be stopped before the next sun falls. And you will be killed."

So he said and the captors laughed at this, but the one who tied his limbs with rope examined the prince's dagger. He saw that it was a blade of splendour, made by only the most skillful of ironworkers, and it bore the mark of the King. This struck fear in the troop. If their captive spoke true, it would mean great trouble for them. They examined their other captive, but as this one was a slave, he carried only an ordinary knife.

So they left the prince tied on the ground and they shackled his servant to their caravan, and they walked out into the night. The prince yelled to his friend, "You cannot forgive me," he said, "but do not forget me!"

"I will come for you! I will not forget you!"

When the caravan had gone from his sight and out of earshot, the prince wept on the roots of the tree. By then, the stars were fading into the dawn. How could he help his friend, his brother? How could he even help himself, bound as he was? He called to the distant stone walls of his home, but that was no use, as the walls of the city were beyond earshot, and well beyond sight. He called for help to anyone who would hear, but if there was anyone on the savannah, they did not heed him. When he had called until he was hoarse, he whispered to his ancestors in the ground, and then he drifted into sleep. In the morning, he awoke to the tickle of breath, and he saw the snout of a small beast come up from a den amongst the roots of the tree where he'd laid his head. This beast was called Mongoose, and as the prince looked on him, he noticed his dagger in the animal's jaws. Mongoose came close to the prince's face—close enough for the prince to slowly open his mouth and take the dagger back with his own teeth. Bit by bit, he cut through the ropes that bound him. When he had done so, he looked on the beast that had come to him. He put his dagger on the ground.

"Receive my dagger as a gift," said the prince to Mongoose. "Will you help me take back my friend?"

At this, Mongoose responded, "You have slept long and your friend is beyond the horizon. Not I nor a hundred lions can take him back now."

And at that, Mongoose went back down to the den amongst the roots.

"Please," said the prince. He crawled on all fours to the opening of the den and spoke with his cracked voice. "Help me," said he, "and I will never stop honouring you. I will honour you for generations."

There was only silence and breath from beneath the roots.

Meanwhile the young slave walked through lands beyond the horizon. One night, bone tired from marching, he fell deep into a dream that he would remember the rest of his life. He lay on his back and gasped in fear, unable to move, pinned to the ground—this time not by men but by a snake that coiled around his chest. Just as the snake leaned back to strike, a small beast pounced and broke the snake's neck with a twist of its jaw. The man watched as this small beast sat on his chest and tore the snake apart with its teeth.

"Look for me," said Mongoose to him, "and you will not be lost."

Each day, the man looked for the Mongoose. He looked as he walked in the slave caravan, day after day. He saw many strange places and many different lands, but no such beast. The farther he was marched, the more he began to fear that he was lost indeed, and that his dream meant nothing. He was sold across the sea to a new land, where he gave up all hope that an old god of the savannah would ever help him.

One day, in the slave barracks of his new master, a snake appeared. The man did not flee. He took the snake up in his hand, and broke its neck.

The next morning, he looked over the fields into the trees,

and saw Mongoose looking back at him. The beast stood still, and so too did the man. His heart began to pound. Mongoose ran, and the man saw him darting through bush, up, up, and up the mountain.

The day after, he took his knife and went up the mountain himself. The new master never found him, and he lived long and well.

That man was my mother's father. The old god of the savannah—Mongoose, so he is called there on the other side of the world. Here, in this land, he is known as Marten.

Remember this, for it belongs to you, Lensinda Marten.

And it is not done. Listen close.

It is a dark morning, thick with falling snow. A girl, barely a woman, treads on the snow with shoes, home-fashioned, that keep her from sinking deep. There is whistling snow and wind all around her and deep beneath her. Deeper still is ice, and below that is water, rushing strong enough that the woman can hear, even through the wind. She walks south, knowingly, and the wind is hard on her left side. When she is across, she looks back and sees no sign of her passage, only a white plain dancing with wind, growing whiter with the light of day.

The light, it seems, comes not from the sky but from the

ground. Around her, there are trees, and among the trees the snow calms, and she can see. The trees are silent and crippled with the weight of the snow, and there is a small beast they call marten, waiting for her. He scurries over snow that is as deep as the ocean, and she follows. The land is quiet, asleep. She walks in the land's dream.

There is a wild force in the tread of the girl.

She walks, following the marten through grove and thicket, until she stoops and lifts up layers of cloth, and feels water between her legs. She walks still, following the tracks of the marten. Snow is no longer falling, and all around is bright. There is no difference between land and sky.

She comes to the marten, throttled at the neck by a snare set at the trunk of a big pine. She crouches by his sleek body at the base of the tree under the canopy, where the snow is thin. His body is still warm. She lifts him, pulls off the snare around his neck, but he only lies, until the snow begins to swallow him.

The girl tries to stand and encounters a pain. The pain is a tolling bell that rattles from her loins to her skull and does not let up until she lies gasping, gripping the trunk of the tree.

She takes hardtack from her pack and eats. The pine boughs hang low and are a womb around her. She eats snow.

The bell tolls again, ringing from her core until her teeth gnash.

She puts the snare in her mouth. She growls like a beast and grinds her teeth into the cord until she retches from the bitterness. Her body rents itself and the snow between her legs grows spotted with blood.

She feels fear then. And then a pain so complete, there can be no fear. The bark of the tree feels good to hold after. It flakes off and clings to her face. She rests. And the fear returns with another wave, slow and cruel.

Night begins to fall, and the cold deepens with it. The girl begins to welcome the warmth that each wave of pain brings. Darkness comes, and her spirit goes black.

The pain awakens her. It is black above, but she is warm, and she smells burnt sage and cedarwood. There is a fire, and across from it are people. Three women, two young and one very old, and two children fast asleep in cradleboards. Their cheeks are full and brown. The girl feels her belly still swollen, and gives thanks in all the languages she knows. But the women hush her, and take a kettle from the fire and wet her lips with a cloth.

She feels their hands on her belly, her knees and shoulders. With a gust of purpose she lifts herself to a squat. She sees the marten hanging on the other side of the fire, gaping at her. She grips furs beneath her feet and pushes until the world inside her spills onto the ground. The women catch the children, singing, and the girl sinks into the earth. There is one baby on her chest. Then another. There is warm water pouring over her middle, and her children are with her, black-eyed and bobbing on her breasts.

She rests for a time, feeling weak and uneasy. Day and night seem the same. The women chatter in a language she cannot understand. They feed her stew and bread. The younger ones unwrap their children from the cradleboards and show the girl how to nurse. And just, it seems, as her breasts swell heavy with milk, a Wolf stoops into the hut. He is white with snow, and he greets the women as an old friend who visits on a whim.

She knows who he is, and her heart caves in on itself.

He looks on her and she does not break his gaze. Her children rise and fall with her breath.

"Know that it is you," he says to her. "You and only you I hunt."

The children are small but contented. And the girl, their mother, does not run. She looses them from her breast and delivers them asleep to the arms of the women who caught them. She touches a hand to each of their small heads and utters the names that occur to her in that moment.

She vows to return. One woman tells her she will care for the children. The girl says she will repay her tenfold for doing so. The very old woman says the children will never forgive her for leaving, and that they will grow strong, and violent. She will be right on all counts.

When the girl sees her children next, more than two years later, they do not believe her to be their mother, and for many years thereafter, they defy her in all ways.

It was fully dark now, and cool, and the streets outside the walls were quieting. I would have no means to return to Dunmore that night, and would have to wander the streets and guard myself.

Cash had finished her tale and I could only just make out her face in the dark. I heard her hand sifting through the basket.

My mouth was heavy. There was something I needed to say. It was unlikely, so unlikely that I would have normally scoffed and got up and left. But I had not left, and it was late, and there I sat gaping in the dark. The old woman glanced up at me and plucked her hand from the basket with a triumphant grunt.

"My father, Dred," I said.

She was chewing and grunted again, affirmatively.

"He was one of those children."

She smacked her lips and gulped loudly.

"Which, I suppose, would make you my grandmother."

"It would, wouldn't it," she said, and I heard the smile on her lips.

"You've always known, haven't you?" I asked, and I felt my face set in its scowl.

She hummed and patted my knee.

"How?"

"Oh, there are many ways to know such a thing," she said. "Your name. Your eyes, yes. But mostly, unlike you, I do not ignore my spirit when it speaks to me."

In the shifting dark, I could not unsee the features of my father, my brother, even, in her eyes and the slant of her brow. It was as if with each glance she appeared to me as someone I had always known and forgot. And for the first time that I could remember, I found myself yearning for my family.

I thought of my father and saw, as if before me, his eyes, the sly glance that I had always seen as a look of hardened circumspection; now that visage peeled away to reveal the sheer apprehension of a child who did not know his own mother.

"Oh, girl, it's all right. It's already done."

I looked to her and became aware of the utter sorrow rising in my throat, welling in my eyes. She was consoling me. And then and there I was weeping, for the second time that day. I wiped the tears once, and again. Cash's hand was on my knee— and then my hand was on hers, and I could feel a soft, supple vein that yielded to the tremor of my fingertips against it. And when I knew I could speak without stammering:

"And my father's twin? I never knew he had a twin."

"*Has* a twin, in all likelihood. She was just as furious, and smarter too. Dinah. You will hear of her, before the day is done."

I squinted as the image of a woman's face, long and fearsome, appeared to me, peering from between two darknesses.

"How did you repay those women?"

She brought the currants in her palm to her mouth and chewed, looking out at the dark courtyard.

"I took some goods from a big canoe."

I recalled the tale Cash had told, a lifetime ago, it seemed, of the man and woman arriving at the swamp village. The boat full of goods buried for the ancestors.

She nodded and hummed. "But I must let you go, yes? Come, help me up, I will call for our turnkey."

"It's my turn."

She raised a brow at me, pausing with one knee bent. "Is it now?"

"Be seated, Grandmother. And listen now, while I unburden my heart."

I took a deep breath, but as I did so the heavy door to the pen creaked open, and we both looked toward the noise and a burgeoning light.

"Forgot about you lot out here!" said the turnkey. He held a lantern that lit up the doorway and made the whole building loom dark above him.

"James!" said Cash. "How could you? Leave two ladies helpless in the dark like this. . . ."

She kissed her teeth and I helped her to her feet and began to gather my things.

"Oh, do forgive me," said James.

We made our way to the door, and I instinctively reached for Cash's shoulder as we walked. I felt her bone under my hand. I was disheartened at having been cut short, and would have liked nothing better than to stay in jail, strange as that compulsion was.

"She knows the way," said James, beckoning both of us into the black ahead of him.

As we went, there was the chatter and howl of the men from down the halls, and a chill went up my spine. I did not relish the thought of a night alone outside.

As we neared her cell, Cash grasped my hand with both of hers.

"Thank you for this day, child. May we have another like it. Just one, I think, and I will be ready for my swift drop."

I squeezed her hand tight, refusing to laugh at her morbid humour. "More than one," I said.

She hummed, and I saw the glimmer of her teeth before she turned and went past the iron bars.

I went with James through the halls and to the front, where I retrieved my knife. I tucked the sheath up my sleeve and curled my fingers around the pommel.

"Careful now," said James, eyeing me suspiciously. "Wouldn't want to see you come through here under different circumstances."

I grunted and bade him good night, shouldering my satchel and pulling open the heavy wooden door. Outside, the street was emptier even than I had imagined. I hesitated, unsure of where I would wander to find refuge. Perhaps to the root doctor's office. He'd seemed harmless enough. Or perhaps to the outskirts of town, where I could find rest unmolested under a wide tree. I looked west, down the road.

A low whistle from across the street made me jump. I squinted, trying to make out the shapes on the road. There on the cobbles was a small coach, and in front of the hind wheels stood a woman in a long white gown.

"That her?" came a voice I recognized, from the driver's box.

"Better be," said the woman, and she stepped across the street toward me, her footfalls echoing off the walls.

"You look like you need a ride, sister."

Her voice was familiar too, though I couldn't quite place it.

I peered hard until she was nearly at the base of the court-house steps and I could make out her face, and a smile of relief came over me.

It was Emma, the old woman's confidante. She was tall and wore her hair in a tight plait that accentuated the long slant of her eyes. Jim vaulted from the driver's box and trotted up behind her, extending his long arms.

"Damn, Sinda, what took you so long?"

Emma told me of how they came to Chatham. The coach was Circe's; I'd forgotten she had one of her own. When Arabella saw I wasn't on the last omnibus into Dunmore, she'd fetched Jim and gone to the tavern to inquire for the coach. There she found Emma, who volunteered to come for me so Arabella could tend to her house.

Emma was a sober woman, nearly as yellow as I, but her voice and the way she held her jaw were so firmly Negro that I hadn't noticed her light complexion before.

I recalled when I had found her at Simeon's cabin the previous day. The beds in the room behind her were sloped with clothes and fabrics. She'd sifted through them until she lifted out an old quilt and glanced at me sidelong as she unstitched a seam, from which she pulled a small parcel—John's journal.

In the coach I struggled to take bites of a meat pie Arabella had sent for me as we went down the bumpy country highway. Emma allowed me some silence as I tried to eat.

"How is she?" she asked after a time.

I pondered the question as I chewed, unsure of how to answer.

"I know she is hard," she whispered, bowing her head slightly. "Lord, how I know."

Her brow was creased, but she let a half smile creep on her lips.

"She told me before being taken, not to fear," she went on. "She said each night she would rip through the mortar of her walls and walk."

This made me chuckle, and Emma's smile became fuller, revealing a slight chip in her front tooth.

"But from what I understand," said Emma, turning pensively to the dark window, "there are men in these woods who would make that prediction more than poetry."

This sobered me. It was true, I thought; it wouldn't be the first prison bust, either by forceful mob or a clever picklock. But the risk of such an action would put many more lives at stake.

"I wouldn't push for that," I said, finding her eyes again. "Now that she is there, her case may sway the courts."

At this, Emma raised a haughty eyebrow. Court justice was not a likely idea for an American Negro. Perhaps it was naive even for me, and I felt stupid for saying it. But justice or none, it only took so many unruly acts before a Negro town would be driven to extinction.

We rode for some time without talking after that, and I finished the pie and listened to sounds of the hoof steps and felt the cart wheels drumming over the ruts in the ground.

"Did you know?" I asked finally.

She glanced carefully at me. "That you are her granddaughter?" I nodded.

"I suppose I did. She told me. Though I didn't believe it until you took so long to come out tonight," she said, and smirked faintly. "You are the child of her first." And then, before I could confirm: "So we are cousins, I suppose."

I squinted, not sure if she was speaking colloquially.

"I'm the child of her last daughter," she said, briskly now. "Not from the same father as the rest. My mother's name was Pearline, and she was born and died in Kentucky."

I felt my eyes grow wide as I took this in. So there was yet another chapter to my grandmother's life. Another child . . . we were a lineage torn to pieces and scattered far and wide.

"I'm sorry for your loss, Emma," I said, and she nodded.

As I looked on her, her features seemed to become a mirror to my own. Was that haughty brow what others saw in me? That stiff shoulder?

"Your father must have had you late in life," she said. "Is he alive?"

I nodded, looking away politely, not wanting to stare.

"He is, yes," I said, and my gut clenched at the thought that I did not really know if that was still true. I'd sent a letter two years before, but no reply, only the silence of time.

Emma made a humming sound, similar to but subtler than

the old woman's, and looked at me directly for perhaps the first time.

"So you know," she began slowly, tentatively. "You know how she came to Kentucky?"

I met her gaze, and seeing the aching that filled her eyes, I felt my own well up in an instant, though I didn't know why.

I shook my head and Emma inhaled as if to begin to speak, but I stopped her with a soft hand on her own.

"I'll wait," I said, "to hear it from her."

Emma hummed slightly in approval and we held each other's eyes for a moment, the night air shuffling between us as the coach jostled at a grim pace through the cricket song and the land.

Chapter IX

The next morning a prodding at my leg awoke me, causing me to thrash and whip myself up to a sitting position. It was pitch-black in the study, and all I could perceive was the sound of my own breath, ragged from whatever dark dream I had come out of.

I felt another prod at my foot and I shrieked, drawing my legs up and casting my blanket downward.

I heard a giggle from the foot of my cot.

"I'm sick, Sinda," said a small voice.

Fanny.

I sighed, releasing the tension in my chest and flopping my head back onto the mat.

"What the hell is going on?" I said, and immediately glanced toward the door to make sure no one else was within earshot of my profanity. It was still dark, and I heard footsteps patter down the stairs.

"I shan't go to school, Sinda; I must stay and help you wash."

"Must you?"

The door swung open and weak light from the hallway revealed Fanny to me, crouched quite a bit nearer to my face than I imagined, with the blanket held over her like a cloak.

"Fanny, get out here, you little sneak!" It was Chloe, the eldest. Her shoulders I glimpsed in silhouette, as upright as Arabella's already. Fanny didn't budge.

"Get, Fanny, or Pa'll whup you."

"He won't," said Fanny, staring straight at me, as if to reassure me.

Chloe grunted.

"It's all right, Chloe," I said. "Is breakfast made?"

"Not yet," said Chloe, glaring at Fanny. She turned abruptly and went back down the hallway.

I swung my feet to the floor, fully awake now, and went to the wardrobe to change from my nightdress. I glanced over at Fanny, who was still crouched like a gargoyle by my cot.

"Fanny, will you gather an armful of wood from out back for the fire?"

Before I could second-guess sending her, she was gone, my blanket trailing her like a cape.

I cooked hominy and bacon for the house. It was Monday, and I gathered they had been up late at festivities the night before because everyone was groggy and ate quickly and silently. They were soon gone to work and school—even Fanny, much to her annoyance. Arabella lingered for a few minutes before she and Velora were off to market, the invitation to which I promptly denied, citing work for the newspaper as my pretext.

"Well, soon enough we will have the story of your long day

in jail," she said, wagging her finger at me and winking before she did up her shoes to leave.

I nodded absently—the happenings of the long day had been running through my head all morning.

"Oh," she blurted, "almost forgot—this afternoon, six o'clock, a meeting at the tavern. Greaves and Markham are in town."

"The tavern?" I asked.

"Yes." She nodded and widened her eyes restlessly. "Yesterday was the church, today the tavern—you know the politics."

She and Velora were out the door already, and I held it open behind them.

"Come, Mummy, let's bustle for the carriage, I hear it!"

I waved them away as they went, hand in hand, up the lane. I watched the dew darken the hems of their skirts, until a ray of sunrise came through the foliage of an oak across the lane, causing me to squint and turn away, back into the house.

Greaves and Markham, I thought to myself. Lawyers—no, preachers . . . maybe one of each. I could never remember.

I meandered back to the study and drew back the curtain from the window, letting in the light. I surveyed the desk, the modest library, my cot, low and unkempt against the baseboard. The scene was dispiriting in a way that always became more marked when the house was empty and silent—well, never truly silent because the mice took advantage of this quiet time to conduct their affairs in the walls and the ceiling around me. Even then, I could hear them begin to scurry. I felt the urge to flee, whether from the study or from all of it, I couldn't be sure.

But now, at least for the moment, I had a purpose. The events, the tales of the day before sifted into my mind, and my chest swelled as I remembered. I had a name, or more aptly, I had a story of a name. One that I could claim. And with it, a grandmother, yes, and a fierce one at that, I thought for the first time and smiled, imagining her looking down the barrel of the bounty hunter's rifle. Yes, although I might not tell anyone yet, I would very much like to talk more with her. Would very much like to see her free.

I sat at the desk, lost in thought as I positioned my instruments: my pen, several clean sheets of paper, and the leather sheath of my knife, invaluable for hurling at the nearest region of mouse activity if I really needed a moment's silence.

There was a knock at the front.

The mice heard it and silenced their movements. I rose and went out of the study, squinting at the door, trying to imagine who it might be. As I approached I heard footsteps going down the porch steps. I swung it open.

Saison was already trotting on the lane back up to his house. He looked over his shoulder and saw me and waved but didn't stop.

"For the woman!" he said, and kept on, his thin frame ambling easily on the grass.

I leaned out of the doorframe and looked at the floor of the porch. There was a large basket full of raspberries, glistening ruby red with dew, and beneath them the mottled green skins of several pawpaw. I thought to take it inside but decided against it—for now the porch would be as cool as anywhere.

Back at the desk, I began jotting down notes. Everything I

could remember from the tales of the day before. As I pieced together the stories I found myself faced with a narrative problem I had not anticipated. Cash had been enslaved in Canada. It was a simple fact at first glance, and for a Negro reader this detail might have made for an interesting and rare piece. But as I considered it, this article, if I understood my job correctly, needed to do more than generate interest. It needed to inspire men to action. The article, I thought to myself, was a document that needed to serve as a testament to black civility, and subsequently a reminder for the abolitionist that he was a power for good in an evil world. Perhaps the whole newspaper needed to do as much, I realized belatedly. The abolitionist need be reminded that he held a position of morality that stood in sharp relief to the brutality of the slaveholders. The fact that she had been enslaved here well before she had ever stepped foot on an American plantation—this made things complicated. It could still be done, perhaps, by way of a narrative of redemption: more potent, after all, is the light that emerges from the dark, the power of purity when one has known sin. It could be done. But the politics of it, as Arabella would say, were delicate.

And then there was the fact that Cash had murdered a dozen innocent men to secure her freedom. . . . It made my stomach wrench to think on it. To shoot down a solitary bounty hunter was a small order after that. It need not be mentioned in the paper, obviously, and in truth I didn't even know what Arabella herself would make of that one.

There was all that, and still I didn't know how she had come to slavery in Kentucky. Her story was yet incomplete.

Another knock at the front. I groaned in irritation but didn't move this time. There was a shuffle on the porch and then foot-steps clapping the wood and away.

The mice picked up again, a gnawing sound up and to my left, behind the cornice at the ceiling. I hurled the leather sheath and it pounded the wall panel with a satisfying thump and fell on my cot.

Silence, for a moment. I looked to the mess of papers on the desk and plucked the top pieces—my draft of the article I wrote after my first visit to the jail. The final version was missing, sent already to the printer. I paused for a moment, my hand covering the words on the top page as I felt the tension of competing urges. I rarely enjoyed reading my writing—there is, after all, always a word or phrase, more often than not a paragraph that I would revise if I could. And these particular words were likely being printed at that very moment, not so many miles west of where I sat. So it was too late to look, and no use to berate my-self over what should have been written a different way. If there had been others in the house I wouldn't even have thought of perusing my old work. But I was alone, and the idea of reading my words as though they were coming from another mind—there was a brute temptation to it, like an itch.

For nearly a decade now, refugees from slavery have been under the terror of the fugitive slave act, putting them in peril of their lives at every turn in their native land. This act has driven thou-sands into Canada, and now it is not only the fugitive but the fugitive hunter who makes bold incursions into British domain.

On the 27th of July last, an American, one Pelham Beall, came to the town of Dunmore. He was hunting several fugitives from the slave state of Kentucky. Beall abducted a stable boy who is employed at the Dunmore inn and tortured him, hanging him by the neck until near death in order to obtain the whereabouts of the fugitives he sought. When he came upon them at a neighbouring farmer's field, one such fugitive, an old woman, shot him with his own rifle, whereupon he perished.

These events exemplify a harrowing truth that we must face: enslavement is an evil that forces humanity to choose between the lives of the downtrodden and the lives of those who condemn them to suffer. It is a condition that precludes peace. An enlightened man understands that slavery is no less than the a priori theft of life. An escaping slave is by definition in a state of retreat. And thus the act wherein a slave strikes down his hunter is perhaps the purest act of self-defense. The man seeking to capture or return another to bondage is victim not to the hand that smited him, but first and foremost to the circumstances that induce him to act in service of an unjust law.

The presence of supporters for the case is requested at the public trial, which will take place at the Kent County courthouse fall assize, at the 13th of September coming. A petition to the Crown to demonstrate the opinion of free inhabitants of Canada West will be circulated before trial.

Let us send a message clearly to all who would sustain the vile trade in human flesh: there is a land where tyranny ends, and there are men who will defend it!

I snorted at that last line. There was a zeal to it that was not me—not my voice. It struck me that I had learned to write in a tone that I had never heard myself utter. It was a contrived medley—something between Arabella and my old tutor, Frost—but definitely not me.

It is your voice, girl . . . a tenor that you have only had the courage to let loose from your hand, and not yet your belly.

I snorted at that idea too, and got up from the desk to walk over to the kitchen. There was an inkling I had had since breakfast, but it had been too dark, and I too tired to confront it. Now, in the light of the morning, I saw the room clearly. It had the semblance of cleanliness, but it was no more than a thinly veiled squalor. This is what happened when I was absent, even for a day. The floor hastily swept, bits of food crusted on the butcher block and on the stove top. And what was worse—the soap dish scraped nearly empty. I felt hot air come out of my nostrils, and I grit my teeth with uneven fury.

I went out back and added wood to the embers in the pit, muttering curses. Tending to the house was one thing, but I saw no reason why it couldn't be kept when I was gone. Had it always been this way? Did people always become slovenly once they hired help? I hung a cauldron above the fire and drew a bucket of water and poured it till the cauldron was half full. I emptied the ash tin therein and the water clouded and swirled and the grey dust rose above it. The fire crackled and the wind pressed me with a waft of soot.

As the lye came to a boil I swept spitefully through the whole house, drawing out piles of filth from between each seam in the floorboards. When it had been bubbling quite some time I put a cloth around my mouth and nose and carefully strained the liquid into a smaller pot. To that I added lard and some wintergreen for the scent, and let it thicken to a soap. Once done, I took a mop and rag with a dash of vinegar and went over all the floors, trim, and countertops.

I finished in the kitchen and stepped out once more to the backyard to survey the smouldering pit and the full brightness of the afternoon. There was an ache between my shoulders and my fingers were swollen and soft from wringing the mop, but there was a grim satisfaction in my breath.

I arrived early at the tavern, quite ravenous. Circe was behind the counter dipping candles and the tallow wafted through the entire room.

"Afternoon," I said.

She gave me a long glance and a grunt.

"You look hungry," she said as I neared the counter. "Leftovers are in the root cellar."

I thanked her and went out back. Deacon was sawing firewood and paused for a moment to nod to me. I greeted him and scrounged a sausage and an apple tart, which I ate outside on the grass, listening to Deacon's long pulls on the bucksaw, watching the main road. When I was nearly done I picked up the distant sounds of a coach and then too, the yips of the dogs, but they must have been in the kennel for there were none on the road or down the lanes.

I walked back into the tavern.

"So someone talked Yarrow into locking up the dogs?"

Circe huffed. "Guess."

"The duchess herself?"

She smiled.

"So," she began, narrowing her eyes at me from behind the dripping twin strands of candlewick, "late night last night?"

"Oh, Circ'. I don't know. Wouldn't even know where to begin." And then, impulsively: "Do you know sometimes I dream of being elsewhere?"

"You mean running away?"

I gave a mirthless snort, sensing the irony in her question. Running away from a runaway town.

"See, that's my problem," I began. Circe didn't wait for the next clause.

"No, sugar," she said, dipping her candlewicks again. "Your problem is that you ain't got nothing to run from."

I began to glower, but footsteps on the ceiling interrupted me. The steps carried onto the stairs, sending faint creaks into the floorboards at my feet.

I squinted, questioning, at Circe.

"The buckra," she said.

A man walked into the main room. He wore ordinary trousers and a cotton work shirt—common wear around Dunmore, but on him they stood out. I would've expected breeches.

He approached me frankly, extending a hand. I offered mine, not thinking much, and he took it and kissed my knuckle briskly.

"Nathaniel Greaves, how do you do?"

I faltered, taken aback by this entrance. He was younger than I'd expected, and not whom I'd pictured—if we'd met before, it had only been in passing.

"Sinda here does all Arabella's writing for her," said Circe.

I cleared my throat.

"Oh!" said Greaves. "Oh."

"Not exactly," I said, finding my voice somewhat.

Just then, the front door swung open and Simeon stepped in, and held the door open with one hand—the other gripped a sack of burlap. Nathaniel stepped past me and around a table to greet him with a handshake and a compliment for the meat on his hogs. I guessed they'd been acquainted at the festivities the day before.

Jim appeared beyond the threshold of the door lugging a large crate full past the brim with carrots, speckled with soil.

"May I help?" said Greaves, and he reached over to Jim and took one end of the crate.

They shuffled it over to where Circe was dipping candles and hoisted it onto the counter. Simeon followed suit with his sack, bowing slightly to me as he passed.

"Thank you, boys," said Circe. "Y'all staying for the meeting?"

"Oh, I don't reckon," said Simeon, placing a hand on Jim's shoulder. "Still daylight out. Though"—glancing at me—"I wouldn't mind a bit of news if there is some."

"Hear, hear!" exclaimed Greaves, a bit out of breath from

his manoeuvre with the crate. "You were with the woman yesterday—pardon me, what was her name?"

I could feel everybody go silent in their movements, and my face grew hot under their gazes.

"Her name is Cash," I said.

I heard Greaves whisper, "Cash," to himself.

And then, because I could think of no reason not to, I gave them the reveal.

"Cash Marten," I said portentously.

Greaves, who did not know my last name, said the name back to me again, louder this time, and then began to speak. Simeon, Jim, and Circe were still staring at me, the question in their faces.

". . . of course, a distinctive name; I remember it from the extradition request."

This took Circe's attention, and she whipped her head to face Greaves. "Extradition?"

He nodded earnestly, and with this motion I noticed a grey sheen to his hair.

"It can't be," said Circe.

"Of course it can," I said, hearing the cutting edge in my voice. "That's what happens when you make front-page news," I continued, and could not help but glance at Simeon.

"Well, it won't be," said Circe, with even more sharpness. "Believe that."

"Hold up, Sinda," said Simeon, softly. His narrow eyes had not left me this whole time. "This woman kin to you?"

I nodded. "She's my father's mother, I believe."

Simeon shook his head and slapped the countertop.

Circe snorted quietly. "There's a word for that, you know, sugar," she said and raised an eyebrow at me.

"I'll be," muttered Jim, one hand on his chin.

"Wonderful!"

This was Greaves, smiling encouragingly at me. I could only manage a grimace.

"That bodes well for the case, I mean."

"I'm sorry, Sinda."

Simeon this time. His hand lay atop his head as though protecting from punishment above, and his weary expression nearly melted my indignation. I shook my head at him in an ambivalence that contained as much forgiveness as discontent.

"And was she born into bondage?" Greaves again.

"No," I said. "Well, it's complicated. The fact is . . ." They went quiet again, and I almost relished their attention. "She was taken from Canada."

The reaction to this surpassed that of the first piece of news— even Circe's jaw dropped.

"Incredible," mused Greaves, shaking his head. "So she's Canadian. I'd daresay that makes it easy! Is there record of that? Could we get your father to testify?"

"You might get him," I said slowly. "You might also find record of her in a Montreal port ledger, or in a newspaper notice for a runaway slave."

Silence as the weight of this sunk into the room.

"Still . . ." said Greaves, his eyes wandering in thought, his pointer finger at his nose. "That might do it, if she was illegally procured."

"*Captured* is the word, honey, and what difference does that make?" Circe squinted menacingly at Greaves as she spoke.

"Of course—forgive me. Well, if she was purchased, one could make the argument—well, I don't know, it will take some thought."

"The argument—what, that she belong a slave?"

They carried on, but my mind had begun to wander. For the rest of the night I was distant. Simeon and Jim never did leave, and Arabella arrived soon thereafter with the church folk and Markham, who was a preacher after all, and a loud one at that. I let others speak, interjecting only briefly when I was called on.

I excused myself before the meeting was done and walked home. The night was not yet dark, and I could see the grass beneath my feet. I breathed deeply, and the hoots of the barred owl over the meadow brought a smile to my lips. I'd forgotten about Saison's fruit on the porch. There was also a folded pile of clothes on the seat of the chair, and on top of that a bundle of wax cloth about the size of a loaf of bread.

Arabella had asked if I would stay and help her distribute the newspapers that she expected early the next morning, but I declined. I would go back to the jail. There was a story I needed to tell my grandmother.

Chapter X

M y original sin was pissing like a man. It was an old woman, Hestia, who taught me one afternoon as we picked Saint-John's-wort and wild plums along the lush path of Mr. Frost's land.

"It's a matter of lift, pull, and thrust," she said. "Good for a wench like me, too old to squat."

I was aghast, but completely interested, and when I hoisted my skirt in my first attempt, I began laughing so uncontrollably that I wet my legs, and Hestia guffawed and led me down to the creek. There I rinsed myself, resisting the current by gripping with my toes in the sharp, rolling sand, and I cupped my hands in the water, lifting gulp after gulp to my lips, so that in short order I could practice again.

I reckon it was this talent that first induced Charley to begin peeping on me, in the midnights when I would leave the cabin to relieve myself in the garden. Pissing in the garden, of course, was also due to Hestia's influence.

"Piss on the soil," she would whisper to me with a wink and a full grin. "Makes the pumpkins sweet."

And so, at that encouragement I was much in the habit of

waking in the middle of the night and meandering into the garden to relieve myself. I never did like the slop jar. And unless it was necessary I would avoid the stink of the privy.

One night, I recall marvelling at the sky as I pissed. I almost stumbled as I arched my body to take in the spillage of flickering stars. And as I followed the sky downward to where it disappeared in the outlines of spiking treetops to the west, I noticed the Russet cabin, right next to ours. Farther down the cabin, I saw the back door open a crack, and a dark blot that came up from the floor about the height of a boy. I had never noticed their door sitting ajar before, and it was still spring, and cool, and folk hadn't begun to sleep with doors open.

Something about the slowness with which that door closed gave him away. It was as if I could see his impudent lips clearly in the dark behind the wooden slats. He was bumptious. A jester much in the habit of making folk laugh, and then moving slowly, with a face completely vacant of expression, which would make his audience laugh all the more.

Had he seen me? For how long had he been spying, the little sneak? What interest was it of his to watch me at this private moment? Amusement? It can't have been, else I would have been teased about it by that point. So then what? What did he covet in witnessing?

And, strangely, it was these questions that awoke the heat in me. Strange, because I couldn't always tell if Charley watched. And after a time, I realized I didn't care. I was sumptuous with my own secret beauty. I did not stop. I did not blunt the edge of my desire. My midnight sojourns became more prolonged.

It was in this way, in the quiet of hot summer nights, clad in only my long tunic, that I began my love affair with the moon. There was a curious ritual I found in the lilt of my hips beneath the cotton. The forest struck up a chorus that seemed to mount as I did. Skeeters hummed a hungry, nasal tone. The moths and fireflies flitted in circles of dark and light, undaunted by the killing swoop of bats. The air grew thick and sweet and caressed the insides of my breasts.

It was with Charley that I revisited my old haunt in the hollow of the tree up the escarpment. I would call it an act not of love but of nature, perhaps, that we undertook as animals would, in earnest silence. We were two of the same class, in the same place, happening to come of age at the same moment of late summer. And I think because of the spontaneous animalism of the act, it never occurred to me to speak of it. Charley, however, apparently did not feel similarly inspired to silence.

Not two days later Mary and I crossed paths as she came up the eastern slope to visit her mother. We were a long way from that Emancipation Day on the steamboat, years earlier. In our young adulthood our friendship had hardened; the trust had melted away little by little and all that lingered was the intimate familiarity. I still cared for her—admired her, even. It seemed each time she ascended the hill she was more urbane and womanly. That day she had on a printed cotton dress with white-work embroidery, a cashmere shawl draped over her shoulders, and satin shoes that looked, perched on a rough log of the corduroy road, like the softest things in the world. I was on my way to town to go shopping for Mr. Frost.

"There she is!" she exclaimed as soon as we were within a few paces of each other. She was breathing heavily from the uphill walk. There was no one around, just some children playing in the woods at the top of the rise, but she spoke as though she were crying to the town.

"Here, ladies and gentlemen, walks a grown woman."

More heaving breaths.

"I don't know what you mean."

I'm sure one could hear in the nervous timbre of my voice that I knew exactly what she meant.

She laughed breathlessly. "Well, be that as it may, I'm prepared to be the godmother."

This flustered me even more. I hadn't even considered the possibility of being with child, and Mary saw this in my face.

"Ooh, so it's true! But don't fret, girl—when was your last blood?"

I shook my head, trying to remember. "A week, maybe."

"Oh . . . Well, maybe fret a little. But—if the next bleeding doesn't come, talk to Hestia—she'll fix you up."

And with that she began her ascent again, patting me gently on the shoulder as she passed by.

I was completely discomfited by this exchange—I wanted more from it, or none of it at all. I turned to look at her, her back to me now. The boning of her dress gave her body an imposing shapeliness that seemed both alien and natural to her. She had always been such a thin girl. I found myself caught up in the machinations of a theory I'd been half-consciously brooding for some time. I had been her anchor in school, I think. I was already half-literate by virtue of my father's profession, and so her friendship with me allowed her some measure of academic advantage—an advantage that ultimately served to extend our girlish disavowal of boys further than it might have gone otherwise. When I left the schoolhouse to pursue study with Mr. Frost, not only was it an abandonment of Mary, but it came along with the bitter death of our childhood fantasy as we reached courting age and came to the hard realization that because we were common girls, and Negro girls at that, our only chance at life was in the service of men. And while I excelled under the patronage of a harmless old scholar, Mary, who had no such opportunity, turned to the gritty underbelly of the Spancel port. She had witnessed her father brutalize her mother, and perhaps for that reason, marriage simply was not an option in her mind. It might have been for me, but Spancel Narrows was small—the Negro quarter even smaller—and because of this there were few options to begin with. Mary was beyond options now. She wielded a power that was as fascinating as it was frightening to me. I remember trying to emulate her when we were young, and I would see her sharp wit cow the boys and make them frustrated and impudent. Now that same tongue disarmed men and honed their desire for her to a hungry, keen edge. And she knew it too, though she was as aloof with them as she was with me. The only clue I had that she still envied me was that she was so thorough in her disinterest.

"Oh," she said, pausing and turning to face me, showing no

sign of surprise to find me staring at her. "And on top too," she said, and winked. "It's the heathen in you."

And with that final cut she was truly gone, up and away.

Around this time, I went with my father to town.

He strode quickly despite his limp, and with a swagger he bore only on Sundays, before posting the notice. I tried to make conversation as we rushed, shifting my unruly hair from my face. A stout wind bumped us along, wrapping our excess around us.

Two squares were the bosom of town. The bustle of the levee spewed sailors and stevedores right through the middle, which, by consequence of the constant traffic, always seemed to be deep with cloying mud.

We passed the tavern in the first square, and Pa stopped me with a tug of his arm as a drunk in sailor's garb teetered in front of us. The wet ground gulped up one of his feet and he fell flat.

As we skirted him we heard a yell from across the street.

"Dred!"

It was Thomas Montgomery, lowering his head beneath his stovepipe hat as he stepped carefully toward us.

"Steel yourself, Sinda baby, the man can signify like a monkey," said my father out of the side of his mouth as we stood awaiting Montgomery's approach.

"A word, Dred," he said, and then looked to me: "Morning, Lucinda, nice to see you."

I gave a half-hearted curtsy.

"Tell me, Montgomery, I am at your service," said Daddy, though his grey eyes darted around the bustle of the square.

"You'll see on the notice, Dred, but I am letting you know as a gentleman, I am putting the lots up for auction."

Daddy took a moment to nod to a passerby before replying.

"That's all fine, Montgomery," he said. "It will be known the land is for sale. . . . It will also be known that my land is occupied and won't be vacated."

Montgomery chuckled and I could tell he had more to say, but Daddy gave an aloof smile and a nod and stepped away. In that region there is a saying that some men will parry with you but won't tarry with you. Daddy was such a man. His was the stature of a denizen. Spancel was known as the town with the darling refugee bellman, and though he was here before any whites, he rarely mentioned that, the old fox. He was altogether too slick to get caught up in conversation of oh, ain't you happy to be here Mr. Martin, or, oh you musta had it awful hard down south Daddy. He might nod or wink to something like that, and with a cluck or a pat on the hand he would be off, not even looking your way, though you were inevitably impressed by the sneaking notion that even though he wasn't looking at you, he watched you more closely than you watched him.

"I hear it said you're nearly full-blood Indian," came the voice of Montgomery behind us, and my father turned slightly—imperceptibly—before he caught himself.

"Which means you'd have a fine parcel of land waiting for you on the cape!"

Daddy smiled and waved his cane in the air, but continued on his way. I stayed in place. I knew he would notice but not let on—he was about his business.

"Crown land will be bought for what it's worth!" shouted Montgomery.

He could signify indeed, this man.

I kept my face stony and turned to go back across the square.

I saw the flash of Montgomery's wide smile as I marched. I stepped over the sailor beached in the mire and a stevedore leered at me from under the crushing weight of his cargo. I glared daggers at him before fixing my gaze on the door beside the tavern.

I took the brass handle of the door and drove it inward. The stevedore behind me whistled and I slammed the door on the noise. It was dark in the hallway and I blinked to shoo the light patches out of my eyes. I scuffed my boots on the mat and listened to the muffled singsong voices above.

I went up the stairs and steeled myself for battle as the voices grew louder and more confident, it seemed. I pushed open the inner door to the parlour. It was bright with colours within and there was a window open in the back, and I could see the water, and smell it. The view of the burnished blue lake was so completely stunning it held me for a moment before I remembered my mission. Three of the girls were eating, reclining on a settee that curved like a gentle wave. They looked at me silently for a moment, as if from a painting. Auntie was seated at her great red chair by the window, smoking and reading.

The thin temples of her glasses disappeared into her massive head wrap.

She was not my aunt, of course; Auntie was how she was called by everyone.

Mary, on the settee, waved to me with slender fingers. I did not pay her the courtesy of a greeting.

"What right you got sharing my family's business all up and down the levee?" I said as I walked toward her, until I was only a pace away.

"What business that be, sugar?"

Mary had an air of relaxed authority in her shoulders that I would have admired had I not been so enraged.

"Since when did you become such a saucy wench?"

I was goading her to retort. She looked at me with polite shock before raising her eyebrows at her friends who shared the settee. I trembled with spite. We had once been friends. Now what were we? Her silk blouse that lay upon her chest as if it were no more than a breeze. My frock of rough cotton and dirt. I was not worth a response.

"Come sit with me, Sinda baby."

Auntie's voice was deeper than any other woman I had known.

"I don't feel much like sitting," I said to her, still glaring at Mary.

"Have a tea, child," said Auntie.

Her voice was hypnotic in its pull. I looked to her, and back to Mary. I shook my head. It was a mistake to have come. If

Mary had been my friend once, she wasn't now. Auntie was elegance and power. And for all my fervour, I was impotent and forsaken.

I came back outside into the rush and noise of town.

Daddy's booming voice had begun to call the news across the square and the crowd was around him, keen and bustling.

"Look here!" yelled one of Montgomery's cronies over the hubbub. He pointed to me as I closed the brothel door.

"Say, Dred," shouted the crony, "are you a bellman or a fancy man?"

This drew laughs from the crowd, and many turned to face me. My father paused, lowering the notice he read from, glancing out at me and at them. How I wished I could disappear in that moment. But if my father saw me, he did not let on. The crowd chittered and hooted cruelly. My heart pounded in panic as I walked away. But there was no hurrying through the mud of the streets.

"Peace!" I heard him yell out as the crowd calmed. "The people of Spancel need the news. We do not all have the luxury of Montgomery, whose personal town crier lays beneath him six days a week!"

The crowd erupted. I turned to look. There were faces of mirth and scandal. They were cruel, but they were poor. And this was a rare occasion. The uproar was far louder than the previous one and Daddy nodded silently before bellowing, feeding them:

266

"The rest of us must be content with my hobbling legs until we can all afford such pleasures!"

Back at home I described the scene at the square to my mother and to Junior, but my father interrupted me.

"You were not to give them cause," he said.

"Oh, hush up," said Mother, her back to us, as she had turned to ladle me a bowl of soup.

Daddy was broodsome and silent for a moment, his face set, but I could tell his spirit was churning. I looked at him and then to Junior, who was stripping nettle stalks and piling the strands in a thick, bunching mess in the wicker basket. Junior had remained quiet throughout, which didn't mean he wasn't listening. Mother brought me the soup and placed her hand on mine, stopping me from bringing it to my lips. I was hungry, but I waited and let the rich garlic and green flavour waft into my face. The heat of it in the bottom of the bowl was pure comfort on my hands. I closed my eyes.

Mother went to the hearth and drew out a smoking juniper bough like a crackling mist in her hands, and she bathed me in it, and in whispers of her tongue, which rolled like water over me. The green of the soup was taken over by something fresh, yet old and mountainous, and I closed my eyes. She finished the saining and returned to the fire, and I brought the soup to my lips.

I saw from the corner of my eye what I might not have heard, because I never have known anyone to step as light-footed and swiftly as my father. In an instant he donned his hat, grasped his bell and cane, and was gone. Junior looked at me, eyes wide for a moment, and then picked up his own hat from beside the nettle stalks and followed through the open door. Mother stayed by the fire. I grunted irreverently and continued eating, content to be only in the presence of her.

But as I sipped my soup I heard the bell. This was unusual. As you've never been to Spancel Narrows, I must explain: The bell was a thing of town. The eastern slope was normally out of earshot of most town noises. The bell was to call out news: royal proclamations, sales, meetings, and bylaws. On the eastern slope, we shared news, of course, but there was never need for anything as formal as a bell—one only had to send a child from door to door. The peal of the bell was alien to the slope, and it dashed over me like a bucket of cold water. What in all hell was he doing?

As I shot out the door and looked around I saw old folk hunching and peering out their doors; women with furrowed brows scurried from the firepits behind houses, their aprons painted with soot. Children dropped like imps from the trees, and men sauntered curiously from the woodpiles, axes on their shoulders. All moved steadily toward Daddy, who stood on the corduroy road in his white breeches, Junior beside him. Daddy's head was covered with the brim of his stovepipe hat as he sounded the brass, and he seemed to shimmer, to expand and tighten with the rise and fall of the ringing bell. His sounding hand was all that moved. The wool of his beard rested on the stiff collar of his coat, and he looked weary.

I made my way down in complete fret, with my mother in tow. I was not the first to reach him, or perhaps I would have questioned him. He was solemn, scuffing a log of the road with his heel. He waited, head down, until the assembling band grew hushed.

"As you well know, they trying to sell the land that we settled all that time ago," said Daddy. "They seem to disagree with the Queen, and are of the opinion Negroes don't have the legs to squat same as white folks."

Folk chuckled and glanced at each other knowingly.

"That's right," Daddy went on. "Won't nobody build nothing while we live here, but they will try by means lawful and nefarious to persuade us that we should not live here."

He paused to survey the group before him, and I saw his jaw clench.

"I suspect that the peace of our hill will be breached tonight," he said simply. This set off a buzz, a murmuring of questions, protests, and fear.

"All may stay with me," said Daddy. "Bring some food if you have it."

With that, he set off, back up toward our house. A child, Phyllis's middle one, began to cry and blabber, and she picked him up and tried to hush him. People shot raised eyebrows, curled lips, knowing looks. No one dissented, though, not even Victoria. And none met my gaze, not even my mother, though she clutched my hand, hard.

That night was the first I can recall silence on the eastern slope. No sounds of cooking, shouting, singing, storytelling, or lovemaking. There was only the wind and it rushed all the louder in the quiet. Daddy, Paul, Henson, and the Ayre boys smoked on the porch. Daddy cradled the barrel of the rifle in the crook of his elbow. Junior and a couple of young men circled and scouted. The rest of us huddled inside and lay out on the beds, on the loft, or on deer hides on the floor. Folk chattered and ate, and others stared at the soup bubbling on the embers. I stood at the threshold and looked out at the night. The treetops of the hillside cloaked Spancel Narrows. The stars were a curtain above the trees.

We smelled the smoke before we saw it creeping gently up the stars. And then we heard the shouting from down the hill. It must have been someone's shack near the bottom, closer to town. There were only a handful of people it could belong to. One of them, a newer arrival, Esther, began to wail, and Victoria went to her and held her head, trying to comfort her. Hestia, who lived with Henson higher on the slope, muttered to herself with increasing intensity. She held a fierce pride in our quarter. Finally, she stood and reached into the hearth and pulled out a long, half-blackened log. The people who were huddled near the fire recoiled as embers fell from her, but she paid them no mind and walked off the porch and commenced down the hill.

The men on the porch faltered in Hestia's wake.

"Hes!" someone yelled. "Don't be a fool."

"She'll hold up," said Henson.

But the men began to follow her, taking up their weapons: three axes and a hoe.

"Junior," said my father, "fetch my lash."

"But the rifle, Daddy," said Junior, already down the porch steps.

"I'll fetch it," I said.

Daddy almost looked at me. He nodded. "Hurry," was all he said, and he grasped the gun like a cane and pushed off the porch after the others.

I did not delay.

The bullwhip hung in a loop on a stub of the log wall, right above the candle box. I swept through the cabin and those on the ground clutched each other and gasped wretchedly, as if taken aback by my haste.

The whip was cowhide, handsome leather, brown as the wood. The hide was plaited tight around a bone handle. The tail of it, three thin strands, protruded from a small oiled knot that held a piece of lead shot. I reached high to grasp the handle and let the tail fall like an angry asp behind me. The wretches shuffled out of my path on the heels of their hands.

Mother, on the porch, lunged at me. I snarled, thinking she meant to hinder me, but then I caught her eye and she caught my hand and pressed a small pouch into it, pushing me gently on my way. I was down the steps in a bound. I could hear the men. The shades of them were not quite lost in the dark fold between the trees and the road.

My heart was in my throat and I heard my breath as the air swept it past my face; a sob. No. Not that yet. My father and I were once inseparable, I thought. I heard a sound like a growl escape my throat. Those thoughts had no place now. Then.

I nearly stumbled on my gown, and I hiked it high. The whip

still trailed my hand, faithfully. This whip; we'd spent countless hours with it at the rotting poplar in the woods. I would
snatch it and run outside shrieking and my father would always come. Before the poplar I would prance with anticipation and fling a rock or a stick, and his body would tense and
his arm swoop like a gust of wind. My breath was always short
at the sound. The way it broke the air. Everything hurtled into
the canopy before it touched the poplar. The forest echoed with
the boom of the lash and my shrieks of delight. "That," he would
say, "was a cut shot." And I would beg him for a flay shot. He
would pretend to object. Smile slyly as I covered my ears. Then,
a deft turn of his body, and chunks of wood would fall and quaver on the leafy ground.

These memories flashed frantically through me as I rushed
down the slope. Where the road continued lazily skirting the
forest, I heard them—they had cut through the bush. Quicker
to descend, and better under the cover of the dark and the trees.
I wrapped the whip around my hand so it would not snag.

The fire glowed through the trees, and I could hear the voices
of other men. Not ours.

I passed Henson stumbling over deadfall, one hand on his
stupid billycock hat. The forest at this hour is treacherous for
an old man. Branches trip and reach, and a wanton slope emp-
ties out under you.

Beyond him was Stephen Ayre, chopping at a branch in front
of him like an idiot. We aren't clearing a path, you wayward ass,
I thought to say to him. We're going to battle. His shoulders
jumped as I passed him.

And there he was, Daddy, breathing hard, stopped for a moment with the butt of the rifle on the crook of an oak. I handed him the whip as I leapt past him, and I heard him press downward behind me. Neither of us said anything; there was only my broken breath, the damp air.

Charley was seated at the foot of a tree at the edge of the clearing and Junior and Paul had stopped and knelt by him. I came upon them. Charley was rubbing at his head; his hand came away damp and glinting.

"What's gotten into her?" said Charley.

"Where is she?" I asked.

"Hell if I care!"

No. He couldn't have let her. I looked out to the glimmering beyond the trees, and I ran. I burst from the curtain of forest and saw the foot of the cabin aflame, smoke huffing up and up.

There were four men. One, with a rifle slung to his back, shook an oil lamp on the clapboard, and danced away and hooted as the flame licked at him; another, a lanky boy, laughed and flung a shock of hair back as he balanced on a pitchfork thrust into the ground; a third—I recognized the lean of his broad back—stood holding a tall wheat flail. The grey-white wooden staff extended above his head and the iron-link chain dangled the clublike head off it. The fourth, nearly obscured on the far side of the cabin, held a torch and an axe.

And approaching them, marching past the stone well, was Hestia.

My throat closed before I could holler for her. Even then, none of them saw or heard her and she was only paces away. I

273

began to run. The flames were already crackling loudly, and Hestia came from darkness. They were not expecting ambush. She yelled and clubbed the boy with the pitchfork square in the ear and he crumpled, yelping like a dog. I ran headlong in the grass between us and clutched at Mother's pouch. I heard Junior holler. I didn't look back, but ran; ran hearing only the close gasp of my breath and the pounding of my heart.

The man with the flail shouted—the boy was his son, was he not? He bore down on Hes and swung the flail in a massive blow. She raised her log, but the shackle of the flail curled around it and the head swung into her back and I saw her break. Heard her. She fell slowly, like a tree.

I screamed and the man turned to me in time to see my pouch hit him square in the forehead. The impact exploded a small cloud of the powder. He shook his head and dropped the flail, his hands going to his eyes. And then I was upon him myself, clawing at his throat. Ripping at his hair. Gouging, gouging. He fell and I tumbled with him. The man with the lamp dropped it and yelled as he came toward us, hands at the ready. He tore me off by the shoulder of my gown, ripping it. I spat in his face and kicked him in the groin and he backed away, moaning and stooping. I saw the stock of the rifle as he bent over, and I thought to grab it. But I was distracted by the sight of Junior and the fourth man running to meet each other in front of the rising flames. They slowed as they neared and circled each other like bulls. The man struck at Junior with the axe and I gasped, but Junior parried with his short-handled hoe and turned swiftly, pummelling the man in the chest, sending him reeling. The broad man grabbed at my gown and I was plunged back into battle. I turned to strike him but my blow glanced off his shoulder. He roared and flung me by my garment, and my head hit the ground and my stomach felt sick, and my arms lost their strength.

The fire on the house was a true blaze now, and it lit our bodies in burning detail. The hairs on my arm wilted and my skin seared. The broad man pawed the ground for his flail and I could see the flesh at his neck reddened and scraped from my strikes. He found his weapon and stood, lumbering toward me. His eyes were nearly closed, swollen already and streaming.

He said something vile and raised the flail high. Then, there was a boom and his head cracked to the side and he keeled over, stiff. My ears rang in the silence after the sound.

The man with the rifle swore and drew it. Daddy turned his body with force and the air cracked open again and the man dropped the rifle and came to his knees screaming through clenched teeth, clutching his hand.

"That was but a cut shot!" I yelled from my elbows, and in the next instant the third blow came across his jaw and he slumped face-first in the grass.

The boy, hand still on his ear, tried to scamper, but Daddy cracked the lash and it whirled around the boy's ankle, tripping him, and Paul ran over and held him up.

Junior was locked, grappling and grunting with the man with the axe. Daddy tossed the lash to the ground and picked up his rifle, cocking it in the same motion, and the man with the axe glanced at it and stumbled, and Junior clubbed at the back of his head once, twice, and the man lay still on the ground.

Henson knelt by Hestia, moaning and sobbing pitifully as he tried to rub the chill from her hands. As if to rub the life back into her.

Stephen had drawn a bucket of water and grunted as he dashed it as close as he could to the heat. But the flames were by now roaring at the pine-bough thatch.

"Don't be foolish," said Daddy. "It's just a shanty."

He turned to the boy, who snotted and quivered.

"You stay here with your fellows," he said quietly. "The sheriff will come in the morning."

Someone went to fetch rope and they bound the four of them to a tree. Then the young men took Hestia up the hill, following the road this time. Henson wailed behind.

I packed that night, right in front of the few women and children who had not left to see Hestia. I thought only of the objects. My hands around them. Grey linsey-woolsey. My father's knife. My fingers like dog's teeth gripping the handle. Pouches of herbs that rustled as I grasped them. My body was a shell with a dark storm inside. If I let it burst I would wash away. A wrap of dried venison. Money. Not all of it—half of the army bills and seven Spanish dollars. It was summer and there would be enough food. They would curse me but they would live.

I left through the back and went north into the cedar grove on Mr. Frost's land. I tripped and fell, which caused me to break open, sobbing. I took the knife and stabbed the ground over and over, first with the blade, then with my fingers. My nail caught in a root and tore. I retched, and screamed into my shallow pit. The keen of a banshee. I hoped they heard. Then I hoped they did not.

Chapter XI

~⚶~

I noticed my hand shaking as I finished talking. I hadn't told
that story to anyone in Dunmore, not even Arabella, and
speaking it now made my bones rattle. I realized suddenly that
this was the reason I had never read the papers that contained
Chiron's narrative. The day before my departure from Spancel
I took those papers from Frost's library. And I could never truly
look on them without recalling the fire, and Hestia.

The old woman was pondering something, her face now dark
in shadow, one hand holding in front of her nose a packet of soap
I had brought her. The new basket of gifts from the townspeople
was before her. I sat on the stool this time, across the iron bars
from where she sat in her cell. The hay now had a rank smell to it.

"What was in this pouch your mother gave you?" she asked.

"Powdered Guinea pepper."

"Ah. Oh."

I couldn't help but laugh, seeing the cunning grin that came
over her.

"That woman—Hestia," said Cash, and paused, softening her
smile. "She did right by you."

Yes, I imagined she would find some glory there.

"If only we had done right by her," I murmured.

"Such are our battles," she sighed, and peered at me for a long moment, a question in her eyes.

"You left that town that very night, yes?"

I nodded.

"And took up with your pirate lover?"

I smiled but did not answer.

"And he brought you to the swamp?" she asked.

"Not directly, but yes . . . he was quite enamoured with the idea of free country. And I was ready, I suppose, to be in a Negro town. Not a quarter, or a street, but a whole town."

Cash hummed with a curious lilt. "And will you go back to your family?" she asked.

I looked at her crossly, and she disarmed me with a frank expression, almost comical in its credulity.

"I don't know," I said.

She nodded and pursed her lips, looking past me to the stone hallway.

"You feel shame," she said abruptly. "If you returned, perhaps they would have cast you out."

She was lively now, and animated her words vigourously.

"They would have been wrong for it, my girl. You know this now; yes, I can see that in your eyes. But then . . . then you didn't give them the chance. You did not have the mettle to stand and face their judgement."

I felt my mouth opening to retaliate, but I had nothing. She had pinned me, unveiling my most shameful truth, leaving me mute and trembling.

"Let me tell you a tale," she said. "It's my turn, no?"

I did not reply. My hands still shook, and I clasped them and did not break the old woman's gaze. She had a warm smile that I refused to match.

"Tell me," she said, "what do you know about 1812?"

I looked to the ceiling, trying to shake off my humiliation. I thought of all I had pieced together from the tomes of military history that I had skimmed over in Frost's library years ago.

"Come, girl. Scholar that you are."

I huffed.

"What is there to know?" I began. "That we British Canadians won. Fought back plundering Americans. Won glory through the daring of Isaac Brock and the Indian warrior Tecumseh."

"Yes, yes," said the old woman impatiently. "So tell me, since we won, what did we gain by it?"

I was silent again as I tried to recall. There was a treaty, there were borders drawn, but land gained—if there was, I knew nothing of it. I shook my head.

"Come now, girl," she hissed. "Any victory of war has winnings, yes?"

I scowled, growing irritated with her sass.

"Nothing to speak of," she muttered, as if to herself. "Whoever heard of a victory such as that?" she went on, and I tried not to roll my eyes.

"All that has changed for me," she said slowly, prodding her finger at the ground, "is that now I am here, jailed, when once I lived free and well on the marsh you call home."

She sighed restlessly and I heard a crinkling from the waxed paper that held the soap in her hand.

"This makes my blood hanker for battle. But I'll settle for a tale of battle. Here. Listen good."

———————

The night we claimed our freedom, my husband and I sat behind tree cover out of view of the sea and one by one we weighted our victims with stones and lashed them to a log of driftwood, and swam them out past the waves where we untied them and let them sink into the depths. We dared not take the canoe back on open waters.

The next morning we sorted through the goods and calculated the value of my children. We chose things that were the smallest and most valuable. Powdered vermilion, the deepest red I've ever seen, in a carved lacquer box; four looking glasses, freshly silvered and small enough to fit in the palm of a hand; and seven long knives with smooth handles of horn with brass filigree. These we hid in a carrying bag underneath our provisions before setting foot any farther.

Inland was a swamp with several running creeks too shallow to paddle, but with enough water to tow the canoe. There were dense thickets of ironwood like arms reaching out from the ground, old gnarled black gum trees, and mats of grass that dipped underwater with each step. It was bright, brighter than under cover of the forest. We walked in the water, our feet plunging into muck, finding hold on twisting roots, and our skin became welted from thin broken branches and the sting of insects. We bathed in pools that made a deep plunging sound as the water dropped from one height to the next, and we made love on an old log thick with moss.

When we reached the village—but do you recall the tale? We offered them the canoe and its contents in exchange for sanctuary. John spoke their tongue haltingly, and I heard the quiver in his chest. I too was overcome with fear—looking between him, the many eyes, and him again. The carnage we had wrought was so fresh upon my hands, I thought that everyone would smell it. There was an old woman who sat and watched us very closely. I believe she did sense our story. I caught her eye, and there was a silent sly look, nearly a mischief, that stopped my breath in my throat.

We slept underneath the canoe on the outskirts of the village the first nights. That same old woman spoke to the village and had them burn the canoe in front of the burial ground, and bury its contents. I wagered she knew it was not worth the trouble it might bring for the living, and so gave it to the dead.

And then, before the embers had cooled we were shown to our very own hut. And there we were. It had all happened so quickly, it didn't seem real. We were alive and well and with a home and people around us who were neither masters nor servants. Nor friends, yet. That first year was strange and haunted. I did not sleep except to dream fitfully, and awaken with the echoes of my wailing children in my ears. They clambered up from the cold black earth, up through cedar boughs, and atop hide mats. Asleep, I would feel a claw on my chest, and then the creaking wail. I was trapped to the ground by the weight of my own breath, my husband dead asleep beside me. And my children, their eyes black as marbles, crawling up my shuddering chest.

But we had a plan. The swamp, as you know, is not even a day's journey to Detroit. And so Detroit was where the village was accustomed to conducting its trade. Their business was good—but only as good as it could be without the eye and the hand of a merchant's clerk. John believed he could double the selling price of the pelts in Montreal. He would lead a small fleet of the men downriver and deliver them to a reward that was well worth the extra time. All he asked in return was to make a brief stop on the outskirts of the town called Caughnawaga, where a girl had left two newborn babes during a deep snowfall of late winter.

Though my heart had never stopped aching in the year since I had birthed my children, we waited another three seasons for good measure, and John grew his hair long. I then shaved his scalp clean to the skin above his ears with a shard of obsidian, and the old woman marked his face in ink with a thorn, so that as he walked with the other men of the tribe, adorned in buckskin and quillwork, he would not be recognized.

With my husband gone I nearly lost my spirit in loneliness. I spent my days by the creek. There is still a creek, yes? Do you know the big rock, shape of a bird, where the water bends south? There I was used to singing by the shore when I washed. To hear my own voice, I would sing any song that came to me, slow first, and then pick the rhythm up and go quick, matching it with my push of the cloth on my ragged rock. I liked to make the soap froth, to work it up into a bubbling muck, and then drown it and feel it wriggle in my hands with the pull of the water. The cloth would come out dripping and cold and free, and I crouched to wring it with my feet wide and my rump strong.

The old woman liked to join me and dance slow to my song, bouncing on her old, creaky knees. She would come and burn sage all upon me and babble with her big face that went from foolish to solemn in an instant. Then she'd pinch my rump and throw back her head and laugh hard. When I smiled back she would caress my cheek and look so deep in my eyes it made me tremble.

The men returned triumphantly not two months later, the children already well disposed to them. When I saw them—one atop the shoulders of a man I didn't know, the other walking next to John—I fell to my knees and wept. I reached for them and tried to hold them to me but they wailed and scratched at my face, and I wept all the more.

The next morning I awoke to the strange chatter of these two children, who glared menacingly at me and would neither understand nor heed my tongue. I went with them about the village, seeking any cloth that needed washing to bring to the water. I was in search of service, of a way to pay for my presence there. The old woman came and spoke to me. She was chiding me for working alone, though I didn't understand at the time. The children took to her and followed her trail. I was left no

choice but to follow them. So it was I came to the women softening the pelts. The old woman rejoiced and beckoned me into
the circle. "I don't know how," I told her, again and again. She
hushed me and put two fingers on my head.

"We are one mind," she whispered—the words I hear in my
dreams still when I sleep near a good fire.

This was how I healed. Scraping and pulling hide around the
smoke. Gossiping. Word by word I learned to holler with the
bunch of them. Nohkomis, my children called the old woman.
They learned the language faster than I did. Only later did I
find out it wasn't a name but a title: grandmother, it means.

In my memories there, the fire is always alive and there are
gurgles of children and the big-bellied laughter of women and
always the aromas of smoke. Sweet wisps of tobacco, big, moon-
white clouds of sage, and the wafts of roasting meat. There, each
changing of the winds brought a labour. As the berries emerged
on the bramble we went among them to harvest. As the men
brought game from the trapline, so too we made stew, and
worked the pelts until they were brown and supple. My children
grew and new children were born from the rhythm of that land.

I remember distinctly when the nature of our work began to
change.

Traders came on canoe one night. Two sacks they carried up
to the fire while our men brought out bale after bale of peltry
from the cellar. After the greetings I went up with Nohkomis.
She lost the traders and their cargo in a fog of sage smoke, holding the herb in a massive ormer shell in one hand, the other with
her eagle feather, billowing the smoke forth like a god of the

swamp. Her prayer finished, she put the shell down and with her sly smile opened up those sacks and plunged her hand in rough, like a child playing in water. She let the finely polished shells fall out of her fingers and the white and violet twinkled and clattered in the firelight. She hummed real happy and held one after the other up to her eye, checking the holes and winking at me.

From that day for about a month, I worked with Nohkomis and two other women to weave a great belt from those shells.

I busied myself with twisting sinew. Everyone knew to give sinew to Nohkomis, whereby she had several baskets of the stuff needing to be pounded, frayed, and twisted into thread. This was my labour, and day after day I crouched and twined like a spider. From my fingers came coils and coils of the strand, thin as the stem of a leaf, strong as ship rope.

Nohkomis inspected the beads that the twine did not fit. She had with her a pump drill with a copper awl on the tip. She put the beads in a rock bowl filled with water and held them with the tips of two fingers. With the other hand she pumped with the drill until it creaked and the awl hummed in the water. She caught me looking and beckoned me over to try. I placed the tip of the drill in the bead and gave it one pump before it jumped out of the water and I shrieked. The women chuckled and Nohkomis laughed hard, leaning on my middle daughter, Nibi, whose face clamped up like her father's when she laughed. She was almost marrying age by then, and my husband had been dead four years.

I contented myself with twisting sinew. That was a task none could do better, because none had the practice, like me, of twisting Negro hair.

We made pemmican early that year, using up the winter stores of fat that sat in copper kettles. We took also dried meat, and huckleberry and plum. To make the work go faster I took two logs of cedar, and with a hatchet and coals from the fire one night I made up a mortar and pestle. I remembered this from my childhood. The next day I used it to mash up fat with the dry meat and berries, and the women were so happy they clapped and made a song for me.

One day, Tecumseh, the Panther, came to the village with his band of warriors. His moccasins were pretty with porcupine quills, and he walked softly, as befit his name.

This was the man who was gathering the tribes to form a new nation. I presented myself to him.

"I hear you call Matthew Tillings your father," I said, and the people grew quiet around my voice. "There," I said, pointing to my son. "There sits my boy, now a man eager to fight for you, and fight well. And when he was still a boy, Tillings laid his lash upon him and would have used him as a bondsman. When you have your nation, will the son take up his father's habits?"

I heard some whispers as they translated my English tongue for those who didn't understand.

The Panther looked at me gravely and I held his eyes.

"Sister," he said to me, "I have lived among them. I have even loved them. But I am not them. Our land will be tended without slaves."

I held his gaze for a long moment more, before nodding and taking my seat again. I had to ask, so that when Nohkomis gave him the belt, we would be of one mind.

She draped it on his arm that night, and with that gift, we were at war.

There was a cycle of duty. My clan started at home, and another went to Fort Malden at Amherstburg. We stayed back and stocked the food caches. We sang our way through brambles of berries; we stooped in the shade of the nut trees and we went out among the fields to pluck beans.

Dred and his sister Dinah brought in fish as well as fowl, which they butchered each day, and they smoked the meat each night.

And then, just as the corn began to ripen, the first clan came back hot with unspent fire. There had been no skirmish yet, and it was our time to go.

We paddled into Bois Blanc Island, just across from Fort Malden. The land was thickly wooded, and it sat right in the strait with full view of the American side. The river there has a light blue in the water that carries on through the sky.

After a night on the island we took direction from the Panther to cross and join the scouting parties. The Americans, who we called the long knives, had raided the British side of the river and retreated, leaving plenty a white man, French and Briton, ready to pick up the musket where before he would have sooner hidden out in his fields. Those fields and the barns were now empty, and those farmers were hungry for vengeance. The Americans only had one way to get supplies. And that was straight from River Raisin and through us. We had word there were two hundred carts of pork and flour, fresh from Kentucky and Virginia farms, and all of it was sitting in River Raisin waiting for the long knives army to come and get it. And right they were to wait, for we were also waiting, in the quiet about the trackways, with keen, sharp blades.

We went to the Indian village they call Brownstown. The Panther had convinced the people there to leave and set up their village on the British side. The corn they left behind was tall and perfect for the scouts to lie in.

I took to climbing trees like I used to do as a girl. I wasn't fit for battle but I was fit enough to climb.

From the heights of an oak tree I saw the battle at Brownstown. We were outnumbered twenty to one but we were fierce and sent them flying back up to Detroit. Them long knives could run too. Dropped their knapsacks, threw their muskets, and ran like hell! They knew that once fired, their guns only served to weigh them down and snag on branches and vines. I saw Dred and Dinah take off in hot pursuit. Like they just couldn't wait to kill.

We erected the bodies of their dead on stakes and let them rot.

Three days passed, and I gathered medicine for my pouch and harvested corn, most of it still half-green but good enough to roast in embers. We cut sprigs of basswood for the volunteers without uniforms to put in their caps so the Indians could tell them from the long knives.

Men spread out to camp, so as not to step in each other's

shit, and to make the enemy scouts think us more numbered than we were, when they looked at the smoke of our campfires.

On the fourth day a scout came running. "Long knives come down through the woods," he said.

"How many?" asked the British captain.

"Many as the mosquitoes in the swamp," said the scout.

Fear spread among the whites at that. The captain butted the ground with his musket and called his men to quiet. He looked around him for the Indians. We were already among the trees. I mixed two pans of birch bark, red ochre and black char. The warriors came to me to paint themselves half one colour, half the other.

There was drum song, and all danced and shook their heads like beasts. They yipped and pushed up against each other. And when they all got the spirit in them the Panther began to jog light through the woods. All followed, and the forest threw a hush. Even the birds were quiet.

I ran but couldn't keep up, and I had to hold my medicine pouch in one hand and hatchet in the other to keep them from clanging against me.

I found a tall white spruce and started to climb as I heard the first sounds of battle. I couldn't see the field but I heard the cannon spray at the British. The long knives were trying to mow them down in the moments it took the two sides to meet. As I climbed I heard the pop of musket fire and the clang of sabres, the yell of a man stabbed with a bayonet piece. I kept climbing, though I was getting tired. The cannon boomed again, and the clamour of many shouts kept rising, fading, rising. And I reached a branch where I could see the Indians attack from the flank like a serpent that bites and recoils.

Another Indian strike, and I saw what the Panther was doing: drawing away a section of the long knives. Opening up the body for the British to pierce again. It was working, but the long knives were too many, and with each wound the body of their army slowed only to swell—more and more coming through the woods.

Then my children came into view. They were small and darting, from the height of my perch. I knew them only by their hair. My heart leapt about as I saw them sprint and lunge and strike, and men fell at their blows and did not rise from the ground. I watched them follow each other and disappear into the bush.

For indeed, at that moment, the horn sounded from the river and the British began to retreat.

Once the Americans saw that, they commenced to whoop, and I heard a far-off thunderclap.

Now it was we who had to run and hide.

By the time I nearly reached the tree bottom I saw a British soldier half carrying a young volunteer, a Frenchman who owned a storefront in Amherstburg. The Frenchman had caught lead shot in his leg.

Behind them was an American on a big tawny stallion. The horse had some trouble in the bush, bucking at the sharp branches that gouged at it, but the man was too brazen to dismount. He flailed his blade, sending splinters every which way, drunk with war.

The two men hobbled beneath me; I stationed real still, close above them. The Frenchman was wide-eyed and frothing at the mouth. The soldier whispered to him, heaving him over roots and moss.

I grasped my hatchet.

It was that same hatchet I'd used to make my mortar and pestle. It was small, like a pipe tomahawk, but with more heft— heft enough to cut big boughs for a lean-to. For when I needed a piece of deadwood for fire, or a thick green sapling for a splint. I had Dred keep it sharp for me, passing the whetstone after every use. So when the American came whooping and bobbing through the woods, his felt hat blocking me from his sight, the white plume of it quivering like the tail of a deer, I sank the hatchet in his head like it was a stump of wood. The man froze up and fell slow into the branch of my tree. The horse kept trotting and the man was pulled for a moment, a branch hooking him by the coat arm, and the horse pulling his feet out with the stirrups, before the stirrups prevailed and he fell bent and heavy on the crunch of spruce needles, and the horse kept dragging him.

I climbed down quick and chased after him to take back that hatchet.

I stuffed clay in the Frenchman's wound, and pressed on his mouth and felt it squirm and clench. He started to weep.

We hid while it thundered and rained.

"We are lost," said the soldier.

"We are not," I said. "With this rain, they won't last another day in the bush."

In the dark of the storm we took the boats across the river. The water was black-green and jumping with the clap of rain. In the lightning, trees were silver. Yarrow whipped at the shore. My clan stopped again at Bois Blanc, and I started a fire, having some wood kept dry in my lean-to. The rain stopped and there was a sawing, a shaking darkness. Waves of chittering insects and frogs that sounded as full as the stars. I took my blade that I had tucked away, careful as a part of hair, and we feasted on the bulbs of river lilies.

Chapter XII

C ash was seated cross-legged against the wall of her cell. She reached over and pulled her basket of delights onto her lap. Her hand settled on a green pawpaw blotched with black veins, and she sniffed at it suspiciously.

I pondered her tale from the other side of the bars. She had removed her head wrap during the course of her telling, and I was struck by the smallness of her skull. Looking at her, it was as if a carapace peeled back, and I saw those same nostrils pulling air as she jostled past the low limbs of a forest. Her skin the same hue, but quickened—

"I've been thinking," she began, cutting short my thoughts. "We've abandoned Chiron's tale, well before it is done."

I nodded.

"We have indeed, and I have it with me. But I have questions."

She looked up at me, raising both brows.

"Do you still speak the Indian tongue, then?" I asked.

"Oh, hardly," she said, and sunk her teeth into the fruit in her hand.

"Hardly enough to turn an Indian tracker from foe into friend?" I asked.

She glanced up with a questioning glare, and sucked noisily at the yellow innards of the pawpaw.

I returned her look with a subtle grin as I waited for her to remember the events that had brought her to jail. We were a world away from Simeon's fields, and from the bounty hunter and the Indian tracker whom she had seemingly converted from slave hunter to abolitionist in a moment.

I saw the memory come to her and she nodded and grunted vigourously before spitting out a wet black seed on the hay. "Ah," she sighed with a devilish grin.

I blinked expectantly.

"Will you tell me what you said to him?" I asked.

She smiled and took another bite of her fruit. I rolled my eyes.

"I don't recall my very words," she began, still grinning, her mouth full, "but sometimes the tongue is more important than the words."

I snorted. "Should I say so to all these abolitionists seeking to change the hearts of slave owners?" I quipped. "Tell them to learn to speak American—then they will be heard, yes?"

I was mocking her, and she responded with a contemptuous fluttering of her eyes.

"Smart as you are, girl, do what you do best: hush up and read."

I smiled and crossed my legs primly, reaching into my satchel for the papers. It seemed my silence fed the old woman's ire.

"Yes, read me the rest of Chiron's tale," she went on, flinging a strip of pawpaw skin at my feet, "for both I and these stones have had enough of your saucy lip!"

I didn't restrain my smile as I sorted through the papers and found where I had left off. The mirth left me then, as my eyes found the first line, and I sobered myself for more bloodshed.

As fate would have it, the 1812 war saw me take up arms for British Canada. The first I saw battle was October 1812, and in the evening following the bloodshed, the men of my company went upriver apiece to a place where the water eddied. They went to sing and wash the blood from their bodies, and from their spirits too, I suppose. Though it was autumn it wasn't too cold yet. And the men had a special bond with this part of the river, where one could hear the thunder of the great falls and taste the mist. For it was in those waters that a number of them did hit upon their freedom for the first time in this life. It seemed strange that the land of freedom was not above, but below and down: down the thundering falls.

I elected to sit watch by the camp, where I made myself comfortable on a knoll in a log of driftwood at the fire, and warmed my ration of Jamaica rum. I was bone tired and rubbed my head to soothe it of the grisly specters of that day. At that time my mount was a tough sorrel quarter horse named Claude, and he stood beside me, stooping to munch on his evening oats. The baritone wavering melody of the men wafted to us through the mist and between the trees.

The whole company had survived this first proper battle of the war. And the action was hot. None could say now that this fight would be a mere matter of marching. None could say either that Negroes were only fit for construction or other subordinate work. No, sir. We had proved that, along with the Indians, we fought each with the worth of three men.

We had trained diligently in the woods and the plains around Fort George for most of the previous three months. The men who did not already know were taught how to move with the quiet only enabled by moccasins. We studied how, in the briefest of manoeuvres, a man could reload a rifle and fire thrice in less than a minute. We practiced how to run low to the ground between tufts of long grass, and how to drop and crouch, shoot and roll. How to move in twos, each one covering the other.

Our captain was a quarrelsome old drunk, and most of us believed that the Brits had assigned him to us so as to not risk any white militia. But luckily, we had Richard, who was everything a captain could be and more. He was an old man, born in Africa soil. He was many years older even than I, and I was not a young man by then. He was tough, and a smart fighter. He drilled us, day after day, in the manner of the Butler's Rangers, with whom he had served some thirty years previous. When I heard that fact I assured the men, as I knew more than most, that we had been granted a chance better than any other battalion fighting for the Crown. I had heard tell of the Butler's Rangers all the way back in Kentucky when I was a boy. During the American Independence war they seemed to be the only company fit to trounce the Yanks again and again. The rangers didn't dress in red coats like the regulars, but instead in green, and they fought in the Indian way. They emerged from the bush for a moment, sharpshooting officers, breaking up the enemy line with quick, hard strikes. They didn't mess around with the blunderbuss. No, for them—for us—it was simple: a rifle with bayonet, a tough pair of moccasins, and a blade for close quarters. No lining up to get shot at. Strike, disappear, strike again.

During battle, as our movement allowed us perspective on the enemy's position and weaknesses, Richard would write up a note and I would go to Claude and the two of us would be off at breakneck speed. I thanked the Lord my legs were still strong enough to ride like that. And I thanked Claude, who, at fourteen hands was sure-footed as a goat and could sprint like the devil was chasing him.

I do believe he saved my hide on a number of occasions that day, having the sense to run jagged and dodge cannon fire to and from the fort and the heights.

I thought of this, looking at Claude from my seat by the fire. Suddenly, he bristled and lifted his neck in the way that he does when he scents a man.

"It's only the boys, Claude," I told him wearily. After all, the battle was good and won. A thrush sang high from the tamarack on which my pack hung. I find nothing more soothing than the whirling call of a thrush. It was the violet dark of dusk, and I marvelled at how such a bloody day could end in this peaceful blue.

"We seen men tore clean in half by cannonball, Claude," said I, "and still we here, fed and well. Still here."

Claude grunted. He looked at me urgently from one side of the white blaze that marked his face. He had been born wild, a mustang. And as such his sense was a fair deal sharper than most.

"Do he answer you?" said a voice from the trees.

My hand went to the rifle that rested on the blanket beside me and I gripped it and crouched, looking into the stand of tamaracks before me.

I quietly cursed myself for having agreed to make camp here. The sound of the river and the falls beyond made it too easy to sneak on us. The battle may have been won, but the danger was never over.

"The skirmish is done, private," said the voice.

With that, a man stepped from the dark between two trees. He held a full-length bow and a leather quiver in one hand. The fingers of his other hand held the notch of an arrow loosely. His face was long and handsome, with the lower half painted black. His head was shorn on one side, and a top lock of hair fell in a long braid on the quillwork of his tunic. He was strangely familiar to me, but I could not say from where. My eyes fell to the dangle of several scalps, tied by their own hair to his belt. He saw my gaze upon them and he smiled.

I heard footsteps quickening in the bush, and in a moment I saw another figure appear, this one shorter than the first. He held a long rifle in one hand and a wicker basket in the other. He was clad in a moose greatcoat and a tight head wrap of blue broadcloth. This face I recognized as he brushed quickly by his companion. It took me a moment, for it had been some years. But sure enough it was young Dred, son of my old friend John, from whom I received the runaway family in Detroit, nearly five years earlier.

The first man muttered something to Dred, who replied in turn, looking over his shoulder as the man walked away silently, back into the forest.

Dred turned back to me and approached the fire, laying down his rifle and basket so as to clasp my hands in his.

"Do you know me?" he asked with a smile, still clasping my hands.

"Of course, young Dred," I said, giving his hands a hearty shake. "Of course."

"Don't mind Dinah," he told me with a wink. And at first, I failed to understand. Dred sat down next to the fire before the meaning struck me. The handsome face, the cruel smile.

"Damn," I said, glancing at the woods and then back at him to see if he was serious.

He was looking at my horse from his seat on the ground. Claude had bent down all the way to sniff him, and he reached out a hand, bound with a strip of cotton damp with blood. Claude widened his nostrils.

"You hurt?" I asked him.

He shook his head and reached in his basket and pulled out a small speckled trout.

"Damn," I said again, taking my driftwood seat, still pondering Dinah. "I suppose she was always tough."

He smiled thinly and drew a knife from his moccasin and began to dress the fish. The scales and guts fell into the embers and hissed.

"I knew it was you," said he. "Soon as we saw that horse fly from the woods like a cannonball. The Yankees shot each other trying to get it in their sights. 'Only one man ride like that,' I said to Dinah."

He chuckled and passed me the end of a stick with the trout splayed out on it, ready to roast.

"Brought supper," he said. "We saw the bum pork they feed you, and thought you might want some real food."

"Thank you, Dred," I told him, and I retook my seat. "Wasn't expecting to see you here; I didn't think this was your tribe."

"They're not," he replied. "But we got friends here. Folk who took care of Dinah and me when we were babes. When we got word that the six nations entered the war, we came down posthaste."

By then, he had another trout splayed out, and we took a moment to place our fish just right, above the embers.

"How 'bout you?" he asked. "Last I saw you, you were mounted guard for the other side. I worried I might cross you on the field."

"I'm more worried about that sister of yourn," I said, and we both chuckled.

"True enough," he said, poking the fire. "So it goes with many of my countrymen. It's a rage that goes deep, and white men don't understand it, but they do fear it."

He looked at me. His eyes were dark, and the skin of his face was the same brown as the tamarack bark.

"Our rage is a bridge to peace," he said.

I sighed and turned my trout. "I pray that to be true."

He scoffed, and this raised my ire. He spoke intelligently, but like many young men, he held more certainty in his bearing than he had earned.

"There will be a new nation," he whispered, leaning toward me, his eyes bright with firelight. "When we win this war, Chiron. A new nation that will span from the inland seas to lands south of the Ohio. All Indian."

I nodded. I had heard as much, and at the time I had no doubt they would get it too. Though then and now, I did not know what such a nation would mean for me.

"That sounds real good, Dred," I told him. "I pray for your victory. But you must know, friend, new nation or not, you ain't gonna get peace with brutality."

He regarded me with a sly, hard look. I went on:

"Come, brother; up on those heights, once the Yanks were all outta lead and fit to surrender, I seen a young private sent out running with a white cravat—all they had left to serve as a flag. The boy didn't make it two paces before an arrow went straight into his skull. Reckon that was your sister. Same happened to the next man, waving a tore-up, dirty tunic. That ain't any way to peace."

He smiled and shook his head. "I would think you know differently by now, Uncle. But tell me, what is the way to peace?" he asked.

I would have answered had I sensed sincerity in the question.

"I hear you now work for slave owners," he said, pinching

off a small bite of his trout and chewing, staring into the woods. I felt my ire rise to my head again. I am not quick to rage. But this boy was brash, and now he would not even meet my eye.

"Is it true?" he asked, as if to the fire.

I let his question wait in silence for a moment. Let the sound of the fire and the warbling thrush cool my head.

"It was true," I said, and he nodded.

I waited another long breath more before continuing. "Three years ago I took my family from their master. We rowed across the straits in a skiff at midnight, and got to freedom not even an hour later. It was simple; I cursed myself for not doing it sooner. I needed work, and the slave owner you speak of needed a man to drive cattle. He paid me well, and gave my family good lodging. I figured your father would not approve."

Dred lowered his head, as if bowing to the fire. "My father is dead five winters now," he said and looked at me finally. "Some folk say it was from a parcel of gifts laden with a white man's sickness."

Poor John. My anger left me with a breath and I wanted to console the young man before me. I could see in him the fury, and I knew that most men will seek a villain in an effort to soothe their grief. But I did not say that.

"That is a great loss, Dred," I told him.

I uncorked my flask of rum and poured a splash on the ground at the embers of the fire between us, and a blue flame hiccupped. I offered him the flask but he shook his head.

We breathed deep and followed the sparks of the fire up past the yellow rush of tamarack and into the patch of sky above where they shimmered like the first stars of the evening.

"Is your family well?" he asked.

"They are. They work at the fort. My son is too young yet to fight, though he wants badly to come with his daddy."

"It may be a good battle to cut his teeth in," said Dred. "I scouted these boys all down the Wabash, the Susquehanna, the Maumee. I tell you, I don't know how they have the heart to fight by the time they get here. I seen a man get so cold at night, he decided to pull up his brush pile on the coals of the fire and fall asleep like that, even as he started to smoulder. Asleep, I tell you!" said Dred, and he closed his eyes in a show of theatre, drooping his head and letting out a snore. In a moment he jerked awake, slapping his leg and mumbling oaths till it made him chuckle, and me too. The laughter felt good in the belly.

Once he caught his breath, he resumed.

"Winter is coming, and they're leaving a trail of dead men. Dead from the ague, the pox, lake fever. A man can't survive these marches soaked to the bone with naught but hog gristle and whiskey."

"Well," I said to him, "the worst is still to come. Word from my lieutenant is that they're bringing a detachment of Kentucky militia. The Kentucks don't balk at a hard fight."

I went silent for a spell remembering the sight from earlier that day up on the heights, when I took aim at a man—a boy, rather. He was young and pockmarked. He clutched his Brown Bess rattling over his heart and at the sound of our whoops he turned and ran to the heights. Perhaps he imagined being scalped, or roasted, or any manner of slow death. He tossed his rifle and ran, and my hand reached as though he was within my grasp. And then he was gone, and there was only the sparse grass of the cliff top and his rifle, and the roar of battle around me.

"How you mean?" Dred asked me.

"Look here," I told him, shaking my head out of its reverie and reaching forward to turn my trout. "Ne'er a man down in Kentucky who ain't come up sharpshooting squirrels."

I sat back and watched the steam seep from the broken red flesh of the fish.

"You ever tried to shoot a squirrel with a rifle?" I asked him.

He smiled, seeing the mirth in my eyes.

"If you can shoot a squirrel, you can shoot a man," I said, holding a grave look for as long as I could. My smile overtook me, and we both laughed again, and I hoped it would sustain a peace between us.

That winter was well and calm, and not until the following spring was everything lost.

I don't remember the day, to be exact, but word from a British messenger is that the thunder of the battery at Niagara could be heard from York. That I believe. The Americans came in hot with schooners and tall ships sounding an orchestra of guns. The move was so bold that they took the beach without too much trouble and sent us hightailing west into the low country.

I thanked my stars that Anne and the children were not at the fort; they had gone to visit Dred's family at a camp secreted in the woods. The Americans marched on us and we retreated, haunted by their ensign high upon their man of war, and the rasping melody of "Yankee Doodle" whistled by fifes.

I rode ahead. Claude's hoof steps pounded the lanes. We skirted farmland and soared over the streams and freshets that laced the woods. I delivered my dispatch to the horrified general at the westward fort, and then I went straight to the magazine. Most of my company was out of powder and shot, so I secured a barrel of each along with a ream of paper, and set about rolling cartridges while Claude feasted on an untouched meadow of clover.

Most troops arrived late that evening, and groups of civilians continued to pour in through the night. Among them was an informant, a scrappy farmer boy who was yammering about the American camp. He was sent to the general's tent. I got word of it and went a few feet from the canvas to listen. The boy had managed to glean the location of the American camp, as well as their night watch code, and then made his way straight to us. As I listened to the muffled sounds of voices through the canvas, I heard in his voice the excitement at the knowledge that he may have found himself with just the right stuff at just the right time; just right, that is, to become a legend before the day broke. And though he had not yet seen battle, they gave him a corporal's sword and summoned all, posthaste, to follow him eastward whence we fled, into the brutal black of night.

For this skirmish, I left Claude, whinnying and uneasy, at

the fort livery. There would be no use for him in what was to come. We marched to a broil.

The rangers jogged through the bush alongside the Indians. I found Dred and Dinah and ran with them. We saw the flicker of the American campfires in a clearing between two creeks, overflowing with freshet streams. This was good. The purling sounds of the water masked our approach, and the light of the fires illuminated them, while the woods kept us in darkness.

There were hundreds of men in the clearing, and when they awoke to the British attack, some of them managed a peppering volley before we were upon them. We rangers and Indians held fast in the trees on the American flank, waiting a moment, then another moment more for them to be fully drawn into the fray. We listened to the pop of muskets and the screams begotten by the goring bayonets.

"No, this ain't no shooting battle for me," said Dred, clapping my arm. He handed me his rifle and drew two tomahawks from the sling at his back. Dinah shouldered her bow and leapt up to the first branch of the great tree under which we crouched, and continued climbing. After a moment she was only discernible by an occasional rustle.

The men around us began to run, and Dred was gone with them. He bayed like a hound in the charge, and there, with two rifles, I crouched in the forest's teeth. From high and low, Dinah and me cut Dred a path. The horde of Indians met the long knives with a clatter. A man lunged at Dred with a bayonetted rifle, and he parried, trapping the blade in the jaw of his tomahawk, and then dropping to turn with a furious movement, hacking the man's leg. The man fell to his knees, using the butt of his rifle as a crutch. I took aim, but an arrow from above me plunged over the charging horde and went into the man's neck. I found Dred in my sights again. A large man drew a cutlass and ran at him. He raised his tomahawks and stood his ground. I shot the man in the belly and he jolted. Dred chopped his sword hand, and then sidestepped a man who vaulted toward him and stumbled to the ground. An arrow buried itself next to that man's face. He scrambled up and ran back toward Dred, who had plunged even further into the melee. I shot the man's heart through his back.

I reloaded both rifles hurriedly, keeping my eyes on Dred as he hacked and tore into his foes. I had learned to move deftly with the powder and lead between my fingers and teeth, the rifles in the crook of my arm. By the time I had loaded, Dred was deep in the fray. Too deep. He was meant to come back within our range, to attack and retreat like a viper, but instead he pressed on. He ducked the swipe of a flailing sword and I took aim, but he was far, and his assailants were too close upon him to get a good shot. I ran out of my cover and into the field, looking through the fray. Dred was backed against a roaring fire, encircled by three men who jabbed at him. He swiped at one but another thrust the point of a bayonet into his knee and I heard his scream above the ruckus of the melee. I saw a man in the corner of my eye, felt his footsteps pound the ground toward me. I maintained my aim and shot the back of one of the men encroaching on Dred. I saw the other men club him with the butt ends of their muskets, and my gut clenched with panic.

I turned to the man charging me and threw my rifle like a spear. The bayonet pierced his stomach and he lurched and stumbled, a pace away from me. I drew my blade from my belt and stuck him in the neck. His eyes were wild and trembling. I saw another man point to me and begin to sprint with three others. I ran back toward the cover of the trees.

I reached the tree where we had begun the battle and crouched with my back to the trunk while my enemies approached. In the dark of the woods I could handle them. I had forgotten Dinah was above. She dropped like a cat on the first man as he trotted under the boughs. He was a burly fellow, so when she fell on him he did not collapse. She sprang from him and drew back her ball-head cudgel. He dropped his rifle and clutched at his neck, and she circled him toward his companions, who had slowed and raised their bayonets. The big man reeled and fell to his knees, loosing a terrible gurgling moan. It was only then that I saw the scalping knife clutched like a dagger in Dinah's left hand. The next man yelled and raised his rifle to slash her. She pounced and the iron stud of her cudgel buried in the man's jaw. The third man ran at her but his head was in my sights and his body fell hard. The fourth man fled.

I reloaded and then followed Dinah down into the field. By then the Americans were in full retreat and Dinah was looking at the faces of fallen warriors on the ground. I ran up to her and

put my hand on her shoulder. She shrugged me off and continued scouring the bloody grounds. There was grisly celebration
around us.

"Dred will not be found here," I told her.

"You don't know that," she snarled to me.

"I do," I said softly. "Indians they kill; Negroes they sell."

The Americans retreated all the way to Fort George that night.
We British went up the escarpment to form strongholds so that
when day broke, we would look down on them like hawks.
Once I had lodged my stuff with my company I roamed to find
the Caughnawaga troop, so that Dinah would show me to the
hidden encampment where my family had gone to stay.

At the base of an enormous white pine I dismounted Claude
to greet a sentinel, a stout, jovial man with long greying hair and
a slash of knotted scars that crept up one side of his neck. An
unlucky pass of blunderbuss shot, I guessed. I did not allow my
eyes to linger. We clasped hands and I greeted him in his tongue.

"Seygo," I said, as I had heard the Mohawks utter at the start
of encounters. The man laughed and replied with a babble of
words that sounded to me like the drumming of a grouse through
the bush. He waited expectantly, still clasping my hand firmly,
our thumbs entwined. I grunted and nodded, feigning understanding, and we both laughed and began our walk into camp,
other voices and forms gaining shape as we plodded up the rise,

and I ducked Claude under low-hanging branches. When we came to the rocky plateau, my guide waved to men roasting meat by a fire. The men looked up at us through the flames and dancing shadows. The grey man clapped my shoulder and gestured past them toward where I guessed Dinah lay.

She was brooding under a lean-to roofed by a beam of dead wood and leaves that formed a hovel between the roots of two thick beech trees. She was set atop a bed of young pine boughs covered with a deer pelt. With one arm she tended her own small fire. In her other hand she sipped from a pot of Rhenish stoneware. The dark sea blue of it glinted off the firelight between her fingers.

"I have spoken to my lieutenant," I said as I approached her, and crouched. "He has agreed to—"

"There is nothing he can agree to," she said, and looked to me. Only then I noticed her bloodshot eyes. "I have been to the camp where my mother and sisters lay hidden," she muttered. "They are all taken."

My heart sank so deep, and I had to put both hands on the ground, as it felt as though the slope would fold me into it.

"Anne and my children . . ." I know I faltered; I know I could not have spoken plainly. But in her eyes I saw she already knew. If her family was gone, so too was mine.

———⋘———

I was there to see Washington burn, and white folk running every which way like vermin from the smoke. I saw the same men and women over and over again, milling about and hollering. They weren't used to running and didn't know how. Lucky for them it wasn't a proper pillage, else the lot of them would've been dead a hundred times over. There wasn't a Negro in sight by the time the battle was over. I slaughtered several who'd been left to station the battery while their white officers fled. I left their blood on the garments of white folk I grabbed hold of as they flailed in the streets. I asked where to find slaves; where were the prisoners. All I got was snivelling nonsense.

"Oh, we don't know nothing 'bout that—please!"

"We hardly had any servants round here, officer!"

They could barely look at me before begging to scuttle away. I saw my dark form loom in their eyes. I wouldn't find what I sought. Not in Washington, anyhow. So I fixed to go to the only place where stories that don't exist can be found. I took five cutlasses from an abandoned smithy and a side of cured hog from the burning cellar of a republican, and I told the men if I wasn't back in three days they were to leave me for dead.

I put all my cargo on Claude, who was safe in the stable of a farm that we had taken during the siege. He looked at me darkly as I packed his saddle, as if he knew the blood I had spilled. The daemon I had become on this campaign. We heard an explosion from the city and he whinnied softly but he was no longer made frantic by the sounds of war.

"Cumon, young buck," I told him. "We going to the woods, deep."

We rode in to where the low country began to rise to the Blue Ridge. We went slow, and I looked for the markers of the route I had taken with Monk all those years ago. We travelled at night, and once near, we stayed off the paths. In those woods, before long, the ground might fall away swiftly, leaving one to plunge to ironwood spears, as if into the fangs of the earth itself.

At night, one might hear a whirring noise. The sentinels of the underlands were slingers. No gunshots. Just a quiet whirring as they whip around a leather strap like a dark halo. And one might not even hear that, 'cause all they need is a clear shot to bury a hunk of basalt in a skull from fifty yards.

One might hear too a rhythm of drums, like the night itself was dancing.

And if one had the eyes for it, one might see at certain spots the forest floor aglow, real faint.

Me, though, I just followed my nose. Tried to smell through the soot of Washington still on me, and the rust of blood. I came across a wisping aroma of hot meat and tubers, strange in the cool scents of the woods.

I sang atop Claude as we made our way, ducking at branches. Sang a song from Africa soil that Monk taught me, and I let the cutlasses dangle and clatter together. There was no reason to try and go undetected in this land.

I only stopped and shielded my head when I heard the whirring.

"I bring gifts for the King!" I said from beneath my arms.

Nothing struck me. It was only a warning. I patted the hog on the saddle behind me and held the blades aloft, shaking them to clamour among the trees.

I heard footsteps in the leaf cover in front of me, and in a few moments two shapes came from out the bush. Two men, glaring silently at us. One of them neared, stepping softly and quickly. The other one remained several paces away, turned to the side, his sling at the ready. They were both painted with clay, grey as storm clouds, clad in a bandolier and dark pantaloons that reached below their knees. They held the long leather straps of their slings like protractions of their arms. Claude tensed as the one approached us, and I calmed him with a hand on his neck. The man stopped and cocked his head slightly to the side. His hair was long and braided tight to his scalp, and I saw the glint of a blade in his bandolier.

"Drop the knives," he ordered. His voice was young and harsh.

I obliged and the cutlasses plunged, looped together through their handles by a twine. They stuck in the ground with a noise like a grunt.

"Dismount," said the man.

They left the hog on the saddle and took the blades and my rifle before covering my eyes with a band of leather, and leading us a ways further into the woods. Brush clawed at me as we walked, and I felt the men turn me more than once. After some time they took off the blindfold and we were under the foliage of a huge wizened elm. Here, they tethered Claude to a low-reaching branch and had me strip down to my breeches. The man with the braids handed me a hunk of wet clay to paint myself, and when I was finished, feeling pleasantly cool in my new adornment, he beckoned to me and crouched among the long roots of the elm. I went to him, and in the dark I thought my eyes were failing me, for he promptly vanished, swallowed whole by the ground. I stood, uncertain of what I was to do, until the other man grunted from behind me. He passed by me, holding the cutlasses and the meat. He too crouched, and fed the blades into the ground. I came closer and leaned in, seeing a blacker dark beside a root the breadth of my leg. He held the side of hog by its trotter and lowered it down into the dark and then looked up at me, and stood, tall and lithe.

"Go on now," he said.

I lowered my feet into the black. It felt wide open below me. I scraped my chest as I passed down, and then I dropped deeper than I expected, and landed, crouching. The world was black; there was no difference between eyes open or closed.

"Walk forward," said the voice of the man behind me.

I went, guided by my two hands on the walls to either side. I felt the cool dust of clay and the wisps of roots on my fingertips. My guide's footsteps sounded far away, yet I could smell the hog he carried. After some time I looked back and saw, or thought I saw, the shape of him. Monstrous and shifting, a dark layer upon the dark itself. I heard my breath, close, all around me. And that was all. Until after what felt like a long time I heard other voices, and singing, and I saw some light ahead. For certain, there was light growing like the moon behind a passing cloud. Light that allowed me to see some of my own body, strange and earthlike with the clay. I walked faster. After a few moments, I came to a curtain of many strings of hanging seeds, and bones, and shells, and they scraped over me like a rattle. I came into a hall, much wider than the tunnel we had emerged from. It was still dark, but there was light from candles sitting in many different heights dug out all along the walls throughout the long room, giving the place the feel of a cathedral. On one side was a pit of embers that glimmered softly. The smells of hot spice and meat made my stomach tighten and lurch. My guide left the hog there and stopped a moment to talk with the hearth keepers. I looked around. In the middle of the hall was a long earthen table where folk lounged and ate, talked and laughed. Their dark bodies seemed like moving extensions of the ground itself.

It's said that King Cullin was an architect back on Africa soil. He dug the first tunnels by himself, and built the main hall with locust wood and stone. He vented the place in mountain caverns and through the hollows of half-dead trees, such that one could be below and never feel stifled. He took to raiding plantations at night, and taking away livestock and people. And eventually, he didn't have to raid. At least not for people. Folk just came.

My guide beckoned me forward, and I went to the end of the hall, where I could make out two passageways. I went toward one on my left, from where I heard a sound, the spattering and flowing of water.

"Not that way," said my guide from behind me.

We passed through four such halls. More than I remembered from my visit when I was young. The fifth was quiet and a darker black. I didn't know to recognize King Cullin, again not able to see, but I figured he was before me. The sentinel passed by me and I heard him lay down the blades. I heard, also, the sound of teeth on meat. Tearing at flesh, and chewing. I caught a glimpse of dark movement, or perhaps I felt the change in the air, and footsteps again, as the sentinel returned from whence we came.

He may have looked at me, I couldn't tell, but after a few moments he spoke.

"I recollect you," he said, and gulped. "You Monk's boy."

How he knew me in that utter dark, it being my first time in the underlands in twenty-odd years, I can't fathom.

"I am," I said.

And, as if he'd read my mind, he chuckled and spoke again.

"You is indeed. You did learn to walk like him, you know. And I smell the horse off you."

His voice was rough, but warm. It filled the space when he spoke, but it only echoed in the mind. I squinted to make him out, and I thought I could see eyes shimmering, ever so slightly, before fading into undulating darkness, and I could see only memories of the shapes we'd passed on the way through.

It is said he had been enslaved as a young man in a Virginia lead mine. That's where he learned to see in the dark, unforgiving folds of the earth. That mine—a series of explosions collapsed it with most of the slaves and overseers inside, it is said.

All this I recalled as the faint shimmer of his eyes appeared to me again, and I imagined the shape of him around it, shifting, like a huge snake.

"Good night to you," he said. "And by that I mean: take a

seat, young man, and eat. Night ain't nothing but niggerday, but you know this nearly well as I."

He paused and chortled heavily, and I heard the clink of iron. I imagine he was inspecting the blades I had brought. I felt around in front of me, and my hands crept up another earthen table. I felt heat at my fingertips. Gently, my hand found something that fit warmly in my grasp. I crouched, and the dirt beneath me softened to my heels. It was pleasant and cool, and a draft of air pulled at my back. I bit into the thing in my hand, and steam and subtle sweetness overcame me. A yam, baked to tenderness.

"You come to me for a story, like everyone else," said King Cullin, smacking his lips as he ate. "And you've brought a good gift. The blades are well wrought. But your story is a hard one. I'll tell you that right now. Though I could see by the dark in the back of your eye that you know that already, or your spirit do anyhow. Despair not, young man. Don't mean there ain't nothing to be done. *They* speak about destiny like it come from above."

He paused, swallowed, and cleared his throat.

"Destiny," he muttered, "ain't nothing but a hole in the ground. Nothing but a path made by night."

—————

Hear now what you came for, a story that doesn't exist.

Last year there was a large parcel sold underground. No papers. Word was they were two mothers, each with children, taken down from the frontier of battle with the British. There was a time it would have been difficult to sell slaves without papers. Not now, though. These days all the slaves of the bay been sneaking off to the British warships like water going out to tide, and ne'er a one planter this side of the mountains will say no to cheap black flesh. Papers can be written up sooner than the plants go sour in the field.

So it was that the whole lot got snatched up by the first tobacco gentleman to get wind of the fresh cargo at the barracks. Old Dr. Sylvanus, you know the one? Yes, I thought you would; there are few parts of the state one can get to without going past or through Sylvanus land. He's one of the better ones, from what I hear. Or at least one of the smarter ones. Smart enough to know that men will work better if they can at least pretend a life of dignity. Pretend not to see the lash if it is judiciously used.

This, as you well know, is the most chance circumstance in which the group could find themselves. All together, in a cabin, on the land of one of the more sensible planters in the tidewater. But among the new parcel was a young man who had not known bondage, and he could not bear it. Under nightfall he set about at once to scout the woods and the waterways that would secure escape. The mothers begged him to wait. Wait patiently until they could not only know the land but also know whom to trust. But such an idea does not hold bearing for a colt that has not known the pen. And besides, a young man could make good an escape, especially if he was comfortable in the woods. But it requires patience and study to secret away a large group of women and children. Patience that this colt did not possess. And so one night he was gone to join the British, who promise the chance to wreak havoc on white men and be rewarded for it with fertile land in the Canadas, or the lush West Indies. Or even to Africa soil, some have said. That is but breath and wind, if you ask me.

Old Papa Sylvanus presented himself aboard the British warship where a number of his slaves were employed in smart uniforms and top hats. The British do not deny the planter the opportunity of an audience with his former slaves. There, on the deck of the man of war, he gave his speech. His line was simple: his business was suffering, and he implored his former workers to return and to help him. Help him, for if he could not count on the labour, he would surely have to scatter many of his current slaves to the winds.

Out of the many Sylvanus men on that vessel, only one came away with him that day.

Perhaps the colt knew what fate awaited him, but more likely he was too used to being treated with honour, and he had no idea. Old Sylvanus had the colt tied to a locust tree in view of his family. And he had him lashed until he nearly perished. Then he sold him south, and sold his mother westward, and there was another boy, child of the other mother, who had done nothing, but he sold him away as well, for good measure. Only the girl children he let stay, with the remaining mother.

It was foresight, one might say. Ever since no more slaves coming from Africa soil, young slave women are the top crop. Young slave women who have been taught to fear are the top of the top, for they also teach their children to fear. This, old Sylvanus has foreseen for quite some time.

What he did not foresee was one such as you.

You're Monk's boy. So you won't fool yourself. The ones who have been sold south and west are gone, and if you go for them, you will not return. This will make an emptiness in you for many generations.

You will not see them again, and you know this, though it looses an ocean inside you.

Let it bury you like the tide does the shore. Now and when it comes again. And again.

Remember the ones that remain. The ones that remain are within your grasp.

Listen close.

You will become a ghost that haunts the tidewater.

You will lay in wait in the woods for as long as you must.

You will study the waterways and the grounds, and not make yourself known, even to your own family.

If you are waylaid by dogs or roving patrollers, you will kill them swiftly and silently.

You will steal what you have to, in order to secure a boat big enough.

British promises may be full of wind, but it is the wind that carries the enchantment.

You will take your family one night, as if in a dream.

You will take your family away.

And if you really are Monk's boy, then you will also take the children who are not your own, and you will give them another life.

That is as far as I can see.

Chapter XIII

I cast down the papers hurriedly, blinking hard at the dark ahead of me.

Cash was rocking back and forth and an awful moaning came from her as though she was the hull of a sinking ship.

I was on my feet.

"Cash!" I said urgently.

She waved a hand at me that seemed as though it were meant to reassure me, but I remained distraught at the bars between us. She inhaled, shuddering as though choking.

I stood, one hand on the pitted iron, watching my grandmother break apart.

She began to slow her breathing and I stayed at my post, wishing nothing more than to go to her. To put a hand on her back.

"You don't know," she said softly, finally, her voice wet. "You don't know *how* that was."

I stared at her and quietly took the stool again, my own breath high in my chest.

"Thank you," she said, holding my gaze. "I cannot speak— cannot say . . . the peace you have brought me with this tale."

She paused, and I felt my eyes widen as I began to imagine

what she meant. Chiron's tale. It bent my mind to think that I had had this, my father's story, in my hands these years, and not known—never read it.

"I've never heard of what came of my children after I was sold away," she said, and the broken sounds that still echoed in my ears gained meaning. "Never in these, what—fifty years. All my prayers for their safety, and never having known."

Her eyes met mine, and sorrowful as they were, she smiled peacefully.

"Our time will not be long today, child," she whispered. "But first, I will speak to the tale we have just heard."

She took another long, calming breath, and then began.

<hr/>

That camp, out in the bush by the bend of a stream. The water was cold by that time of year, and there was a place where the shore dipped in and made a small pool.

I had the children bathe near my scouring rock where I washed and the current was stronger. There I had them wade in while I watched with Nohkomis.

"Why must we all go, Mama?"

Nibi sat on the sand beside Nohkomis and pouted.

The youngest, Jeannie, left the water, her lips blue, her skin alive with whisper hairs on her back. She grasped around her body with stick-thin arms and tripped and splashed as she walked back to land. Her big head of hair pushed out drops of water as she shook the few steps to Nohkomis, who stood beckoning on the shore, all draped with blankets.

That was where I first heard the cannonade, and everything shook well.

Early the next morning, I awoke from a light slumber. Yes, I heard them before I saw them, and Nohkomis also rose to join me. We clutched each other as they came up through the bush, too slowly to be kin. I did not flee. I saw them dragging my boy like he was a half-broke mule. Limping and seeing out but one side of his face.

And the band of renegades. They had a wondrous look, like they couldn't believe what they were doing. Couldn't believe it would work. But they had just chance enough. Chance enough they caught themselves a Negro in a skirmish. Lucky enough that they found an Indian willing to save his own hide by telling them this Negro got five Negro sisters and a Negro mama, ready for the taking. Lucky enough that if they made it through the night, they could sell the lot of them for more money than they knew what to do with. This I saw in their faces beneath their caps, and in their cautious swagger, and in the tightness of their hands gripping muskets.

"I'm going with my children, Nohkomis."

She shook her head fierce and yelled and struck me on my

chest. I would not see her harmed for me, though. So I bound her wrists tight with cord and tethered her to a tree.

My spirit knew the moment would come, I think. Knew I had got more than my time. And my children, they were ready, though they didn't know it yet.

Freedom, you can't get and bury, and keep it and keep it so it won't ever go away. No, child. You got to swing your freedom like a club.

Anne and her two children ran. They did not make it far. I rounded up my girls and ushered them to bondage. All my daughters.

"We go with the white men," I told them. "They near killed your brother and we got to take care of him."

I took my boy's bent face in my hands and did not look sullen upon him.

The iron felt familiar on my wrists. As we walked away into the morning, I swear I heard the wails of Nohkomis for miles.

Yes, even now it is in my ears.

Don't look so upon me, girl; it will do nothing.

I didn't know what to say.

The old woman sat in the cell, her eyes shut firmly, her face glinting in the shadows.

What could I say? Her world had come apart so long ago. And yet she and I were here somehow, seated paces away. I could hear her stammering breath. I looked to her, but her eyes remained clamped shut. I became aware of my open mouth, the emptiness of words.

And there were footsteps coming down the hallway already.

"I wrote the article, you know," I said, breathlessly. "In the paper. I wrote it last week. It came out this morning. I'll bring it for you."

"I would like to hear it one day," she said, her eyes still closed.

The footsteps were upon me. I could see James from the corner of my eye. It was so soon, it felt. He stood beside me in the corridor, dangling the keys impatiently. I stood, gathering my things.

"I imagine it is well writ," said the old woman. Her eyes were open now and swollen. She looked like a different person.

"It is," I replied. "It is a pity, you will never be hanged at this rate."

She scoffed and looked away, raising a hand as if to dismiss me.

I walked out in a daze. James was sullen and said nothing to me. The weather I could feel already from inside the jail. It was muggy and heavy; a storm was brewing. As I walked out, over the threshold, I gazed up at the turmoil of clouds racing in above the town. A voice from the street rang out:

"There is a land where tyranny ends!"

It was then I noticed the guards on the steps ahead, their backs to me, and beyond them, spilling out on the road, was a crowd.

"And men who will defend it!"

Another voice; I couldn't see the speaker. Someone started to cheer, and then there was applause. I stood on the courthouse steps, stunned, and then afraid of what might be happening. I saw Arabella at the head of the throng, with her unrepentant smile. As I looked further, I saw the faces of Simeon, Cass, Emma, Jim, and many others. I caught the eye of Circe too. And Greaves, near her. There was another loud whistle and it made me flinch. Simeon took out his kerchief and bowed his balding head deep toward me. Others did the same, waving hats and newspapers in the air. My face felt full with heat and sorrow and jubilation all at once. The wind blew warm as a gust of breath, and I smelled soot and sweat and the stink of the hot road. I stepped down to stand with Arabella and the cheering grew louder. She lifted my hand and I noticed its shape, slender and looming in front of the walls of the courthouse. I felt my own voice in my belly and heard it join the roar of the people around me. I hoped the old woman heard our clamour.

Acknowledgments

I give thanks to the planet for continuing to teach and nurture me despite my slow path to reciprocity. I give thanks also to my ancestors, for much the same reasons. To my family: you taught me how to love, and how to love stories, and in so doing gave me everything I needed to begin this work. There are many people whom I encountered through oral and written histories who inspired this work, most notably John "Daddy" Hall and "Old Man" Henson of Owen Sound. To them and to the countless others, I give thanks for the inspiration. When this novel was a frail, experimental thing, Frank Wilderson, Charmaine Nelson, David Austin, Chanzo Greenidge, and Dionne Brand wrote letters of reference that were instrumental for me to get into school and secure scholarship money. Thank you for believing in me. Thank you to the creative writing MFA at the University of Guelph, and to all my peers and teachers who gave the program life and meaning. The Constance Rooke scholarship, along with the Edward Y. Morwick scholarship, the College of Arts Travel Grant, and NSERC (CGS-M) provided me with the means to research, study, and write, and for that I will always be grateful. Thank you to Waubgeshig Rice for your sound advice, and for reminding me that it is a good thing to *enjoy* writing. Thank you to Shani Mootoo for putting me on track in the task of giving structure to the manuscript. Catherine Bush, your notes were most pertinent, and to you I owe the title. Catherine Tammaro, your support as a friend and elder was instrumental in finding the soul of this book. To Peter Meyler: gratitude to you is gratitude to all those who do the sacred, quiet work of bringing forgotten history to light. Thank you Lynn Brown and Kaitlin Littlechild, for your attentive notes and recommendations. Sam and Chelene, thank you for being thorough and passionate agents who guide me in making a career out of this. Lara, Laura, and Abi, you are kind, thoughtful, and precise editors, and the book is much better for it. And to all the people at the publishing houses who helped get this novel out there—thank you, your labour is appreciated! To my partner, Brooke: thank you for teaching me how to find my truth—I don't think anything could be more important. To my children, this book is for you; may you find the stories that inspire you to carry your world forward. To all those who have helped me in this work whose names are forgotten or lost, I also give thanks.

Author's Note

As a young man, I worked as a tree planter to pay my way through university. It's not an overly uncommon job for a student—seasonal, hard labour, good money, and a built-in adventure to a remote part of the country. For me, a city kid with a strong yearning for nature, it was perfect. The summer I was twenty, I travelled to a remote British Columbia town. My bus had been delayed and I arrived alone and exhausted at three in the morning. There was a park next to the bus stop, and I lugged my gear to a secluded place and slept. A few hours later I was awakened by a pair of police officers, their hands on their holsters. They told me I couldn't sleep there, and watched me until they were convinced I wouldn't continue to do so. As I sat on a bench afterward, my body shaky with adrenaline, a man who had seen the whole thing approached me. I presumed he was Indigenous by his features and his manner of speaking. He welcomed me and pointed me to the different places in town I could go for food and a hot shower.

It would not be the first time I feared for my life in a police encounter—also tragically not an uncommon experience, particularly for young black men. But moreover, it was one among many times in my life that I felt welcomed to land by Indigenous people. I had already begun to reflect more broadly on my relationship to the Indigenous people of the lands I called home, and to wonder how other black folks had experienced and thought about this.

I yearned for nature, as I mentioned, but that yearning was beginning to crystallize as a desire for a meaningful connection to land. And land, I was learning, is rarely void of human belonging, even if it seems that way to the untrained eye. I began to understand my black identity as an inheritance of enslavement, yes, but first and foremost of the theft of African peoples' connection to land—in other words, the theft of indigeneity. How intriguing the relationship might be then, between black and Indigenous peoples—peoples whose relationships to land had been profoundly interrupted by colonialism in parallel yet distinct ways. But why had I never seen or read anything about this?

I was steeped in stories of various colonial formulations: I knew and had seen many stories that were concerned with the relationships between black and white people, and similarly, between Indigenous and white people. And of course, between whites and any other people of colour. But I couldn't think of a single story I knew that meaningfully explored black and Indigenous relationships.

A few months later, I came across a photograph of John "Daddy" Hall, a man of African and Indigenous descent who has an incredible story. He had fought in the War of 1812, been captured and survived decades of slavery in Kentucky, and escaped all the way up to Owen Sound, Ontario, where he became the town crier and lived to be over 115 years old. It was a story that brought together several corners of history I had never truly examined: black-native alliances in slavery-era Canada, Indigenous sovereignty, the Underground Railroad, and the politics of free black settlement. I dove deeper and deeper into these chapters of history—reading books and primary source materials, talking with Indigenous and black elders such as my friend the Wyandot faith keeper and artist, Catherine Tammaro, Tuscarora historian Rick Hill, white historian Peter Meyler, and Merikin Maroon leader Akilah Jaramogi, to name a few. I read and heard the stories of countless black people who held remarkable knowledge of the land they inhabited, and who had deep and complex relationships with not only the whites but also the Indigenous people around them. It became clear that the history was written and alive in ways that I was encountering and even experiencing. What was missing, I realized, was the stories in narrative form. With a burgeoning passion for creative writing, I set out to write a novel. My goal was to conjure a world that was very close to the "real" world, yet different in some of the ways that fiction allows for. Readers well-versed in the period will pick up the people and places in the novel that are amalgams of historical figures and locations. Dunmore, for example, the town populated by refugees of slavery in which the novel opens, was not a real place, yet I believe it could have been in the sense that there were many communities like it— some of which, such as Buxton, Ontario, still exist to this day. Others such as the Queen's Bush are now found only in history and myth.

While working on this book, I heard a call to action several times, in a few different forms, from a few different people. If I were to paraphrase and synthesize: we must share the stories that haven't been shared, in order to bring healing to our world. It's an idea that has motivated and inspired me through the years and many drafts that have birthed *In the Upper Country*. It is a story I am honoured to write.